For
Peter

Keep on
reading,

Nancy Swing

W9-ATZ-534

Malice
on the Mekong

Nancy Swing

PARK PLACE PUBLICATIONS
PACIFIC GROVE, CALIFORNIA

This book is a work of fiction. Names, characters, places, and incidents either are products of the author's imagination or are used fictitiously. Any resemblance to actual events or persons, either living or dead, is entirely coincidental.

Copyright © 2016 Nancy Swing

All rights reserved under International and Pan-American copyright conventions. No part of this book may be used or reproduced in any manner whatsoever without written permission from the author, except in the case of brief quotations embodied in critical articles or reviews.

First trade paperback edition March 2016
Designed by Patricia Hamilton
Manufactured in the United States of America

Published by
Park Place Publications
Pacific Grove, California
www.parkplacepublications.com

ISBN: 978-1-943887-3-2
Printed in U.S.A.

"I'm Just Wild About Laos" sung to the tune of "I'm Just Wild About Harry." Music by Eubie Blake, lyrics by Noble Sissle, 1921.

Short quotations from "I'll Take Romance." Music by Ben Oakland, lyrics by Oscar Hammerstein II, 1937.

Cover photo of Wat Sokpaluang, Vientiane, Laos courtesy of Alex Bunjes.

Artwork of Anousavari and boy with buffaloes from the Map of Vientiane, Lao P.D.R, published by the Women's International Group, 1993.

In Memoriam

Ann Swing Williamson
June 8, 1910 - February 28, 1997

Leonard C. Swing
June 8, 1910 - December 27, 1998

How they loved a mystery.

Acknowledgements

This book was 20 years in the making. When I first started to write it, I was too close to the experiences that inspired it. More importantly, although I'd written all sorts of non-fiction, I soon learned that I didn't know how to write fiction. So when I could fit writing workshops into our international life, I participated in several, most helpfully at University of California, Los Angeles, University of Iowa and University of Winchester, U.K.. Meanwhile, we continued to move around the world, jumping from Hawaii to Central Asia and then Italy. Wherever we went, I kept seeing similar patterns of behavior in the expatriate community, reinforcing my initial impressions. Finally, we retired and moved to California, where this story continued to haunt me. I realized I had to finish it.

After all the years and all the venues and all the revisions, it's impossible to acknowledge by name everyone who read and commented on the book. But they all have my gratitude; their feedback helped make it better each time. That having been said, I would like to offer special thanks to:

Russell Sunshine, life partner, who helped me get through the days darkened by women like Sophia, and who encouraged the writing through all the drafts and all the years;

Workshop participants and leaders Susan Taylor Cheak (Iowa), Tara Ison (UCLA) and Sally Spedding (Winchester);

Fellow participant in the UCLA workshop, Nick P. Maginnis, whose comments taught me more about writing than I deserved, especially at that pitiful stage;

Puongpun Sananikone for advice on Lao culture;

Francine Vanderstricht for advice on the French legal system;

Alex Bunjes who granted permission to use his wonderful photo of Wat Sokpaluang on the cover;

Women's International Group, Vientiane, Lao P.D.R. for permission to use artwork from their Map of Vientiane.

Ann Shelbaer Ammons, who kept pushing me to self-publish through all the rejection slips; and

Patricia Hamilton, whose expertise in self-publishing is matched by her grace and gentility.

Any remaining shortcomings or errors in the book are all mine.

A Word about the Historical Setting

This work of fiction takes place in the early 1990s in Vientiane, Laos, or the Lao People's Democratic Republic (Lao PDR) as it is officially termed. Formerly a French colony, the country gained independence as a constitutional monarchy in 1953. Shortly thereafter, a long civil war began with the guerrilla Pathet Lao supported by North Vietnam and the Soviet Union. During the 1960s and '70s, Laos was used as a supply route by North Vietnam in its effort to gain control of the South. Consequently, the United States launched the so-called "Secret War" with support from Thailand. This effort involved arming the Hmong people of the Lao mountains and massive bombing carried out by the United States. Between 1964 and 1973, American planes dropped an average of one bomb-load every eight minutes around the clock, making Laos the most bombed country in history.

The communist Pathet Lao came to power in 1975, deposing the king, who later died in captivity. The country sank into international isolation with consequent poverty and hardship. A decade later, it was becoming clear to the national leadership that a change in direction was called for, and they introduced an "Open Door" policy in 1989. Its goal was to develop a market economy through encouraging foreign investment, attracting official development assistance and promoting foreign trade. By the early nineties, scores of foreigners were living and working in Vientiane, with positive and negative results for expatriates and Lao alike.

There was no Canadian Embassy in Vientiane at the time of this novel. The author created its existence in order to avoid association with any actual embassy in the city at that period. She also took minor liberties with the geography of Vientiane to simplify descriptions of some scenes.

Because the author could not discover how the Lao legal system worked with regard to serious crime during the era of the story, she elected to assume that the French system had been continued after independence.

It has since become common to use the more appropriate term "Laotian" to include all the ethnic groups who live within the Lao PDR. But at the time of this story, everyone said "Lao."

Some Help with Language

A Word about the Pronunciation of Lao

Lao, like Chinese, is a tonal language. Therefore, attempts to transliterate it into Roman typeface are not perfect. For the purposes of this novel, here are a few tips:

- Vowels are long

  - "a" as in "father" (ah)

  - "e" like "-ay" in "hay"

  - "i" like "ee"

  - "o" as in "bone"

  - "u" like "oo" in "boot"

- A "c" followed by "e" or "i" is pronounced like a soft "s" in English; e.g. "baci" is pronounced "bah-see."

- An "h" indicates an explosive sound like the "h" in "hound." That's not too difficult until one reads what would be a dipthong in English. So "Pathumphone" is pronounced somewhat like "pah-toom-pone" not "pah-thum-fone."

- Sometimes transliteration of a Lao name was retained in French spelling, so "Bounxouei" is pronounced "boon-shway." For the same reason, Vientiane is pronounced "vee-en-chan."

Abbreviations, Words and Terms

baci - traditional Lao ceremony of blessing, usually conducted at times of life-transition.

biscuit - British term for the American "cookie."

bodhi - member of the fig and mulberry family, specifically the one under which the Buddha attained enlightenment.

Centigrade - Characters mentioning temperature think in Centigrade. A little help: 20°C is around 70°F; 30°C is a little over 90°F; and 40°C is around 104°F.

cheongsam - traditional dress worn by some Chinese women, high-necked and a slim skirt with slits up the side.

churidar kemiz - trousers fit tightly to the calves and a tunic, worn by some ethnic groups of the Subcontinent.

dependent spouse - official term for a spouse accompanying a person hired to work overseas.

dupatta - long, narrow scarf worn with *shalvar kemiz*, usually draped across the front of the neck or chest, with ends trailing in the back.

elastoplast - British term for the American "bandaid."

expat - expatriate, a person residing in a country not of his citizenship; for example, Americans are expats in Laos.

farang - foreigner.

jerry can - large metal can, 18 inches or so in height, used to transport water and other liquids in East Africa.

-ji - suffix in Hindi used to indicate respect.

kawb jai - thank you.

khan - silver urn central to the *baci* ceremony.

laissez-passer - permission to pass; in this case, government-issued permit to travel up-country from the capital.

kurta pyjamas - loose-fitting pajamas usually made of thin cotton, worn by men of the Subcontinent; often used for loungewear at home.

local hire - an expatriate hired to work while residing in-country, almost always paid at a significantly lower salary than if hired from outside the country at international rates.

Mae Ork - term of respect used by ordained monks for a woman of the lay community.

NGO - Non-governmental organization; a not-for-profit organization like Save the Children, Red Cross, Oxfam, etc.

nop - hands held palms together in front of chest, a salute to the divine spirit which resides in every person.

pa-sin - tube-skirt worn by Lao women, usually woven by hand, often in elaborate designs.

Pathet Lao - communist party which came to power in 1975.

pushpin - short pin with spool-shaped head, used to affix something to a bulletin board.

raita - cooling dish served with spicy foods of the Subcontinent; usually yoghurt with something mild, like chopped cucumber.

Res Rep - Resident Representative, the ranking person for programs conducted by the relevant organization in a given country; as in UNDP Res Rep.

shalvar kemiz - baggy trousers and tunic worn by men and women of the Subcontinent.

Subcontinent - Southern area of Asia including Bangladesh, India, Pakistan and Sri Lanka.

sutra - a saying in Hindu literature; later in Buddhist scripture.

tiffin box - metal container used to transport lunch in the Subcontinent; usually multi-layered with compartments for different dishes.

torch - British term for American "flashlight."

UNDP - United Nations Development Programme, agency of the United Nations which works to improve conditions in developing countries.

USAID - United States Agency for International Development, agency of U.S. Government tasked with providing assistance to developing countries.

wat - Buddhist temple.

Malice
on the Mekong

Barely dawn, and the boys were on their way to the fields outside Vientiane. Perched on the broad backs of the water buffaloes, they watched the Mekong. It was the rainy season, and they liked looking for all the things the rushing river had captured. A brass water pot swirled past, followed by a small boat with a big hole and a hillock of broken branches.

Then they saw something odd, something white caught in a half-floating tree hooked into the bank. The boy on the lead buffalo went to investigate, leaving the family herd in the care of Younger Brother. The smaller boy's nostril's flared, the only sign that he felt torn between the self-importance of responsibility and an almost unbearable curiosity.

Younger Brother dug his toes into the mud and craned his neck to see. Elder Brother was only one year older. Why did he always get to do everything first? Life was so unfair. The eight year-old sighed and looked across the rolling water to the far bank, wondering if the boys in Thailand were going to school.

A buffalo strayed, and Younger Brother tossed a pebble to turn her back to graze with the others. He tried to see what Elder Brother was doing, but the older boy's body hid the white thing captured by the tree. All Younger Brother could see was a familiar back shining with sweat. So he threw a rock into the water to make a big splash. Elder Brother didn't even look up.

Younger Brother caught his own face twisting in frustration. Only babies do that, he thought. Worthy people learn to control their emotions. He tried to focus his mind on the river. Some months ago, before he was old enough to help with the buffaloes, he'd watched his mother mix a cake in the foreigners' house where she worked. That was how the water looked where it tumbled over the huge rocks in the riverbed, like brown batter being beaten for a cake.

He edged closer and looked down the embankment. The Mekong had churned down from the highlands and tossed up so many things—dead birds, a rubber sandal, and that giant tree uprooted by the water's fury. Just then Elder Brother jumped up, and Younger Brother could finally see what was down there. A woman's body was caught in the tree root, her long scarf trailing in the current. He squinted to see more clearly against the sun's reflection, then sucked in a breath. What was a *farang*—a foreigner—doing in the Mekong?

Elder Brother ran up the bank. He slipped, and smelly ooze smeared his legs. His dark eyes showed white all around, and his face was a funny gray color. He shouted at Younger Brother to watch the herd and dashed off toward the temple, bits of gold from the Buddha gleaming in the dark interior.

Younger Brother gritted his teeth. He hurried around the herd, bunching them together. The huge animals caught his frustration and grumbled. He got control of himself, sang a soothing song, and the buffaloes quieted. He tried, but he couldn't prevent his eyes from slithering again and again to the *farang's* body.

Elder Brother re-appeared with the abbot and several monks. Their one-shouldered saffron robes and shaved heads gleamed golden in the rising sun. Younger Brother watched them slide down the bank and wondered if he'd ever get there to see for himself. A few moments later, the abbot climbed back up, leaving the monks to guard the body. He took time to smile kindly at Younger Brother and tell him that he was going to phone the police.

Hours later, after the boys had told all they knew to the officials and told it all again to their family and then to the neighbors, before they had bedded down the buffaloes and then themselves, important people began to take decisions. They wanted to do what was best for everyone.

Anjali squirmed from under her parents' bed and brushed the dust balls out of her hair. Where could Mummy-ji have hidden the chocs? Every week, Daddy-ji brought her mother a box of Bombelli's chocolates. Each evening after dinner, if Anjali had been good, she was allowed one piece. But that wasn't enough. Finding where the chocolates were hidden had become the center of Anjali's eight year-old existence.

She'd spent days methodically searching the huge house, moving chairs so she could look on high shelves, crawling behind couches, scraping fingers on rough locks. Now only the third floor remained. No one slept up there any more, not since the last generation when the family included live-in aunts and uncles. Things were more modern now. Daddy-ji's brothers had their own houses nearby.

Anjali climbed the narrow wooden stairs, careful to keep to the far right so they wouldn't creak. She opened the door of a bedroom and gasped. It was full of boxes and old suitcases. How would she ever work her way through all that clutter?

Hair escaping from her single braid tickled her nose, and she shook her head to free her face. Her eyes fell on an old armoire at the end of the corridor. It was where the extra linens were kept. The perfect place. Anjali ran to twist the key.

The smell of starch and lavender tumbled out. Anjali stood with hands on hips and grinned. Under the scents of fresh laundry was the perfume of chocolate. She lifted each sheet and towel until she found the silver box with the gold-ribboned lid. Then she carefully took one chocolate from each section and rearranged the bonbons so her pilfering wouldn't show.

Tuesday morning, Anjali woke up later than usual. She'd been dreaming of her Bombay childhood. Those golden days seemed so long ago. She counted back. This was '92…more than forty years.

She'd once heard Daddy-ji's best friend call him "a black Englishman." Her father had laughed and said in his impeccable upper crust British accent, "But what else could I be?" Looking back, Anjali had to agree. It was a fair description not only of Daddy-ji, but of the family's entire world.

She picked up a bedside photo taken in Mummy-ji's beautiful garden. With her forefinger, she fondly traced the fading figures. Her parents sat on cushioned wicker chairs. Daddy-ji's mother, in the widow's traditional white, sat regally on a stool to his left. Anjali's three mischievous brothers looked unnaturally tidy in their St. George's School blazers, but her older sister was very much at home in a perfectly draped sari.

In the background of the photo, as they were in life, stood the household servants, from the lowly sweeper to the majordomo. In the center, seated on her mother's lap in a frilly dress, was baby Anjali, lovingly spoiled by doting family and worshipful servants.

Anjali sighed. She was the only one left.

She looked out the window. It was raining again. It was always raining this time of year in Laos. She should be used to it.

She'd lived most of her life in the monsoon belt, following KB around the world. Normally, she didn't give it a thought. But today the rain depressed her. It was her birthday, and KB was up-country. Again. Like he'd been most of their married life.

Another sigh escaped. That's what officers in the United Nations Development Programme did. They went up-country to oversee projects. She pictured smiling children in new schools, happy women using pumps with safe water, proud farmers with increased yields. That was the kind of thing that KB had helped make happen for more than twenty-five years.

He doesn't have to be in the field now, she griped to herself. He's Resident Representative. He's in charge of the whole Country Programme. But after what had happened in Hanoi, he felt compelled to be personally involved in everything.

She stirred, and the cat at the foot of the bed murmured a complaint. Traveller was an old neutered tom, hauled from post to post, a furry comfort, especially when KB was away.

And a pitiful attempt at continuity in a life of change, she recognized.

Anjali felt at war with herself. She tried to smile. She'd known what she was letting herself in for when her parents had arranged a marriage with KB Rao. They'd even given her time to get to know him, to decide if he was right for her. And he was. She'd always been proud of KB and his work. It was just that today…

The phone rang. Anjali reached out a hand and lifted the receiver. "Hello?" Only static on the other end.

"Hello?" she tried again. A faint voice seemed to be shouting down the line.

"I can't hear you," Anjali shouted back. "Please hang up and try again."

She leaned against the pillows and waited patiently. Traveller came to sit on her lap, and she tickled behind his ears, his purr vibrating under her fingers.

In Laos, a re-dial could take anywhere from a minute to several hours. But today it took only a few seconds, and then she heard Anand, her beloved first-born, calling from California.

"Hello? Hello? Mummy-ji, is that you?"

"Yes, my darling, it is. And how lovely to hear your voice."

"I couldn't miss your birthday. Many happy returns!"

Anjali's eyes filled with tears. So like Anand to be thoughtful. He put on the children to wish her happy birthday, although the littlest only gurgled. Then his darling wife offered her wishes. Such a comfort to know how well Anand had chosen when he was ready to marry.

Anand came back on. "What're you and Daddy-ji doing to celebrate the great day?"

Anjali hesitated.

"What is it? Something wrong?"

"No, not really. Your father's up-country."

"Oh, Mummy-ji," his voice sank with disappointment. "How could he? It's your fiftieth. That's important!"

"It's very kind of you to remember, darling. You've made me very happy."

"But why can't Daddy-ji be there?"

"Because he's got a critical project in trouble. He had to go up to Sayaboury to try and save it. I wouldn't have it any other way."

Anand began to protest anew, but Anjali put a stop to it by asking for news of his upcoming promotion. After a while, he rang off with kisses from everyone, and Anjali got up, cheered by his call.

As she did every morning, Anjali stepped onto her mat and composed herself for postures and meditation. Today, warm thoughts of her mother teaching her yoga came flooding back. Anjali couldn't have faced life's challenges without it.

Thirty minutes later, she rose from the mat, refreshed in body and spirit. She took a good look at herself in the full-length mirror. A short, plump Indian grandmother looked back, face a bit wrinkled and only slightly sagging, hair lightly grayed but strong and thick in the braid down her back. Her eyes, which were her best feature, or so KB said, were bright and lively.

She hadn't aged as gracefully as Mummy-ji, she judged, but she wasn't covered in rolls of flesh like Daddy-ji's mother either. Not so bad for fifty, she decided and gave up the last vestiges of gloom.

Showered and shampooed, Anjali padded on bare feet out to the screened-in veranda. Not every foreigner followed the Lao tradition of leaving one's shoes outside, but Anjali's own family had observed this Asian custom. It came as naturally to her as wearing the long tunic and baggy trousers of her *shalvar kemiz*.

Onhta had set the breakfast table with Anjali's normal spartan fare, fruit and a couple slices of toast. When Anjali sat down, Onhta entered and placed a pot of tea before her.

As usual, Onhta was dressed to perfection. Her dark *pa-sin*, the traditional hand-loomed tube skirt, had a narrow decorative border at the bottom. Her short-sleeved white blouse was tucked in with the customary silver filigree belt, and her long, black hair was fashioned into a bun at the nape of her neck.

"Will there be anything else, Madame?" Like most Lao of her generation, the forty-something Onhta spoke French, painstakingly learned at school in colonial times.

Anjali smiled. "*Non, merci.*"

Onhta, impassive as ever, turned and retreated into the kitchen.

Anjali nibbled at the fresh papaya picked that morning from the back garden and tried not to think about her birthday.

She spent the morning at her desk, writing letters to family and friends. She needed to write as much as she needed to breathe. To reach out, to stay in touch with loved ones helped give meaning to a life spent far from the people she cared for. And who cared for her.

"My dear Helen," Anjali wrote and looked out across the front garden. The rain had stopped. Water drops beamed in the deep shade cast by coconut, guava and banana trees. Bending from the waist, his sturdy legs locked at the knees, the gardener Kongkeo was picking up fallen twigs and leaves from the manicured lawn.

Anjali berated herself. What was the matter? She felt so restless. Hard to settle down to what was normally a pleasure. More like duty this morning.

A small bird landed on the garden's spirit house. Onhta had left an offering on the terrace that ringed the fanciful structure—a quarter pineapple fashioned into a small boat. Inside, a pink hibiscus bud nestled on woven palm fronds like a tiny person seated on a mat. Resting on its narrow pedestal, the spirit house was perhaps a foot high, a perfect replica of a Buddhist temple. Its white walls set off the elaborately upturned roof of red and green trimmed with shining gold.

Although spirit houses graced virtually every building in Laos, many foreigners objected to having one in the garden or gave reluctant consent for the sake of the Lao staff. But Anjali believed in a spiritual world. Those small houses on pedestals were a symbol of what is never seen, yet often perceived.

The bird raised the courage to take a bite from the pineapple and flew off to feed her family. Anjali bent her bead back to her own duties, unaware that tonight would change her life.

That evening found Anjali and her best friend en route to Il Ristorante. "Is it true what I heard at bridge this afternoon," Suneeta asked, "Sophia's been wound up tighter than a drum for days?"

Anjali turned to look at her seat mate, newly returned from India and basking in the fruits of her shopping. The gold trim of Suneeta's magenta silk sari glistened as they passed street lamps on their way to Sophia's goodbye party. Neither woman was fond of Sophia, but duty required they attend her farewell event. KB thought highly of Sophia's husband, who'd led a difficult UNDP project to a particularly successful conclusion. And Sophia had done a lot of good in her two years in Vientiane, not the least of which was co-founding WIVS, Wives in Voluntary Service. Everyone had been invited to her party— all the diplomatic wives, all the WIVS members—it wouldn't do not to go.

"I don't know," Anjali replied. "I haven't seen Sophia since she produced The Vientiane Follies. She was very intense at the rehearsals, but that only seemed natural, given it was her farewell effort."

"They say she blew up at every rehearsal."

Anjali wasn't fond of gossip, not even with Suneeta. She glanced at Thongsy. Always correct, the chauffeur sat upright, eyes ahead, driving silently through the night. "I couldn't say," she replied, "I usually came just to recite my little poem and then went home. I never stayed for a full rehearsal."

"A poem, Anjali? You wrote a poem for The Follies? That doesn't sound like you."

Anjali smoothed her second-best sari of green and gold silk. "No, no. Sophia wrote the poem and asked me to read it—some silly thing about diplomatic life. It wasn't too biting, so I felt all right about doing it."

Anjali vacillated about her obligation to help Suneeta's catch up on Vientiane's news. Their friendship went back years. They'd first met while serving on the same International Women's Club committee in Botswana. Their husbands had been assigned there at almost exactly the same time, Suneeta's Raj to a junior position in the Indian Embassy, KB with a similar job in UNDP.

Now they were all reunited in Vientiane. Raj was the Indian Ambassador to Laos, and Suneeta was the perfect ambassador's wife. Anjali and Suneeta had kept in touch over the years with weekly letters, and sometimes the couples had vacationed together. Now Anjali and Suneeta were back in daily contact, nurturing each other with the friendship of decades.

Suneeta rearranged her armful of golden bangles. "What's this about a row with Jackie? Over a tearoom?"

"That happened before you went on home leave. Sophia was going to organize a tearoom in connection with Jackie's craft shop, but they had some sort of falling out."

"Oh yes, I remember now." Suneeta smiled with self-deprecation. "I guess it slipped my mind once I saw my beautiful new grandson."

Anjali pushed a wisp of hair behind her ear. She preferred her braid, but tonight she'd put her hair up, and tendrils kept escaping.

"Probably just another tempest in a teapot. Sophia means well, and she has creative ideas for WIVS-fundraising. But she can be a little bossy at times."

Suneeta's shoulder-length coiffure was perfect, as usual. "At times? Always. What was that phrase Anand kept using when he was at Stanford? Control freak. That's Sophia all right. She has to be in charge."

"Yes, but that's because she wants so much for everything to turn out right."

"But who defines what's right?"

"Well, there's something to that," Anjali conceded.

Suneeta looked at Anjali. "What's the matter? You seem a bit down."

Of course Suneeta would perceived the truth beneath the facade she'd been trying to project, Anjali realized. She longed to tell her friend everything, going all the way back to Hanoi, but it wasn't only her secret. She couldn't betray KB. So she settled on a more narrow focus. "I am a bit, actually. Feeling restless and dissatisfied."

Suneeta put her hand over her friend's. "Now Anjali, what have you got to be dissatisfied about? You've got a gorgeous husband who's still madly in love with you after all these years. One son happily married with two grandchildren to my one. The other son, a grand success at The London School of Economics. And you, you're the most admired woman in Vientiane. Most of the women here would give their right arm to have your luck."

Anjali didn't feel like hearing a recitation of her blessings, but she knew Suneeta was trying to help. "I'm just a bit under-occupied here. It feels like something's missing."

She was relieved from saying more when the car arrived at

Nam Phou Square, the heart of expatriate Vientiane. Thongsy got out, opened Anjali's door and stood erect, eyes not looking but nevertheless seeing, as the women disembarked. Anjali could feel the night's humidity like a living presence against her face. She followed Suneeta under the archway to the city's only true dining experience. Il Ristorante had recently been opened by two Italians who somehow managed to get good pasta, extra-virgin olive oil and other necessities through Customs.

Inside, Alberto scurried forward on perpetually swollen feet and led them to the private dining room in the rear. Suneeta looked at Anjali with questioning eyebrows, and Anjali knew what she meant. They'd expected the whole restaurant to be reserved for a private party.

The smaller room was quite unlike the brick-walled main dining room with its framed posters of Rome, Florence and Venice. Tonight, the simple white room was filled with orchids. Anjali was a bit taken aback. Granted, one could buy five sprays in the market for about a dollar, but this seemed excessive. There were giant vases of orchids in every corner and a huge mound of them in the center of the round table, all in the same pale shades, the merest hints of violet.

Anjali counted the places around that single table—ten. Now it was her turn to raise eyebrows. Suneeta's widening eyes spoke volumes. Where was everyone?

"This is so much nicer. So intimate," a high-pitched American voice said. Anjali turned to see Pam, one of Sophia's long-standing followers. "I'd much rather have it this way," Pam said too brightly. "Quality time!"

Across the room, Sophia was holding court and looking, as usual, five years younger than the forty she'd spent on earth. Her well-maintained body was ideally displayed in a full-length dress of Lao silk, slit at neck and hem. Artfully looped around her shoulders was a long scarf of multi-colored silk batik trailing almost to the ground. Both dress and scarf matched the orchids perfectly.

Which was chosen first, Anjali wondered, the outfit or the decor?

In attendance at Sophia's side was her newest protege, Vicki. Her frizzy, ginger hair and ill-cut linen dress were in marked contrast with Sophia's high style.

Sophia's best friend, Catherine, came forward to greet Anjali and Suneeta. "How lovely you both look tonight. So nice of you to make a special effort for Sophia." Catherine was also in silk, but her dress was old-fashioned, rather like something her mother might have worn in the fifties. She led them over to Sophia almost as if they were approaching a high Lao dignitary.

Sophia gave them a dazzling smile. "Anjali! Suneeta! Two of my favorite people!" She first clasped Anjali's hand between both of her own. Then did the same with Suneeta. "So good of you to come." Her upper-class British accent was at odds with her Canadian passport, but Sophia often said her whole family spoke that way.

Her carefully manicured nails were the perfect shade to match her dress. An opal ring of baroque design ornamented her right hand, balancing the mass of diamonds on her left.

Irony overcame Anjali, and she wondered if her second-best sari were good enough.

Suneeta jumped into the pregnant silence. "You're looking smashing tonight, Sophia. Surely that dress is one of your own designs. I recognize that flair."

Sophia was genuinely appreciative. "How kind of you to say so." Her beautiful face made a small pout, and her large green eyes turned sad. "My last design, unfortunately. The copies have already been sent to the boutique."

"To the good fortune of the ladies of Ottawa," said a voice in French. Gabrielle, the wife of the French Ambassador, had arrived. Anjali and Suneeta moved out of Sophia's limelight.

Pam began immediately to urge everyone to take her seat. The slight squeak in her voice and the restless tossing of her hair betrayed her nerves. Despite the air-conditioning, a sheen of perspiration floated on her upper lip.

Around the table were cream-colored place cards filled out in careful calligraphy. Anjali saw with sinking heart that she was seated on Sophia's right, a nod to her husband's diplomatic ranking no doubt, but an honor she could have done without. Gabrielle was on Sophia's left. The place cards then proceeded around the table by strict ranking. Someone had carefully separated Anjali and Suneeta without giving obvious offense.

As soon as they were all seated, three waitresses appeared with serving plates of antipasti—prosciutto and papaya, cold veal with tuna-and-caper sauce, a frittata with something green inside. Alberto's business partner, the younger and dashing Pasquale, poured the wine, ending each service with a little flourish.

When all the glasses were full, Gabrielle rose. She was the epitome of the well-dressed Frenchwoman—copper-rinsed hair beautifully styled, a little black dress adorned with three strands of pearls, a Cartier wristwatch discreetly banded with black lizard. Gabrielle made a long speech in French. She spoke English perfectly but always used her native language for public occasions. Tonight, half the women around the table had no idea what she was saying.

At one point, Gabrielle paused for effect. Pam started to raise her glass for a sip. She turned rose-red with embarrassment when Gabrielle continued.

Years ago, Anjali had lived in Paris while KB was seconded to UNESCO, so she could easily follow—what a treasure Sophia was, so active in the community, helpful to all in need, talented and artistic, her departure a loss to everyone.

The product of a posh and private girls school, Sophia clearly understood the speech. She sat with rapt attention, gazing up at Gabrielle with smiling eyes.

Eventually the toast ended, and everyone raised her glass to Sophia. She gracefully nodded her crown of braided auburn hair to acknowledge their good wishes.

Pam jumped into the silence as the antipasti went around. "How will all our projects go on without you?" she gushed at Sophia. "You've been an inspiration to us all."

Sophia looked graciously toward the new WIVS president. "Lolly is the perfect person for the job. Three months after I'm gone, you won't even miss me."

"Impossible!" cried Vicki, then caught her faux pas. "Of course Lolly will be wonderful, but we'll always miss you."

Sophia inclined her head and passed the veal to Anjali, who passed it onward. The frittata looked good. There were always dishes in Italian cuisine that a vegetarian could eat. Despite living overseas, Anjali was conscientious about Hindu dietary restrictions.

Pam grabbed back the center of attention. "Thank goodness you've put so many WIVS projects on strong footing. But what about *The Vientiane Voice*? Has Karen found a new editor?"

Sophia smiled with regret. "Unfortunately, no."

"Oh, it's so exasperating!" Pam said.

"I don't want to speak ill of the absent, but it is worrying."

"Of course it is," Vicki consoled. "And after you worked so hard on *The Voice*."

Sophia's nod managed to convey a great sadness. "Yes, I always supported Karen's projects."

"But she never supported yours," Pam simpered. "Never mind. You made a huge success of The Follies without her!"

Well, thought Anjali, at least she wouldn't have to say much if this kept up. She avoided looking at Suneeta for fear of giving her inner thoughts away. Instead, she let her mind return to KB's phone call that afternoon.

"Anju! Anju!"

She couldn't mistake that voice, despite the tinny sound of a poor connection.

"Hello, my darling," she said, feeling a great peace wash over her. She could almost feel his arms around her.

"Happy birthday! I've been trying to call you for hours, but the lines have been down. They just got them fixed, and I demanded to be the first to telephone. The local Telecoms officer very kindly offered me his office when he knew the reason for my call. Happy birthday!"

Anjali had a sharp vision of her lanky husband at a strange desk, squinched into a chair too short for him, knees too high, sweat tricking into temples silvered by the years. She felt her eyes brimming. "I'm so glad you called."

"Anju, you know I'd be there if I could. And my heart *is* there." She nodded silently at the comfort in those words.

"I'll hurry home as soon as this is over," he continued. "Won't be long now."

"Won't be long now," she repeated and felt her heart rise in anticipation.

Finally the goodbye party was over. Sophia rose, smiled at one and all, and said, "What better way to spend one of my last nights here than with good food, good wine and good friends? It means a great deal to me that you cared to come, and I shall always remember your faces around this table." She raised her glass. "To all of you—thank you for a fond farewell."

She threw back her head and drank down the full glass of wine. When she turned her head upright, her eyes glittered, and her mouth trembled. Catherine, who'd been virtually silent all evening, came forward and put her arms around Sophia, whispering in her ear.

Sophia sagged against her friend, and Anjali felt both sorrow and admiration for her. So few women had come. It had to have hurt, yet Sophia had put on a brave show. It must have cost a lot to keep smiling all evening.

Seemingly bolstered by what Catherine had whispered, Sophia pulled herself erect. "Come on everyone. Time to go home. I'm getting maudlin, and that will never do."

The women followed Sophia out into the night. Monsoon clouds covered the skies. It was as hot and humid as when they'd arrived. Sophia settled gracefully into her little silver sports car and smiled gaily all around. She pushed a tape into the player and drove off, air conditioner full blast, Pavarotti singing "Celeste Aida," her batik scarf blowing in the wind.

"Anjali, I need to talk, and you're the only one I can trust."

It was unlike Cyril to be so blunt. Must be some crisis at the Embassy, Anjali decided. He was in a hurry and couldn't speak over the phone. "Where and when?" she asked.

"My house for tea. Today at four-thirty?"

"See you then."

It was such an odd, short conversation for Cyril. Anjali was fond of the Canadian diplomat. A bit world-weary, a tad effusive, but still charming when he wanted to be. We all have our faults, Anjali mused, but our gifts may not be readily apparent. Cyril had many gifts, not the least of which was his loyalty to friends. Well, he needed a friend now, and she'd try to be one.

Besides, she'd been restless all morning. Sophia's goodbye party last night had only fed her fidgets. After breakfast, she'd opened the new book Anand had sent, but she hadn't been able to concentrate. She'd tried to have lunch with Suneeta, but her friend was busy planning an Embassy reception. There'd been no chance of going for a drive, because the Lao Government required an official *laissez-passer* for any trip more than a few miles outside the capitol. And shopping was never an option, because there'd be nothing new to see among the meager goods in one of the world's poorest countries.

Traveller jumped up on her lap and insistently rubbed his head against her hand. She looked down at him and recalled how she used to crawl into her grandmother's lap to hear stories from Hindu mythology, stories of Sita, Rama's dutiful wife, and of Devi, whom no man could tame. Every story always ended the same, "So who will Anjali be when she grows up?"

Anjali smoothed Traveller's fur and smiled. For a moment, she was fifteen again, running down the hockey field, scoring a goal and feeling like Devi. Anjali sighed. Too much Sita in her life. Not enough Devi.

The high shade of old mango trees created a cool oasis within Vientiane's heat. The sweet scent of frangipani led Anjali up Cyril's walkway, lined with red hibiscus incandescent in the half-light.

His house was one of her favorites. Traditionally built with exterior beams and white stucco, it had belonged to a Lao doctor who'd escaped during the war. Cyril's predecessor had renovated it with loving care. He'd retained the usual open floor plan and relied on the Mekong's breezes to cool the house at night.

Anjali tapped the brass knocker, and Cyril's houseman instantly opened the elaborate wooden door. Despite Lao custom, she left her sandals on. Cyril preferred a Western lifestyle, as evinced by his closing and air-conditioning the whole house.

The wide entrance hall was covered floor to ceiling with butterflies gleaming in glass boxes. It was Cyril's only hobby. Wherever he'd been posted around the world, he'd collected, preserved and mounted those exquisitely colored, fragile wings.

Cyril came through a wide archway. He extended two long hands nearly devoid of flesh and captured Anjali's plump one like a prized specimen. "Welcome, Anjali. Bless you for coming on such short notice."

Suneeta had once said that if Cyril turned sideways, he'd disappear. It wasn't strictly true, Anjali reflected, but he was so tall and thin that he almost looked like a walking needle.

"You sounded like you need a friend today," she said.

Cyril led her to a couch upholstered in mauve silk with pillows embroidered to match the butterflies mounted above. He gestured at the elaborate tea on the low table before them. "Anjali, will you pour?"

She noticed Cyril's hands were shaking but made no comment, not wishing to embarrass him. She tilted the blue-and-white pot into matching cups. As was their custom, they both took a moment to appreciate the aroma before sipping their Earl Grey in silence. Cyril seemed far away, lost in thought.

Normally, Anjali would have chatted about inconsequential matters before bringing up an important topic. It was the way things were done in Asia. But she could see the upset below the calm demeanor Cyril was trying to project.

"What's the matter, Cyril? Something to do with the Embassy?"

Cyril started out of his reverie. "What? Oh, the Embassy. Well, partly to do with the Embassy." He paused for a moment, as if collecting himself. "It's probably hard to believe, but when I joined the Foreign Service, I was a young man with ideals. I wanted to make the world a better place, and I thought diplomacy held the answer. I was a bright youth with a bright future."

So typical of Cyril, Anjali thought with exasperation. He never could tell anything without going back to the beginning, even if it was ancient history.

There I go again, Anjali admitted. Devi creeping out. Patience! She took a tomato sandwich and leaned back to listen.

Cyril settled his angular body further into his cushions and crossed his long legs. "Two years of stamping visas in Asuncion took the shine off. Then came thirty years of compromises, not doing something because it was right but because it was expedient. Now here I sit, the number-two man in our Vientiane Embassy, part of me still hoping that somebody back in Ottawa will take my advice."

Anjali didn't know what to say. It seemed such a dreary life the way he told it, so different from KB's rise to success. Her heart sank for a moment. Until that problem in Vietnam. But that wasn't really KB's fault. She caught herself and turned her attention back to Cyril.

"It all sounds very wearing," she said.

"I feel I've wasted my life, ending up on the second string in Laos." Cyril ran his fingers through the few hairs combed over his scalp. "The Land of A Thousand Elephants, they call it. A distant memory, if it ever existed. Thank God my posting's almost up. I need to get out of here."

This wasn't the Cyril Anjali knew. He was effete, yes, but self-pitying? He seemed so downtrodden, like he'd lost faith in himself. Like me, she recognized. Whatever could have happened at the Embassy to make him feel like that?

"No joy in working with the Lao," Cyril said, "Insipid, insecure, intractable and generally maddening to know. What does KB say?"

Anjali shifted on her cushion. "You'd have to ask him, but I think he feels very lucky about the caliber of his Lao colleagues."

"I can hear what you're thinking, Anjali—What a fool old Witherspoon is, racist and neocolonial, tired and useless, not worth listening to."

"Cyril, we're both getting older. We're bound to see the world with different eyes. But don't let whatever happened destroy all your hope. It's not worth it."

He shook his head. "You know what life is like here."

He ticked off his points on the fingers of one hand—the communist government was suspicious of foreigners, frowned on social interaction between expatriates and locals, even expected the Lao to inform on foreign hosts after dinner parties, although that, at least, had changed recently. "Living here means constantly fighting ennui. Am I right, Anjali?"

She felt something resonate within her. Selfish to think about that now, she scolded herself. Concentrate on Cyril. "I think we all feel more restricted here than in some other posts."

"Absolutely right. I've only mentioned the Lao. And the diplomats?" He shrugged. "The Aussies are the only ones doing anything here. The French are still looking back, trying to dominate Southeast Asia all over again. The Russians have sunk to teaching English. And the Americans are only interested in drug interdiction and MIA's."

Anjali was starting to feel exasperated again. Was Cyril thinking of leaving the Foreign Service? Taking early retirement? When would he get to the point?

"Bottom line," Cyril summed up, "the dip scene is pretty flat. That's why the diplomats all loved Sophia. Even the snooty French."

Anjali had a vision of Gabrielle's extended toast and Sophia beaming up at her. What could Sophia have to do with all this verbiage?

Cyril continued, "Her attendance at a diplomatic function just about guaranteed success, didn't it?"

Anjali reckoned Sophia got as much out of those events as she gave. "She's certainly been a fixture at those affairs."

Cyril rushed on, "Sophia would have made a wonderful ambassador's wife. When I was a young man, the wives felt they were a vital part of the Mission. They didn't think it was beneath them to organize functions that contributed to diplomatic goals."

Anjali thought about Suneeta, busy planning just such a party. What were Raj's goals for that event? Information? A trade agreement? Support in the U.N.?

The sun was lowering, and under the deep shade of the old trees, the house was growing dark. Cyril's houseman entered and switched on a lamp in the corner.

Cyril seemed oblivious to his presence. "Remember Sophia's last dinner party? Table decorated with white orchids and little silver animals. Matching orchid in her hair. Dressed in an emerald *cheong-sam* she'd got in Hong Kong. Scintillating conversation led by a gifted hostess."

Anjali tasted a savory pastry. "One wondered how she could be so up-to-date."

"She was a voracious reader. She had magazines and books sent… er…courtesy of a friend with access to a diplomatic pouch." Cyril had the good grace to look a bit uncomfortable at this misuse of his duty-free privileges.

Why was Cyril talking so much about Sophia? Anjali mused.

Had he fallen in love with her? And couldn't face losing her? They couldn't be thinking of running away together. That was absurd... wasn't it?

Cyril glanced at Anjali, a sideways glance as if to see how he was doing. "Sophia was a perfect mimic. Remember her imitation of the French Ambassador on Bastille Day? Totally hysterical."

And indiscreet, Anjali thought.

Cyril must have read her mind. "Okay, it was wicked, but also terribly entertaining. Unlike the boring gossip at the Club on Sunday afternoon, which is a rehash of the gossip from Saturday night's reception. Those dreary events—you must suffer as much as I do, Anjali."

"I think this is where I say, 'No comment.'" Anjali didn't like where this was going. She just couldn't picture them as star-crossed lovers.

Cyril paused and rubbed his jaw. Anjali could hear his fingers rasp on nearly invisible stubble. The natty Cyril hadn't shaved that morning.

"She really should have been an ambassador's wife," he said. "Look how she found ways to benefit the Lao virtually as soon as she arrived. Buying all the vintage silk she could find."

And depriving anyone else of having any, Anjali thought, even the Lao who cherished that heritage. She tried to show polite attention as Cyril continued.

"Used that silk to create her famous dresses and employed whole families in making them. She did the same with the furniture manufacturers, you know. Designed things for her own use, and soon other foreigners were placing orders. We're sitting on the first couch made for someone else. Sophia stitched these cushions with her own hands."

Uh-oh, Anjali thought, what does that mean? Sophia's usual special favors for diplomats or special favors just for Cyril?

"Did you know that, Anjali?" he said. "How she did all that in a private capacity, long before she founded WIVS?"

"Yes," Anjali said wearily.

Cyril speeded up his delivery. "Look at all the things she did to make WIVS a success and Vientiane a better place. The theme parties. The Christmas Bazaar. The Follies. *The Voice.* All to raise funds to benefit the Lao."

Anjali was getting more and more uncomfortable with Cyril's exhortations. What did he want from her?

"Sophia did it all with such grace and style, didn't she, Anjali?"

She decided to give him one more response. Then if he didn't get to the point, she'd give him a nudge. But she wasn't going to agree with that statement. Sophia could be a bully. Still, she had to say something positive.

"Sophia's always been full of energy." Anjali reached for a miniature chocolate eclair. She felt the need of a little pep herself.

"She had more energy, more talent and more *savoir-faire* than any of the wives." Cyril tilted his head. "Present company excepted. One could see many of the women were jealous. But she never let it touch her. She marched to her own drummer, knew what was right and did it."

Anjali tried to look at her watch covertly, but Cyril noticed.

"Let me fix you a drink," he said suddenly. "You've been very patient with a garrulous old man. The sun's going down, and you deserve a gin-and-tonic. I won't be much longer. Then I have a favor to ask."

Anjali's heart sank. He wanted a favor, something to do with Sophia's leaving. But what? She smiled in spite of herself. She certainly wasn't going to hold the ladder while they eloped.

"Is it such a favor that I'll need a gin-and-tonic to say yes?"

"I wouldn't insult you," he said. "Look, I need a drink, and I don't want to drink alone. Will you join me?"

"All right. I'll have a G&T."

Cyril walked over to a traditional Southeast Asian cabinet, gilt figures on black lacquer, now converted to a bar. His hands were like stork feet busy with glasses, ice and liquor.

"I don't mean to imply that Vientiane is without its good points," he said. "It's just that there's so little of everything that one values—so little beauty, so little charm, so little that's amusing or entertaining. That's why Sophia made a difference."

With his back turned, Anjali could finally look at her watch. Nearly six. Get on with it, she thought. She wanted her dinner, Anand's book and bed.

Cyril brought the drinks back and sank into the cushions like he was settling into a lifeboat. He took a long pull on his whiskey. "She was unfailingly kind. I remember walking along, head down, shoulders bowed. Feeling an intolerable futility about my life. Then Sophia appeared out of nowhere. 'How's my favorite man today?' And as if by magic, the world was all right again, and so was I."

He let out a long, shuddering sigh. Anjali didn't know what to make of this. It was unlike him to express so much emotion. She didn't know whether to be sympathetic or suspicious.

Cyril dragged a hand across his eyes. "So that's how I see

Vientiane and how I'll remember Sophia. The one boring, tepid and suffering from a long decline. The other bright, talented and full of life. I'm getting sentimental, but I have to say it—for me, she was the only thing in Vientiane that made life bearable."

He balled his bony hands into fists so tight the knuckles shone in the lamplight. He sat up straight, took a deep breath and said, "All right. I can't put this off any longer."

Anjali held herself perfectly still. She didn't want to interrupt him now, not even with a gesture.

Cyril blurted it out, like food poisoning held in too long. "They found Sophia's body floating in the Mekong this morning."

"Oh, my God!" Anjali felt her stomach jam into a knot. She was totally stupefied. Not something to do with the Embassy. Not a love affair. Sophia dead. Impossible.

Cyril continued. "The police are saying it was an accident."

Anjali couldn't bring herself to accept it. "I saw her just last night."

"As near as they can tell, that's when it happened."

"You mean after her goodbye party?" Anjali was incredulous. She pushed a hand into her stomach to ease the cramp.

"That's what they think."

"How did she end up in the Mekong? Did someone force her off the road?"

"No, no. Her car was found upstream, by that small park near the hotel. I was the Duty Officer, and I took the call from the police. Husband up-country, so I had to identify the body. Oh, Anjali, it was so horrible. Yesterday she was full of life, and this morning, she was just a limp, muddy *thing*. Not a person, not my friend. I don't know how I got through it."

Cyril began to crumple—his face, his body, everything sagged. Anjali looked away. She was full of questions, but she knew how important decorum was to him. She concentrated on breathing long and slow to calm her stomach. It was so like Cyril to tell what had happened in this roundabout way. He was afraid of his emotions, so he sneaked up on them.

When did all this happen? When was the body found? And why hadn't she heard anything? Why hadn't the phone been ringing? Vientiane was a town that fed on gossip.

She forced herself to remain patient until Cyril could regain his composure. Out of the corner of her eye, she saw him square his shoulders and sit up straight again.

"I keep trying to remember her as she was." Cyril's quavering voice got stronger as he went on. "God, she was glorious. It's an overblown word, but she was. Golden skin, masses of auburn hair. Slim and chic, even in those ethnic costumes she liked to wear."

He reached out his thin hand to touch Anjali's plump forearm. "Forgive me for going on like this."

Anjali recognized what Cyril was doing. When Mummy-ji's brother was killed, the only talk Aunty Bela would allow was happy stories. So for one week, the extended family had gathered in that sad house and told stories of laughter instead of tears. Anything to avoid a vision of Uncle's mangled body lying by the roadside, the wheels of his motor scooter spinning and the hit-and-run driver speeding away into the night.

"No need to apologize," Anjali said. "Sophia was your friend."

"Yes, and a good friend, too. Both beautiful and kind." He nestled more securely into Sophia's cushions. "That's a rare combination."

Cyril looked up and out. Anjali's gaze followed his. Light from a streetlamp haloed the antique spirit house his predecessor had been so proud of. Now it was falling apart from neglect.

For one awkward moment, it seemed as if Cyril would lose control, but he didn't. Not Cyril the diplomat, the man who had spent a whole career hiding his feelings.

He gulped the rest of his drink and became more official. "It's been kept very quiet, but all hell's going to break loose tomorrow. The ruling will be Death by Misadventure. Everyone wants it that way. So much tidier for all concerned. But I don't believe it. Sophia was too sensible to walk that close to the Mekong in flood, too athletic just to fall in. Suicide is out of the question. Sophia was full of *joie de vivre*. She would never have taken her own life."

Cyril looked up from his empty glass and into Anjali's eyes. "Sophia must have been murdered. Assassinated by one of those jealous harpies."

Anjali gulped. She couldn't believe what she was hearing. Cyril had to be more upset than she'd realized. Why else would he come up with such a preposterous idea?

"That's what I want to ask you, Anjali. I want you to find out what happened." Anjali's stomach cramped again as Cyril hurried on. "You know everyone, and everyone trusts you. You're the only one who can uncover which of those women killed Sophia. Whoever killed her killed life itself."

To Anjali's dismay, Cyril finally broke down and sobbed into one of Sophia's beautiful pillows. She sat quietly, her hand on his shoulder, looking at the remains of their tea—her plate of crumbs, Cyril's as pristine as when they'd begun. He'd eaten nothing.

She felt confused by Sophia's death and Cyril's reaction to it. How had Sophia drowned? And why couldn't Cyril accept the verdict? Why did he want her to get involved? The whole thing made no sense.

After some moments, Cyril drew out a handkerchief. Anjali saw it was soiled, reached into her bag and gave him a clean one.

"Thanks. Sorry to break down like this. Must be the alcohol."

Confused over what was really happening, Anjali tried to concentrate on what he was saying. And what was behind his words.

"Anjali, you must help." The muscles of his face were absolutely rigid. He could barely force sound out. "Tell me you will. No one else could find out the truth."

"Cyril, this is a job for the police, not some overweight Indian grandmother." But she had to admit to herself she was intrigued. How had Sophia ended up in the Mekong?

"Bother the police. They want a ruling of accidental death so all this can be swept under the rug. The last thing they need is a high-profile murder case. If you don't do it, who will?"

"I wouldn't even know how to begin."

"Just do what you always do. Talk to people. Ask them their views. Everyone bares their soul to you."

"Look at me," he added with some embarrassment.

Anjali was tempted. Sophia's death was an affront to her need for the world to make sense. Beautiful, vibrant women didn't just die overnight with no explanation.

She realized with horror that she hadn't felt so stimulated since she'd presided over the Vietnamese Arts Society. Was she so bored with life that she needed to investigate a death? That was too ghoulish for words. Besides, she needed to keep a low profile in Laos. For KB's sake.

She knew an outright refusal would only result in more pleading from Cyril, so she promised to think about it.

"Oh, Anjali, thank you. I know you'll decide to do it once you've thought it over. You won't be able to stand the injustice of it. You'll get involved, and you'll find out what happened. I know you will."

Cyril's face relaxed, but Anjali's stomach was in tighter knots than ever.

That night, Anjali lay propped up with her bedtime cup of hot cocoa, thinking about the Sophia she knew. Not Cyril's Sophia, but a person far more complex. Sophia had been like a chameleon, appearing now this way, now that, to different observers.

How many Sophias were there? Anjali wondered. And what really happened to her?

Later, she dreamed of Sophia before a three-way mirror. In each panel was a different image. Behind her in each reflection, like a figure seen through fog, was Cyril.

The scenes came alive, and Anjali entered each one in turn, recognizing them as reflections of past events.

The first was the dinner party Sophia had hosted to welcome Anjali and KB to Vientiane.

A bit presumptuous of Sophia to take that role, Anjali thought, looking down at the legions of heavy silverware surrounding porcelain plates on a white damask cloth.

She gazed at Tom, clearly uncomfortable in his dark suit and tie. He was one of UNDP's project managers, she realized, and his wife probably wanted to make a good impression from the outset.

A cream-colored place card had directed her to the seat on Tom's right. KB had the other seat of honor beside Sophia. Around the table sat not the other UNDP project managers, which would have been more appropriate, but the Ambassadors of Canada and India, as well as the Res Reps of other U.N. agencies in Laos. Sophia's guests were all of high diplomatic rank.

The household staff, augmented by their relatives for the occasion, glided out of the kitchen to present platters to each guest's left, oversized Georgian silver spoon and fork perfectly positioned for serving the gourmet cuisine. Sophia guided her staff without seeming to. A raised chin, a slight nod, a glance at water carafe or wine, and everything was done swiftly and unobtrusively.

Sophia looked stunning in a teal-and-gold sari. Even though she probably meant it as a compliment to the heritage of her guests of honor, it felt wrong to Anjali, as if Sophia were borrowing their national dress for a costume party.

At the end of the meal, Sophia's staff poured champagne into crystal flutes. Tom, his sweaty face shining in the candlelight, stood to make an informal speech of welcome to KB.

Then it was Sophia's turn, her upper-class British vowels filling the room. "What a pleasant duty to rise in toast of Anjali Rao. Her reputation precedes her, and we feel honored to have her grace our table and our community. Exemplary wife and mother, legendary hostess, tireless volunteer for those less fortunate…" Sophia cocked her head and gave Anjali a little self-deprecating smile. "…I do hope we can capture that energy for WIVS!"

A chuckle of appreciation for Sophia's winsome plea rounded the table, and everyone nodded at Anjali. Sophia raised her glass and half-bowed. "We welcome you to Vientiane, Mrs. Rao, and wish you only happy days among us."

The dream proceeded like cuts in a film. Without a link, Anjali was in Sophia's silver sports car en route to her first WIVS meeting.

Sophia chattered on about the organization. "One does one's best to make life a little better for everyone. There's so much to do, and so little time, really." She glanced over at Anjali. "I hope we can count on you to take an active role, Mrs. Rao..."

"Please call me Anjali."

A gracious turn and dip of the head, as if a great honor had been bestowed. "Thank you, Anjali. It's so hard to find people one can depend upon, who won't criticize but pitch in and get the job done..."

The scene shifted to the meeting, and Sophia led like a demon. "Now who will volunteer for the set-up committee? Mary, will you chair? And how about you, Khadijah? I'm sure we can't do without you. Who else? No volunteers? Shall I volunteer for you? Elisabetta? Janine?" And so it went until all her committees were filled with volunteers of her own choosing.

Then it was the coffee break, and Anjali was standing near when a small woman with mouse-colored hair approached the WIVS president.

"Sophia? I was thinking, what if we used lime green as a coordinating color for the affair? The markets are full of that cloth right now, and it's ever so cheap."

Sophia stood up and stared down at the woman. Her eyes curled with disdain. "How thoughtful, but it's already been decided to use coral." She paused and smirked. "Besides, it's more cheerful." She turned on her heel and walked away, leaving the woman to gaze out the window, her lips pressed so tightly, they blanched.

The dream-Anjali realized she didn't want to be any more active in WIVS than she had to. It seemed too much like her early years as an expatriate wife, raising small sums of money for projects that didn't really solve problems. And the WIVS discussions had been permeated with condescension toward the Lao. Another thought struck: clever, the way Sophia used her height to intimidate that poor woman.

Now Anjali was in the mirror's third image, the first reception that UNDP held after KB took over as Res Rep. A world-famous expert on Women in Development had been brought in to conduct workshops and serve as advisor to the Lao Government. The reception was in her honor.

Anjali's eyes fell on Sophia, sitting on a stool literally at the feet of the diminutive Indonesian Ambassador, dwarfed by his over-stuffed chair. Sophia smiled up at him. "I have such lovely memories of my time in your country. Borobudur, Yogyakarta, the exquisite batiks…"

Anjali moved on and missed the rest, but not before she noted the Ambassador beaming down at Sophia as if she'd just won the school prize.

Later, Anjali heard Sophia introduce herself to the WID consultant. "Such a pleasure to meet you. I'm a bit of an expert on Women in Development myself. I'm Sophia Powell, the founder of WIVS."

Anjali gasped. Sophia wasn't an expert on WID. She didn't even know what it was. The field of Women in Development nurtured the contributions that local women make in developing countries. If Sophia were a WID expert, she'd have fostered projects that empowered the Lao women, promoting cooperatives, small-business loans, education. But Sophia saw WIVS in a philanthropic role—rather like the society ladies in the pages of *Town and Country,* Anjali imagined. And WIVS beneficiaries weren't empowered. They were dependent on WIVS charity.

Anjali noticed Gale turn abruptly and head for the buffet. So Gale had heard Sophia also. Gale was one of the co-founders of

WIVS, an act for which Sophia had claimed sole responsibility.

Anjali awoke with a start. Why was Cyril in the mirror, but not in the scenes? Was it because he was trying to manipulate her?

She got up and headed for the leftover chocolate cake in the fridge. I need a project, she acknowledged, but not this project. She mustn't forget what happened in Vietnam.

"Ah don't mind sayin' we have quite a few scholarships to hand out," drawled the Tidewater voice of the U.S. Cultural Affairs Officer. "Nothin' would give me greater pleasure than to see some of these fine artists studyin' in America."

He was addressing the first Executive Committee meeting of the Vietnamese Arts Society. Anjali was presiding, and the effort required all her skills.

The French Embassy officer couldn't wait to be recognized. "If you will permit me, Mme. Rao, I would like to remind the members of the committee that France has been providing such assistance to Vietnamese artists for several generations." He paused for effect and looked squarely at his American counterpart. "And we intend to continue."

Probably a Polytechnique graduate, Anjali speculated. No one else would be so arrogant.

Outside drizzled December's cold mist, so fine the Vietnamese called it "rain dust." Inside the Ministry of Arts conference room, the walls and furniture were all in shades of gray. Anjali glanced down at the table. A metal tag was affixed, "Property of U.S. Government." Spoils of war?

Anjali smiled gently at both men the way she used to soothe her sons when they were peevish. "I'm sure there's enough need to go around. In this first meeting, we're trying to define needs and discover resources. I'm delighted to know that both the French and the Americans are so supportive."

The Arts Society had been formed to assist the renaissance of Vietnamese arts now that the communist regime had relaxed controls on outside influences. Anjali had been drafted to serve as its founding president because of similar work she'd done in Indonesia. Her youthful interest in the arts had become a fulfilling avocation as she followed KB from post to post.

The Minister of Arts held up a lengthy document. "Exactly my point, Mme. Rao. We must define needs first. My staff has drawn up a list of what the Ministry requires We have made copies in Vietnamese, French and English."

Hanoi's most respected painter grew red in the face. "But we artists have not been consulted about our needs."

The director of the Hat Tuong troupe raised an elegant eyebrow. "That is so. We must all participate in defining our needs." She paused, and her smile had a rebar of steel behind it. "And in distributing the resources."

Now the Minister was red in the face. These artists would not have dared say such things only a year ago.

Anjali had the same concerns as the artists. For the project to be successful, the Society had to work with and through the Ministry, but the government must not be in control.

"May I suggest that we use the Ministry's thoughtful list as a departure point?" she said. "Perhaps we each could study it and see if we have other needs we wish to add. Then we could discuss it at the next meeting."

Everyone looked mollified except the president of the International Women's Group. The hefty British woman had been genteelly waving her hand for attention throughout the previous exchange. The seams of her short-sleeved silk suit appeared ready to burst. "Our interest is in costume design. We would like to establish a scholarship."

The local director of a French firm jumped in. "Societe´ B.N.L. has been in the construction business for decades. We would be pleased to renovate the Hat Tuong Theatre."

The Hat Tuong director bowed and smiled her courtly gratitude.

"That's only good business practice, isn't it?" said an American firm's local manager. "As a matter of fact, Bluebell Corporation has already drawn up a plan."

"Precipitous!" said the B.N.L. representative.

"Much too soon to draw up a plan without consultation," the Minister opined.

"Rash," agreed the French Embassy rep.

Anjali beamed at one and all. "Another document for our consideration. We'll take it under advisement."

That evening, Anjali sank into an armchair and put her legs up on the matching hassock. Her feet were always swollen at the end of the day. Must lose some weight, she lectured herself.

The houseman brought their before-dinner drinks and set the tray down on the coffee table. KB took a long swallow of his gin-and-tonic, then asked about Anjali's first Executive Committee meeting. It took her only a few minutes to convey the factions and their agendas.

"They're thinking about their need to make a splash and not what the artists need to be creative," she finished.

"I'm so proud of you, darling," KB said. "You'll make a success of this committee, just like you did in Jakarta."

Anjali hadn't missed the light of triumph in his eyes. "And what about you? Something good happen today?"

KB practically bounced in his chair. "I think we've finally solved our procurement problem. We've been trying for weeks to find a qualified Vietnamese to take charge of purchasing the things we buy on the local market. The Admin. Officer brought in a man for me to interview today, and I quite like him. Name's Tranh. We're giving him a three-month trial."

Anjali sipped her G&T. "You look thrilled to bits."

She met Tranh at a UNDP staff party some months later. He looked to be about fifty, hair starting to gray and lines appearing around eyes and mouth. Anjali knew that Vietnamese could be either older than they looked because of genetics or younger because of suffering during the war and its aftermath.

The small, thin man bowed slightly. "It is an honor to meet the wife of our esteemed Resident Representative. Allow me to offer my congratulations on the excellent efforts of the Vietnamese Arts Society."

Anjali was initially surprised that Tranh would know about the Society but then reflected that he was famous for being connected to everyone in Hanoi.

They chatted for a few minutes about the Society's struggle to find supplies.

Tranh said, "Perhaps I may be of assistance. My aunt was a

classical dancer in the old days…" His voice trailed off for a moment, and the barest hint of pain crossed his face. "I know something of the needs of Vietnamese artists. My work with UNDP has revealed many sources not always openly available."

Anjali was disconcerted by his last phrase. Tranh must have sensed it. "I do not mean to imply anything improper," he said. "Only that people are often reluctant to display what they have for fear the government may change its policies." He smiled, and a row of dingy metal teeth reflected the lamplight.

Anjali wondered if he'd been tortured. Wishing neither to pry nor to commit, she thanked him for his offer and said she'd think about it.

When she later mentioned Tranh's suggestion to KB, he said, "As long as he does it on his own time, I'm all for it. The man's amazing at finding things. He's basically working without supervision now. The Admin. Officer and I just have a monthly review with him."

Anjali accepted Tranh's assistance and was soon praised by all concerned for her decision. He was seemingly able to get anything— oil paints, gilt, brocade, cement, someone to copy broken theater seats, old black-and-white photos of traditional costumes. The committee voted to pay him a monthly honorarium.

Anjali sat on the auditorium dais of the Ministry of Arts, the dry smell of dust rising all around. The cleaners had only managed to stir everything up in preparation for the ceremony.

She smiled to herself. Only a few more weeks, and they'd be in New York. KB's outstanding performance had earned him an important post at Headquarters, and she could barely wait to sample the museums, theater and concerts.

The three years in Hanoi had been good for her also. Anjali had learned early in her international existence that life had meaning when she was productive. The Arts Society had provided the perfect opportunity. She thought back over the Society's accomplishments. She owed a lot of today's honor to Tranh.

She shifted in her hard chair and smoothed her sari. The Minister of Arts was winding down his speech. "And now, if Mme. Rao will step forward…"

Anjali rose and glanced at KB. His face was lit with joy.

The Minister smiled. "It is my great privilege to bestow our highest medal for foreigners on Mme. Rao in recognition of all that she has done for Vietnamese arts."

Anjali bowed her head, and the Minister slipped the multi-colored ribbon and enameled gold medal around her neck. "The Order of the Friends of Vietnam."

The entire auditorium rose to its feet and applauded. It was unusual for the communist governments of Southeast Asia to bestow such medals. Anjali looked down at the Society's fractious Executive Committee all cheering with one voice. Tears threatened, and she blinked hard to keep her composure.

Anjali waded through a sea of boxes, some sealed, others partially filled, a few still gaping open and empty. She was supervising the packing for their departure to New York. The furniture belonged to UNDP and would remain, but she'd collected arts and crafts from all the countries in which they'd lived. After twenty-five years, it was a lot to pack up.

She tried to figure out how many times she'd gone through this. It had been a lifetime of packing and moving and unpacking.

She curbed the sense of being overwhelmed. It always looked like they'd never have everything ready by the departure deadline, but they always did. No wonder experts said moving was second only to losing a spouse in terms of stress.

She heard the gate open and KB's car arrive. The long tropical lunch break made it possible for him to come home unless he had a meeting during the meal.

Anjali stepped out under the portico as KB exited the car, his face creased around eyes and mouth. He looked like he needed a little tender care.

"What's the matter?" she asked once they'd got inside.

"Oh, the usual," he snorted. "The auditors are out from New York, nitpicking us to death about adhering to regulations. Damned bean-counters have never worked in a developing country in their lives. They haven't a clue how to get things done in the Third World."

He stomped off to wash his face and hands, then joined Anjali in the dining room, still talking as if he'd never been away.

"They want to know why we used petty cash to buy pushpins. Pushpins, by God! We spend millions to put in safe village water supplies, and they're focusing on pushpins!"

He speared a forkful of vegetable curry. His favorite, but he didn't seem to notice what was on his plate. "Want to know where Tranh got the Xerox toner and why he didn't go through proper channels. Proper channels! If he had, we'd have been out of toner for months. Imbeciles!"

"Tranh?" Anjali asked. "They're concerned about Tranh?"

"They're all over his office. All heated up because he didn't follow standard procurement procedures" KB's face filled with contempt. "I'd like to see them find enough petrol to keep the vehicles running with their proper procurement procedures." He reached for the pitcher of water and poured some into his glass.

Anjali felt something small and cold in her stomach. "Has Tranh done anything wrong?"

He slammed down the pitcher with such force that water slopped out on the table. "Of course not. He just didn't always follow their damned New York manual. Everything's been on the up-and-up. Not even a whiff of corruption. He knows how to get things done here, that's all. We had the same sort of chap in Jakarta. But he was better at filling out forms, so the bean-counters were happy."

Anjali let KB go on for a while. After he'd vented his exasperation, she'd help him calm down and think about how to handle this latest tempest.

Lunch over, she watched his car drive away and placed her hand on her stomach. The small, cold feeling was still there. Tranh had used all his contacts to help the Arts Society too.

Three days before they were to leave, KB didn't come home for lunch. His secretary called to say he'd been detained meeting with the HQ officer in charge of Southeast Asia.

Anjali felt the small, cold feeling creep back into her stomach. Why had Headquarters sent this official out now? She hadn't known he was coming. It was all highly unusual.

She tried to keep busy packing suitcases. Most of their effects had already been removed from the house. All that remained were the things they'd take with them—clothes, toiletries, some reading material, her jewelry.

The bad feeling swelled as Anjali sat waiting for KB to return that evening. It grew dark outside, and the houseman padded through, clicking on lamps. But still KB didn't appear. The cook came to the door with a question on her face.

"We'll wait a bit longer," Anjali said. "I'm sure Monsieur Rao will be home soon."

Finally, after nine o'clock, she heard the gate. The outside lights were on, and Anjali could see KB's profile in the back of the official car. The man who had always maintained the upright, athletic posture of his youth was slumped back against the cushioned seat.

She went outside as the chauffeur opened the rear door of the car. KB sat there for a moment, then emerged, his face ashen. She looked into his eyes, trying to convey that no matter what was wrong, they'd weather it together.

They walked into the house. "We've kept dinner for you," she said.

"I'm not hungry, darling. Do you mind?"

"No, of course not. I'll tell cook to put it in the fridge for later."

Anjali returned from the kitchen to find KB sitting on the edge of their bed. His hands hung limply between his knees.

"What is it? What's happened? Are you all right?"

He stared down at his hands. "I'm trying to find the strength to tell you."

She knelt before him and took his hands in hers. "We'll be strong together. Tell me."

KB looked up, his face sagging with angst. "Tranh's been fired."

Is that all? Anjali thought and felt a smile beginning.

"The auditors discovered he's been taking kickbacks from the suppliers."

Anjali's heart jumped as she recalled how Tranh had recently replaced his gray metal teeth with gold ones. He'd been so proud of his new smile.

The feeling in her stomach grew colder. She sank back on her heels. "How big a kickback?"

"Not much, about a penny on a dollar. UNDP can't tolerate kickbacks. We all know that."

"Oh dear," she said with understanding. Tranh was the sole support of a huge extended family. Then another thought struck her. "What about the Arts Society? Was Tranh taking kickbacks there also?"

KB looked exhausted. "I don't know. Probably."

"Will UNDP press charges?"

"No, the amounts are too small, and they don't want the bad publicity." KB's face drowned in guilt. "Oh, Anjali, I'm so sorry I got us into this mess."

She moved to sit beside him. "You didn't get us into this mess. You did what you thought was right. So did I. You didn't force me to accept Tranh's help. Besides, it's not such a mess."

KB turned to look at her, his face filled with remorse. "I'm afraid it is." He took a deep breath and blew it out. "We're not going to New York."

Anjali felt as if something huge and heavy had slammed into her midriff. She gulped air, and it stormed into her stomach. But her physical distress couldn't match her emotional pain. "Not going to New York?"

"Going to Vientiane instead."

She felt her face fall and saw him see how disastrous it was for her.

"To Vientiane? To do what?"

"To be Res Rep. It's a much smaller post, a kind of probation. If I can redeem myself, we'll be back on track."

Anjali's eyes flicked back and forth, following her wildly careening thoughts. Not New York. Back to a small post. One of the least developed countries in the world. Everyone will know. She couldn't bear it.

Now it was KB's turn to offer comfort. "Look on the bright side, darling. It could have been worse. At my age, they could have given me early retirement."

Anjali shook her head to clear it of negative thoughts. Now was when they'd see what they were made of.

She smiled at KB and took both his hands. "You're too young to retire. And you didn't make such a terrible mistake. They know that. That's why they're giving you another chance. We'll go to Vientiane and do our best. It won't be long before you'll prove once again how terrific you are."

Anxiety fled KB's face, and he pulled Anjali into his arms. His whisper ruffled the parting of her hair. "I can do anything with you beside me."

"Of course I am, darling," she murmured against his chest.

Anjali breathed in his relief and hid her thoughts. She'd have to keep a low profile in Vientiane. No projects for her. Just be the perfect Res Rep wife until they got through it.

Then she rose and finished her packing.

The morning after her mirror-dream, Anjali was still haunted by its scenes. How pathetic, she thought, Sophia so careless, so needy of recognition.

She sat up and looked out the window. It had rained during the night, and water droplets glistened on every leaf and blossom. The sweet scent of the frangipani trees next door filled the room. Such an ugly tree, she mused, but its warty branches showcased luscious, creamy flowers.

The scent brought a revelation. Anjali needed to find out what had happened to Sophia. For her own sake, as well as the dead woman's.

She couldn't believe Cyril was right about Sophia being murdered. Still, the race to close the official investigation was troubling. Sophia had her faults, but she deserved better than being filed away in some dusty cabinet.

Anjali's thoughts turned to her own experiences in Vientiane. Her life out of balance. Ever the dutiful wife, with no project, no identity of her own. Too much Sita, not enough Devi.

For a moment she considered KB's situation and her resolution to keep a quiet profile after Hanoi. She decided it wouldn't hurt to ask a few questions here and there. It would only be natural. Everyone would be wondering what had happened. She could keep it low key. Not even Cyril had to know. In fact, she realized, she didn't want Cyril to know.

That evening, Anjali was dressing to go to a reception. She and KB went to at least three such events a week, sometimes diplomatic, sometimes not. This one was in honor of visiting brass from CARE. With KB up-country, she had to go alone.

As she brushed her hair and twisted it into a simple bun at the nape of her neck, she recalled Sophia's similar hairdo at the first rehearsal of the Vientiane Follies. Sophia was always changing her coiffure, a different style for every occasion and always perfectly done. But that night, it had been disheveled, escaping from the elaborately woven chignon. So uncharacteristic of Sophia to be untidy.

Anjali sat in the front row, waiting to recite the poem Sophia had written for her. She'd arrived in time to see the act before hers, a trio of expatriate wives singing "Three Little Maids from Laos Are We," based on the famous song from *The Mikado*. The adaptation was cleverly done, and for a first rehearsal the women performed well. They had the song down pat, and their voices blended nicely. But they got the stage directions wrong and bumped into each other at the end. The three women stood there, giggling and shifting from foot to foot.

Early days yet, Anjali thought. These things always happened at first rehearsal.

Sophia dashed screaming from the back of the hall. "No, no! Can't you get anything right? You move just like you play tennis. Don't you know your left from your right?"

The giggling stopped, and bright magenta ascended from neck to hairline on each of the offenders. They reached out to touch one another.

Anjali caught Sophia by the wrist as she charged by and said for her ears only, "Easy now. It's the first rehearsal. Give them a chance. They'll get it right next time."

Sophia looked down at Anjali, her eyes wild. She let out an explosion of air, then got hold of herself, literally wrapping her arms around her body. "Yes, you're right. Of course."

Sophia looked up at the women and raised her voice, her anger under tight control. "Anjali's on next. Clear the stage, please."

The three women seemed to look down at Sophia for apology or explanation, but she retreated to her director's chair without uttering another word.

Anjali climbed the stage steps thinking how Sophia's behavior was excessive. There had to be more to it than mixing up stage directions.

Anjali finished her coiffure for the CARE reception and fastened a beaded gold ornament in her hair. She wiped the haze of mildew from her heeled sandals and slipped into them.

Was something wrong in Sophia's life, she wondered, something yet to be discovered?

Twenty minutes later, Thongsy pulled under the CARE Rep's portico. Anjali descended into a cloud of mosquitoes and hurried inside. She walked through the receiving line, murmuring all the expected things, "How do you do? A pleasure .... So kind of you...."

By the time she'd finished, her hand was sweaty from being repeatedly clasped, and her throat was dry. She headed for the bar and an orange juice. She always drank "soft" at official events.

The sweetly acid taste rolled across her tongue. Anjali felt a twinge of hypocrisy about preferring to commit her sins in private. India's Hindu and Moslem religions forbade the consumption of alcohol, but her parents had had a G&T on the veranda every evening before dinner, talking over the day's events. Now she and KB did the same. It was their special time together, and she cherished it.

Anjali sighed. At official functions, she represented not only UNDP but also India. Whether we like it or not, people judge our compatriots by what they see in us. She didn't want people to think that all Indians were slack about religion.

Time to mingle, she resolved, and took another sip. This was the perfect opportunity to start her investigation. She surveyed the crowd, trying to decide which group to join.

A knot of Aussies stood together, their harsh vowels rising above the din. "You hear the latest about Champassak?" said a woman with over-permed and -peroxided hair.

"You mean the dig at Wat Phou?" asked the brunette in the ultra-short skirt and ultra-high heels.

"Is that the temple that's almost as important as Angkor Wat?" asked the young man with "New Arrival" stamped all over his face.

"Right." The blond lowered her head and glanced around, then spoke out of the corner of her mouth. "No one's supposed to know, but it looks like they found something really big."

"They better box it up then," said the brunette. "Before somebody else gets to it."

Interesting stuff, Anjali thought, but nothing to do with Sophia. The flat sounds of a Canadian voice caught Anjali's ear. "Oh, God, not more fermented fish sauce."

Anjali couldn't see the speakers, but she couldn't miss the British response. "Absolutely revolting. However do they eat it?"

Anjali gulped her orange juice. Nothing there either.

Two young Americans walked by, a junior officer from the Embassy and a computer specialist for one of the USAID projects. They were wearing shirts tailored like short-sleeved jackets outside their dress trousers, the usual attire for Western men at formal occasions. In their crewcuts and shirt-jacs, they were almost twins.

"So they're up-country at some drug interdiction roadblock," said crewcut number one. "The Congressman's shouting, 'Take the picture! Take the picture!' But the film's jammed, and the official photographer is literally sweating his job. Then a bird flies over and drops a load on the Congressman's head. Just as the camera goes click. 'Gimme that goddam camera,' the Congressman shouts and throws the whole thing in the river."

"Your tax dollars at work," said crewcut number two.

Anjali sighed. All this was the usual gossip. She edged further through the crowd and heard Sophia's name. Now maybe she'd learn something. She paused near three women clustered around a bowl of nuts.

"Don't tell me she just fell in," said the skinny redhead, her sludge-green dress sagging in the humidity. "That woman was too fit to fall in the Mekong."

"Yes, but what if she had too much to drink?" asked the short one in the silk trouser suit.

The redhead smirked, "That wouldn't be unusual for our Sophia, would it?"

Anjali realized she hadn't thought of that and remembered Sophia downing her last glass of wine in one go. If Sophia had been so drunk that she fell in the river, it would certainly have been a scandal worth hushing up. Anjali lingered to hear what else the women might say. She was close enough to smell their overworked designer deodorant.

The third woman wailed. "What will become of WIVS now?" Her chunky body swelled with distress and her wide blue eyes opened even wider. "Even when she wasn't chairing a committee, she was still the leader."

The redhead took a handful of nuts, ignoring the spoon meant to prevent contamination from dipping fingers. "Oh, it'll lumber along. Someone else'll want the glory. You'll see."

"I always felt sorry for her," said wide eyes.

"You must be joking," countered the redhead. "That woman never wanted for anything. If she saw something she liked, she took it."

"Like Jean-Claude, for instance?" put in the trouser suit.

"Shame on you!" said wide eyes. "She's not even in her grave."

The redhead raised an eyebrow. "No doubt some'll be glad to see her there."

Wide eyes almost choked on her drink. "You don't think she was murdered, do you?"

The redhead raised both brows. "Who knows? I can think of a few who might have considered it..."

"Who?" gushed the trouser suit.

"Karen...Jackie...Philip. And how about a jealous husband?"

"Shhh," whispered the trouser suit. "Here comes Jackie."

So, Anjali reflected, Cyril wasn't the only one who thought Sophia might have been murdered. Several suspects. She wrinkled her nose. But this was all just gossip. She needed facts. She began to work her way across the room.

A tall woman with glasses moved a grudging inch as Anjali tried to slip by. "Suicide? You're joking. She had too much to live for."

Her short companion was more compassionate. "Everyone has a dark side. Even Sophia. I think she kept herself busy to avoid some sadness we never knew about."

Anjali raised her eyes toward the ceiling. Everyone has a pet theory, she realized, but she needed more than that. She looked around the room. Who might really know something?

Anjali felt a tap on her shoulder and turned to see Raj. His sensuous lips smiled. "I could see you needed another." Suneeta's husband took Anjali's empty glass and handed her a second orange juice. "Suneeta's tied up with the Minister for Women's Affairs."

Anjali followed his glance at his wife, standing with a tiny Lao woman in an elaborately brocaded *pa-sin*.

"We're trying to start a joint venture for hand-woven silk, and Suneeta's much better at that sort of thing than I am."

Seeing Suneeta with the Minister reminded Anjali of their first and only real fight. It had happened in Botswana over a similar event.

Suneeta had been chatting up a junior minister at a diplomatic reception, promoting the benefits of importing Indian goods. Later in the evening, she came bubbling over to Anjali, "I've got him! He agreed to speak to his minister about importing Indian cloth."

Anjali was troubled by Suneeta's coup. "To whose benefit?"

Suneeta's sunny smile flipped to frost. "Why both, of course."

"More to India's it seems to me. Botswana needs to build up her own manufacturing."

"But Anjali, you're Indian," Suneeta protested.

"And you're talking from Raj's point of view."

Suneeta looked around at the faces beginning to be attracted by their exchange. "I'm my own woman," she hissed.

"So am I," Anjali hissed back.

They parted before the interested faces could be drawn further in.

Anjali lay awake that night, acutely uncomfortable with the tension that had arisen between them.

Next day, Suneeta arrived unannounced. There were dark circles under her eyes. Anjali warily invited her in and asked the cook to bring tea.

Suneeta didn't even wait for the tea. As soon as she sat down, she blurted, "I feel awful about last night. Maybe our husbands are playing on different teams, but that's no reason for us to be at loggerheads."

Anjali thought about the other expatriate women in Gabarone, how they seemed to devour each other, and smiled at Suneeta. "Yes, let's be friends."

Suneeta grinned back. "The best of friends."

Anjali's attention was returned to the CARE reception by Raj's bright smile. She needed information about Sophia, but Raj barely knew her. Still, it was always a pleasure to talk with her old friend.

Raj's dark eyes shined down at her. "Where's KB? Still alone?"

As they chatted, Anjali became aware that several sets of eyes had veered their way. Raj still looked like a Bollywood star, even if he had put on some weight. His face had filled out since Botswana, but he was thickset rather than fat. His fine aquiline nose set off a full-lipped mouth. Classical Hindu sculptures had such features, Anjali mused.

Tonight, he was dressed in white *churidar kemiz*, his shapely calves accentuated by the slim cut of the traditional trousers. A raw silk vest with a collar in the Indian style was buttoned over the long tunic. Like his hero Nehru, Raj had his usual rosebud in a buttonhole. The whole effect was devastating. A mutual friend had once described Raj as a faithful ladies' man, and the depiction suited him perfectly. Raj loved women and showed it. But Anjali had never had any doubt of his commitment to Suneeta.

That didn't mean others wouldn't be suspicious. Someone was bound to make something of this. KB gone, and she was talking too long with Raj. What a pain. She gave her empty glass to a passing waiter and made a bland excuse to Raj. She felt suffocated in the crowded room and went out on the terrace for some fresh air. Only to be greeted by the whine of mosquitoes.

Moira was leaning against the railing. "Oppressive, isn't it? All the gossip about Sophia."

Anjali brushed the insect-hum away from her face. "Lots of people full of things to say."

"Odd. I never really knew her. I'm not sure anyone did."

"Maybe no one knew her, but everyone's got an opinion about her."

"You know what they say where I come from—opinions are like behinds. Everybody's got one."

The remark was typical of Moira, earthy and direct. But her next comment brought Anjali's senses to full alert.

"There *is* something about Sophia's death that puzzles me, though. It's not an opinion. It's not gossip. It's a fact. About where they think she went into the Mekong."

Other guests came out onto the terrace, and Moira lowered her voice. "I don't want to talk about it here. Let's not fuel the gossip. Can you come for lunch tomorrow? Sean's out of town for a couple days, and the kids are eating with school friends. It'll be just the two of us."

Finally, Anjali thought, somebody with something meaningful to say. She realized she'd never have considered talking with Moira about Sophia's death. Asking a few questions was going to be harder than she thought.

The two women agreed on a lunch time and drifted back inside.

Cyril bustled over. "There you are, Anjali. I've been looking all over for you. Have you made a decision about what we discussed yesterday?"

Anjali was caught off guard. "Ah, well…I've been thinking about what happened to Sophia. We all have."

Cyril leaned closer. The smell of whiskey enveloped her. "So you'll do it?"

Anjali felt crowded physically and mentally. "No, I didn't say that."

Cyril's eyes turned crafty. "But you're intrigued, aren't you?"

"Well…yes."

"I just know you'll do it once you really think it through."

Anjali wondered why he was looking so triumphant. For a moment she was back in her family's Bombay garden watching her brothers play cricket. Ashok had looked just like Cyril when he'd bamboozled the more sober Vikram into hitting the ball that broke their mother's prized urn.

Something jabbed her arm. A mosquito had hitchhiked inside. Her last bite, Anjali thought and smacked her a good one.

"Of course I'll think about it, Cyril." She spoke more curtly than she meant to, but it got rid of him.

Anjali escaped to the buffet table and filled a small plate with local and imported delicacies. Everyone made a dinner of these receptions. Who wanted to eat twice in one evening? The pungent scent of spices mixed with fermented fish sauce rose from the table. She helped herself from a dish of vegetables and green chilis, then added a small pouch of sticky rice wrapped in banana leaf.

Burt was at the next platter, piling spring rolls on an overflowing plate. "Good evening, Anjali. Hot enough for you?"

"The food or the weather?"

"Both. And the conversation too. Who killed Sophia, that's the hot topic for the evening."

Anjali felt her hopes rise. Maybe the businessman knew something.

The two crewcuts crowded up. Anjali and Burt moved away from the table.

"Truth to tell," Burt said, "I never could see why everyone was so enthralled with her."

"No?" she said to encourage him to say more.

"I guess she just wasn't that important to my view of things here," he said. "Oh, she was flamboyant and highly visible. But she wasn't really where it was happening. It's the big guys who make a difference in Laos—World Bank, U.N., companies doing business. Sophia and her WIVS were pretty small potatoes, if you ask me."

Just more opinions, Anjali realized with a sinking heart. Might as well change the subject. She took a walnut-sized lump of sticky rice and rolled it into a ball with her fingers, as the Lao did. The glutinous pearls of short-grained rice absorbed some of the vegetables' spicy fire.

Burt tried the same thing, but he scooped too much out of the banana leaf and then couldn't fit it into his mouth. Easier for me, she observed. Westerners were handicapped in Asia by having grown up with forks and spoons.

"I'm looking forward to your dinner party, Burt."

"Right! KB coming?"

"I'm afraid he'll still be up-country."

"No matter, we'll be even numbers. See you Saturday. Don't dress up. It's much too hot, even with the a.c. on full blast."

Anjali finished her plate and gazed around the room. Across the crowd, she saw Philip looking so haggard and beaten she was immediately drawn to him. He'd recently come back from home leave, his wife and children remaining behind. Probably not that long until his tour of duty was over, so his wife was no doubt getting the household running and the kids started in school. Was Philip missing them that much? What a change from when they'd been together at the NGO picnic a while back.

KB and Anjali had been invited because UNDP had joint projects with some of the non-governmental organizations. Philip and his wife, Frieda, were missionaries. Their pacifist sect had come to Laos with a bomb-disposal project right after the war. Whether because of his religion or his natural disposition, Philip was unfailingly gentle and kind.

At the picnic, a Lao child had fallen and scraped his knee. The small boy tried mightily not to cry in public. Philip scooped up the child and tickled him with his beard. Lao men have little facial hair, and the boy was fascinated. He laughed shyly and twisted his fingers into the long, russet beard. Philip winced as the little fingers pulled, but he gently disentangled them, tossed the boy into the air and sent him back to play with the other children.

Anjali had a strong memory of the white smile lines radiating through the tan around Philip's eyes that day. Now his eyes were sunken above cheeks devoid of color.

"Philip, are you all right?"

"As well as can be expected, thanks." He looked like he was about to have a panic attack. "Why can't they shut up? I don't want to hear about Sophia! After all she did to Frieda, I never wanted to see her again. Well, I got my wish, and that phase of our lives is over, thank God."

Anjali was taken aback. Then she remembered the redhead had mentioned Philip as a suspect. And that Philip's wife had returned to the States early, something about her health.

He looked into Anjali's face with a haunted expression, turned and walked out the door.

Anjali felt chilled. Suddenly, she wanted to go home. She made the rounds and said goodbye, not even pausing for the desserts arriving from the kitchen.

On the way, Thongsy drove past the spot where Sophia's body had been found. Anjali looked out the window toward the Mekong and saw the Lao who drove for Sophia's husband running off into the shadows. She asked Thongsy to pull over.

"Wait here," she said and got out of the car. She stepped over the curb onto ground spongy from the monsoon. Mud seeped over the tips of her sandals and between her toes. It was only two meters to the Mekong's edge. She went to the spot where she'd first seen Tom's driver and peered over the bank.

A single white lotus with a lighted candle was floating away in a boat made from a folded banana leaf held together with pierced twigs.

Anjali stood in the river's breeze, a faint muddy smell blending with the stronger, sweeter jasmine. Overhead, tree branches stirred, and a bird softly protested his disturbed sleep. Far away, a bamboo flute seemed to answer the bird's call.

Her feet felt cold in the oozing mud. What was she getting herself into?

She shifted from one foot to the other, recalling what Mummy-ji had said years ago when her youngest daughter had asked why she was always playing bridge. "To keep my mind alive, darling." Anjali had consciously refused to learn the game, but perhaps that explained why so many expatriate wives, Suneeta included, were devoted to playing.

Maybe she was starting something more difficult than she'd realized when she decided to look into Sophia's death for both their sakes. Certainly tonight's reception had revealed more paths to follow than she'd appreciated. And Philip's behavior was disconcerting. He'd been so full of pain. Now this—why was Tom's driver running off into the night? Did he launch the little boat into the Mekong?

She watched the candle float away and thought about her life. In the end, pursuing an investigation was a lot better than playing bridge. She nodded to herself and turned to go.

The cold mud gave way. Adrenalin soared through her body as she struggled to keep her balance. Her eyes took in the tumbling water and the pierced-leaf boat wallowing in the waves. Her heartbeat jumped to match her rapid breaths. Anjali had accepted that it might not be easy investigating how Sophia drowned. Could it also be dangerous?

The candle on the tiny boat winked out.

Anjali rose from her yoga the next morning feeling more mentally alert than she had for a long time. Yoga was a tool for harnessing the powers of the mind, and she felt on the verge of important discoveries.

At breakfast she found the *Vientiane Voice* beside her plate. The six-page, tabloid-size paper was published weekly by WIVS, which used the profits to help finance their charities. They had a government permit, and printing was done at the official government facility. Had WIVS not agreed to these two stipulations, the *Voice* would never have seen the light of day.

Anjali always looked forward to the *Voice*. It was much improved since Karen had taken over as editor—more professional in look and in writing. The paper focused on events in the expat community, but there were always a couple stories on Lao political and economic affairs. The *Voice* would have been shut down if the government thought the views expressed were not in alignment with party interests, so Karen was careful to report just the facts in such articles.

Today, of course, the front-page story was about Sophia's death. The official verdict was announced, followed by details of where the body was found, where her car had been left upstream and the forthcoming WIVS memorial service.

The mention of WIVS carried Anjali's mind back to Sophia's

goodbye party. She remembered the dead woman slumping against Catherine, and Sophia's best friend whispering something in her ear. What had she whispered? What did Catherine know?

After breakfast she phoned Catherine to commiserate. Then she maneuvered to get herself invited for tea a few days later, when Catherine would be feeling more herself.

Anjali skimmed the article again. Most of this she'd already heard from Cyril. But there were two facts he hadn't touched on—the body had been discovered by two Lao boys, and they had summoned the abbot of the nearby temple. Anjali cocked her head to the side. The two boys and the abbot would be key witnesses in an investigation. Why hadn't Cyril mentioned them?

Anjali decided to walk to Moira's house for lunch. It wasn't far, and she needed the exercise. She rounded the corner from her lane into the larger street and nearly ran into two elderly Lao ladies, their *pa-sins* long and dark, their thinning hair pulled up into high, severe buns. Anjali nodded, and just for a moment, their eyes widened in surprise. In Vientiane, most foreigners drove everywhere.

Need to walk more and eat less, Anjali resolved. She passed a sugar-cane vendor, and the sticky-sweet smell caressed her. Anjali's hand crept up to her waistline. Too many desserts, she thought, too much chocolate. She always craved sugar when facing life's challenges.

Bicycle brakes screeched behind her. Anjali whirled to see Moira dismounting, her black and silver ringlets blowing in the breeze. The Lao were getting their fill of strange foreigners today, Anjali thought, one on foot and one on a bike.

Moira's blue eyes crinkled with mischief. "Ah here she is, en route to a lunch with no drinks. Not to worry, I've just been out to get some cold ones." She opened her bicycle basket to reveal bottles of Pepsi and lemon squash. "Gosh, I really prefer Coke, don't you? Too bad Pepsi got the country-wide contract. Must have made the Lao an offer they couldn't refuse. Oh, well, let's hurry home and drink them before they warm up."

Moira always spoke in long phrases without a break. Anjali often had to decipher where the punctuation would have been if she talked like other people.

Her hostess took Anjali's arm with one hand and precariously balanced the bike with the other. Her enthusiasm swept Anjali down a shady lane to Moira's house. It was a simple house in a simple garden. A battered jungle gym hovered over bare spots in the grass below. Anjali was mildly surprised to see a litter of puppies tumbling over their mongrel mother. Expatriates usually had cats. More portable for families moving from post to post. Anjali smiled to herself. Moira was always taking in strays, even pregnant ones.

Moira seated Anjali on a tattered wicker chair on the unscreened porch and went inside to fix the sodas. Anjali gazed fondly after her retreating back. Moira was one of the few truly good people she'd ever known. She was caring and thoughtful and full of humor. A spiritual person, a nurturer. No wonder she'd almost become a nun.

Moira returned with the drinks and curled her elfin body into another decaying chair. "Now, let's have a good natter about everything that's troubling us."

Anjali unconsciously sucked her lower lip between her teeth. Small talk wasn't for Moira. She always wanted to look into people's souls. She seemed to need that level of shared intimacy. "Tell me your secrets," she'd once said, and Anjali hadn't known what to answer because secrets aren't necessarily for sharing.

Moira smiled and her voice softened. "Last night, I could see you were troubled about Sophia. And I know I am."

Anjali sipped her lemon squash. Maybe this was the right time for sharing secrets, just not all of them. "I'm bothered by this speed to say it was an accident. How do they know it wasn't something else?"

Moira lifted her hair and offered her neck to the slight breeze. "I never felt I knew Sophia. I'm not sure anyone did. Was there ever anyone who kept herself such a secret?"

The sun was suddenly darkened by gathering clouds. Anjali looked up and saw a gecko making its slow, lizardy way across the porch ceiling. Down in the yard, a puppy yelped when the play got too rough.

"How can someone be gregarious and secretive at the same time?" she asked.

"I think Sophia used all that activity to mask who she really was. She didn't want us to know her. Remember the retreat at Wat Sokpaluang?"

Anjali cast her mind back to the huge complex, called a forest temple because it lay outside the ancient city ramparts. Now that the ramparts had nearly disappeared, it sat in the suburbs, surrounded by modern houses, with only a few trees remaining from the old forest.

She pictured Sokpaluang's yearly, week-long retreat—young men and boys coming from all over the country, their heads shaved, taking up bowls to beg food from the faithful every morning. Nearly all Lao males, she knew, served as monks at least once in their lives. For most of them, that period lasted only a few days Then they returned to school or work and everyday family affairs. But for some, it was the beginning of a lifetime dedicated to the Buddha.

Sokpaluang's retreats were open to the whole community. Last year, a group of expatriate women had attended the weekend event. Anjali had gone out of curiosity, but for Moira, with her unrealized religious vocation, it had had a metaphysical dimension.

"Yes, I remember,"Anjali said, "What about it?"

"Remember how we'd planned to stay the whole weekend, but most of the women had trouble following what was being said?"

Anjali smiled. Moira spoke Lao very well, despite the fact that it was a difficult, tonal language. But the majority of expatriates spoke Lao poorly, if at all. At the Sokpaluang retreat, most of the expat women had become bored after several hours of incomprehensible ceremonies.

"So we quietly slipped away Sunday morning and ended up by the Mekong watching the sunrise," Anjali said, wondering what all this had to do with Sophia's death. Did Moira suspect one of those women? Maybe Cyril was right after all.

"And opening our hearts to one another," Moira said. "We talked about really deep things—fears and hopes and dreams, men who'd let us down and churches that hadn't held us up. It was a time of great magic and sharing. It was one of the most spiritual experiences of my life."

Anjali remembered less about the shared secrets and more about watching the sky turn from ultramarine to rose and gold, then to bright blue. It had been very restful after hours of chants and clouds of incense.

"Remember how Sophia held herself absolutely aloof?" Moira asked.

Now that Moira mentioned it, Anjali did recall Sophia seeming embarrassed by the revelations. She remembered Moira asking something like, "Has it been that way for you, too, Sophia?" And then Pam had said, "I'm sure Sophia never has problems with *her* man."

Moira shifted in her dilapidated chair and leaned forward. "Sophia just sat there and said nothing. Her whole body was talking though. It spoke volumes about her misery at being part of something that was so…what? I don't even know what it was for her."

A monsoon squall struck the porch with a wall of water. The mongrel bitch and her pups scrambled for the garden shed. Over the din, Moira shouted, "Let's go inside so we can hear. Pathoumphone must have lunch nearly ready."

They slipped out of their sandals and entered the combination living-dining room on bare feet. Above, the gecko seemed to follow them inside. Moira's house was one of the newer ones in Vientiane, not as well built for climate as the old colonial structures It felt hotter inside, but there was a ceiling fan to stir the air.

Pathoumphone came out of the kitchen with a smile and the news that lunch was indeed ready. She was dressed in a *pa-sin*, but unlike a maid in a more formal household, hers was bright with colorful designs.

Anjali thought about how Western visitors were often amazed that expat families had at least one servant. But that wasn't a luxury. There were virtually no appliances in Vientiane. Those lacking the diplomatic privileges to import duty-free did without. Hands, not machines, did the household chores. Depending on income and station, a family might have many servants. Because Moira's husband worked for a non-profit organization, his salary allowed them only Pathoumphone, who served as cook, maid and babysitter all in one.

Anjali helped herself to *tom yam paa*, a fish soup with lemon grass and mushrooms. Too spicy for some expats, but she loved it. A big bowl with French bread was all she needed for lunch. She wanted to get Moira back on the topic of whom she suspected, but Anjali knew better than to rush it. Especially if she wanted to keep her investigation secret.

She remembered Moira's husband was in Champassak as part of the team working on the preservation of Wat Phou. "When's Sean coming back?"

"Not 'til next weekend. You probably heard they made a big discovery."

Anjali nodded, her mouth full of Pathoumphone's delicious soup. Through the kitchen's open door, she could hear the maid chopping the next course. So much for trying to lose weight, she thought. The Lao felt a guest hadn't truly dined unless she'd sampled many dishes.

Moira continued. "They also found someone's been pilfering artifacts from the temple."

Anjali clicked tongue against teeth. "That always happens. Someone stealing ancient art and selling it to disreputable dealers."

Moira nodded. "And God knows there's enough of them in Bangkok."

"But they can't take the really valuable things, can they?" Anjali asked. "I've seen the photos. Those stone carvings are enormous."

Moira put down her spoon. "I don't know. Sean can't say much about what's happened over the phone, but I know he's feeling pretty depressed."

Anjali thought about how the men were always bringing their problems home. The women tried to solve their own troubles without bothering their husbands.

"I think really Sophia was depressed," Moira said, making one of her typical flights of connection. "Staying busy with WIVS and all her projects. Traveling outside Laos whenever she could. Anything to fill up her life. A sure sign of depression."

"A lot of women get away as much as they can," Anjali countered. "Some wives even refuse to stay here."

"Yes, I know." Moira sounded a bit defensive. "Most of us don't have enough to do, so we reach out for anything to keep us occupied. But Sophia kept herself so busy, it was pathological. And she drank a lot, even by Vientiane standards."

"That can be a symptom of a lot of things," Anjali replied, feeling a little irritated. What had happened to Moira wanting to talk about where Sophia went into the Mekong?

"But it's often depression," Moira said. "Sophia tried to hide her pain, but I could see how troubled she was. Look how Tom treated her."

"Well, yes," Anjali conceded, "I've seen him give her a hard time now and then. When he thought she didn't know what she was talking about."

Moira said, "She should have divorced Tom and moved back to Ottawa. Then she could have been herself, eccentricities and all. It wasn't just Tom. Their son got caught smoking pot again. They're going to kick him out of that fancy academy down in Singapore."

Anjali took a sip of water. She was confused. Moira wasn't one to gossip like this. Or was it gossip? It would be just like Moira to marshal the facts as she saw them, bolstering her view of what had happened to Sophia.

"Every family has its problems," Anjali said. "Why would Sophia be brought so low by a little cannabis? Kids have been smoking it for years. She seemed too strong to let such small things get her down for long."

"Menopause," Moira said. "Messes up your ability to take the punches, makes you depressed half the time, magnifies the problems."

Revelation came at last. "Are you talking about your life or Sophia's?"

Moira's face fell. "Mine, I guess." She paused. "And Sophia's too."

Pathoumphone returned to clear the table, and Moira gazed out the window. Anjali could hear the birds singing again. The monsoon must have let up. The doors and windows were open, but wide eaves had protected the interior. The scent of Laos, at once bountiful and mouldering, filled the house.

Moira let out a sigh. "Now that Sophia's dead, I'm trying to make sense of my own life."

"We all are," Anjali said with a flash of self-recognition.

"I don't want to end up like that, with a life full of empty busyness. I look at all of us, and I see the same thing. We're all stunted somehow. Following our men and always making do, always coping. That's what we were taught."

Anjali recalled her grandmother admonishing her to be like Sita.

"I can't go on like this forever," Moira said. "I need to go in search of myself."

Her words hit Anjali like a jolt of electricity. Me too, she realized. She'd lost the girl she used to be.

"I'm going back to work, even if it's just for pin money," Moira said. "I don't want to end up like Sophia."

"You won't. You're too strong. Despite all her flamboyance, Sophia was really weak."

Anjali's thoughts drifted back to her own life. She'd let the trouble in Hanoi shake her self-confidence. Would finding out how Sophia died bring it back?

Moira said, "I think Sophia hated her life. She kept herself busy to fight depression. But she also kept herself aloof. She traveled a lonely path toward self-destruction, when she could have had friends to ease her pain."

Self-destruction? Anjali thought. What did Moira know that she didn't?

"Sophia drowning," Moira said, "it's tied into how she couldn't connect with other women."

Anjali felt her face move with skepticism. They weren't going to descend into the New Age, were they? Sophia wanted power and admiration, not buddies.

Moira rushed on, "Look at how formally she entertained. Artfully done but separating people instead of bringing them together."

Pathoumphone arrived with the results of her chopping—a flower made of thin papaya slices and ice cream. As usual with any dish made by a Lao, it was beautifully presented. Delicate slivers of bamboo leaf heightened the effect.

For a dessert without chocolate, it was awfully attractive, Anjali thought. And tasted as good as it looked. The papaya had been picked before it was fully ripe, and its tart flavor blended artfully with the homemade ice cream.

Moira said, "Sophia was especially separated from certain people. Like Karen and Frieda. On the face of it, Sophia and Karen should have been fast friends. They were a lot alike. Talented, energetic, cosmopolitan, well-traveled and well-read, devoted to theater and the performing arts." She shook her head. "But those two were separated by a wall as cold as ice."

Now we're getting somewhere, Anjali thought. She'd often noticed the tension between Karen and Sophia. It had always been there, even before the Folkloric fiasco.

"Karen and I are close," Moira continued. "In and out of each others' houses almost daily. I tried to get her to open up about the strain between them, but she wouldn't say a word."

The flicker of the gecko's tongue leaping out to snatch an insect caught Anjali's eye. How could she capture Karen for a talk? One in which Karen would open up and tell what had happened to create such estrangement. For now, if Moira couldn't add anything to what Anjali already knew about Karen, she might as well change the subject. "What about Frieda?"

"She's just the opposite of Karen. " Moira said. "Nothing in common with Sophia. The stereotypical missionary's wife, gentle and shy."

"How did she come to know Sophia then?"

"They sang in the Vientiane Chorus together. Apart from the Chorus, Frieda was terribly isolated. She had four small children to raise, and she helped Philip with project book-keeping in the afternoons while the kids napped. She was so busy she didn't have time for much else."

"How sad."

"I think she preferred a quiet life. But it looked to me like she was becoming too isolated for her own good. So I racked my brain for ways to get her out of the house."

So like Moira, Anjali thought, adopting strays. "And?" she said.

"Finally I thought of WIVS. Maybe Frieda couldn't get away to be really active, but perhaps she could go to the monthly Koffeeklatches, hear some interesting talks, interact with someone other than the two-year-old mind. Pathoumphone could babysit all our kids together."

As if the mention of her name were an incantation, Pathoumphone reappeared with iced coffee and condensed milk, a Lao staple in the heat and humidity.

Moira continued, "At first, Frieda seemed interested. We marked the date on our calendars. I called her the night before to confirm when I'd pick her up. But something happened when I said Sophia was hosting the Koffeeklatch that month. There was a long pause at the other end, and then Frieda said she didn't think she could go after all."

"Did she say why?"

"From the tone of her voice, it was clear I shouldn't ask."

Anjali's irritation flared. Had Moira brought her over here on a wild goose chase? What she had to tell was just a bunch of dead-end stories.

Moira paused as if considering her next words very carefully. Good manners took over, and Anjali waited patiently, looking out the open door. She could see the garden shining after the squall. The rain had turned the bare spots under the jungle gym into puddles reflecting the banana leaves above.

Moira nodded her head once with deliberate resolution and turned to face Anjali. "I've been thinking about where they believe Sophia went into the Mekong. Not where she was found, but where they discovered her car, upstream. It was left at the park where we all sat and talked after the Sokpaluang retreat. Do you think that's important? Should I tell the police? Or Tom?"

Anjali didn't know what to think. She hadn't made that

connection. But what, if anything, did it mean? "I don't know, Moira. Are you saying that someone from that morning might have killed Sophia?"

"I don't think anyone killed her. I can't imagine that anyone who was part of that spiritual conversation could have pushed Sophia into the Mekong. If that spot has meaning, it's that Sophia committed suicide."

Moira speeded up her argument. "She was depressed. She separated herself from other women. She didn't have any support. That park by the river had some meaning for her that we didn't realize. She went back there and sought solace in the only way she felt she had left."

Oh, no, Anjali almost groaned. They *were* descending into New Age psychobabble.

Moira leaned forward. "What do you think?"

Totally unbelievable, Anjali reacted. Sophia was too tough to let life get her that far down. But she couldn't be so rude to her hostess as to say it. "It's an interesting idea, but there's no proof either way. That place had meaning for you, but did it have meaning for Sophia?"

"Nobody believes the official verdict," Moira said. "We're all just waiting, holding our breaths. We need to know why Sophia died." She held up her hands in supplication. "You know how hard the international life is on wives. If Sophia committed suicide, what hope is there for the rest of us?"

Anjali shivered in the heat. "Yes, I feel it, too—this need to know what happened. But I'm not prepared to say it was suicide."

Moira's face fell.

Coming here was a waste of time, Anjali reaffirmed. How could she salvage the rest of the day? Her mind returned to the *Vientiane*

Voice article and the two boys who'd found Sophia's body. Now *there* was a path worth pursuing.

Anjali hurried home through the afternoon's heat and humidity. She realized she was acting just like those Westerners she looked down on. Always in a rush, didn't know enough to slow down in the tropics. No wonder they were always complaining about the climate. But she had to get back to the house as soon as possible.

Once home, she barely stopped to wipe her face with a damp cloth before she started off again. Passing the dining room table, she saw the fruit basket Onhta replenished everyday. It reminded her of the gifts her grandmother had always brought to the Hindu temple in Bombay. Anjali scooped it up and hurried out to her elderly Deux Chevaux.

Like so many vehicles in Vientiane, the tiny 1930s-style coupe´ had been hidden away during the war. But when foreigners started returning after the Lao Government instituted an "Open Door" policy, it had come down off the blocks, received a new coat of wine-and-black paint and been sold for several times its original value.

Anjali blessed KB daily for insisting, shortly after they were married, that she learn to drive. She'd been reluctant to try, but she soon became the first woman in her family to pilot a car. Back home in Bombay, she'd always been driven by either Daddy-ji or the family chauffeur. Now, as the wife of Vientiane's ranking diplomat, she often had to submit to being driven when the situation demanded. But whenever she could, she dispensed with the chauffeur and got behind the wheel of her very own little chug-a-lug Deux Chevaux.

Kongkeo opened the gates to the walled compound, and Anjali nosed her car out into the quiet lane in front of her house. The tinkle of a bicycle bell warned her just in time, and she hit the brakes as a five-person family rolled by—father peddling, mother sidesaddle on the back with a baby on her lap, young son standing on projections from the rear wheel hub, younger son perched on the metal rod connecting seat and handlebar-column. They all smiled and bowed their heads as they went by.

They'd still be smiling, Anjali thought, if she'd hit them. Only in Laos did one find people so gentle that they apologized for an accident when it wasn't their fault.

Anjali pulled up to the curb beside the temple and saw a familiar car driving away. Had Cyril been to visit the abbot? Had he given up on her and decided to conduct his own investigation? She got out of the Deux Chevaux and picked up the fruit basket.

Unlike the ancient *wats* in the city center, this temple was relatively new and certainly insignificant. She didn't even know its name. She walked through a low concrete wall into a bare-earth compound, the ground swept completely clean of debris by novices.

The temple's modern buildings lacked the elegant grace of the traditional *wats*. Its clumsy concrete structures were painted in garish colors of screaming pink, bright blue and tomato red. Anjali sighed, thinking of the muted dark green and cinnabar of Wat Sisaket. Perhaps they'd forgotten how to make the old colors and had to use whatever they could find in the market.

To her right, under a pillared roof without walls, a group of novices sat on grass floor-mats. Their bodies were wrapped in saffron-colored cloth, one shoulder bare. Their minds seemed totally focused on the bent and wrinkled monk leading them in a chant. Not an eye turned toward her as she passed.

Anjali wasn't sure how to find the abbot, but she knew she had to speak with him. She wasn't even sure what the protocol was. She knew women mustn't touch monks, but the men weren't totally cloistered. She'd often seen Lao women talking with monks in *wat* compounds.

A young monk came out of a nearby building and approached. Anjali marshaled her meager supply of Lao and felt vexed with herself. She should have studied more. She wasn't fit to speak Lao except to buy a few things in the market.

The monk placed his palms together in the traditional *nop*. "How may I serve you, Madame?"

Anjali returned his *nop* and smiled. His English was perfect. She felt ashamed. Why should they be speaking her language in his country?

"I wish to talk with the abbot." Surely he would know how to contact the boys.

"May I know what it is about?"

Anjali hesitated, unsure how to respond. If she told the truth, would he send her away?

"I…want to consult him about a death."

"One moment please. I will see if he is available. In the meantime, may I suggest you rest in the shade of the *bodhi*?" He gestured toward a concrete bench under a young tree. Anjali thought she remembered that all Buddhist temples had such a tree, because the Buddha had received his enlightenment under a *bodhi*.

She sat down and looked up at the broad leaves of the fig-like tree with their elongated tips. She needed a kind of enlightenment also, she realized and wondered if she were likely to get it. The chanting novices and the soft breeze stirring the leaves helped ease her tension. She sat quietly and watched a beetle roll a ball of mud over the tree roots.

She hadn't long to wait. The monk returned and guided her to the main building, which housed the Buddha statue. Anjali removed her sandals and followed the monk into the incense-perfumed interior.

When her eyes had adjusted to the relative darkness, she saw an old man kneeling on the floor, his eyes closed, his face toward the Buddha. The statue was only partially covered in gold leaf, another sign of how new the temple was. In the ancient *wats*, the faithful had brought tiny leaves of gold for so many decades that the statues gleamed with a thick patina. This one was mostly black with splotches of gold here and there.

Anjali knew enough to sit down on the rush mat, her legs drawn to the side. A woman's head must not be higher than a monk's, and the soles of the feet must never face anyone. She placed the fruit basket in front of her.

She drew a long, sustained breath to compose herself for waiting. But there was no need. Almost as soon as Anjali assumed the correct posture, the abbot opened his eyes and turned to greet her with palms together.

She responded with her own *nop* and felt instantly humbled. She had never been in the presence of such spirituality. It seemed to flow from his enormous eyes and bathe her in tranquil beauty. His body, dressed in saffron identical to that of the novices, was so thin it seemed without substance. She could easily see the skull beneath his shaved scalp and the fragile bones under the parchment of his hands.

His face was what struck her most forcefully. It was full of suffering.

Anjali knew that the communist Pathet Lao had rounded up the monks and other members of the old regime and sent them to re-education camps. Unlike what had happened elsewhere in Southeast

Asia, the men and women in the camps had reportedly not been physically tortured. But there had been very strong efforts to erase all traces of previous beliefs and substitute faith in communism instead. The abbot's spiritual suffering suffused every line of his face. His features were also full of acceptance and serenity. It was a powerful combination.

The abbot waited politely.

Anjali lifted the fruit basket and put it down nearer the abbot. "Your holiness, I…I have come to seek your…I have come to ask you about the *farang* woman who was found in the Mekong."

Once again, Anjali felt chagrined. She hadn't been so tongue-tied since her first debate for the Lady Wallington School Team. She waited for the young monk to translate her question. She'd never sensed so strongly that she was intruding. She had no right to bring more of the world's suffering to this man.

The abbot smiled and replied, the monk translating. "This is a pointless quest, *Mae Ork*."

Anjali frowned at the use of the Lao term, and the abbot seemed to perceive her lack of understanding. He gestured for the monk to explain.

"*Mae Ork*," the monk said, "it is a term of respect for a woman outside the ordained community. 'Lay-mother'—that is the closest I can come in English."

Anjali smiled her appreciation, and the abbot continued with the monk translating. "It is a pointless quest. The woman is passing on to another life. It can do no good to investigate her death. Let her spirit rest."

But what about the spirits of the living? Anjali thought. We cannot rest.

She knew the answer. A Buddhist would counsel her to accept whatever life brought.

The abbot spoke to the monk, who said, "The abbot would like to give you his blessing."

Anjali's heart sank. She should have realized the abbot would never tell her what she wanted to know. He wasn't concerned with the things of this world.

Then she remembered how she used to be a fighter, like Devi. Maybe this was another dead end, but she had other avenues to explore.

She accepted the temporary setback and bowed her head over palms-together hands. The abbot began to chant a sutra. The words sounded familiar. He was chanting in Sanskrit, the ancient language of her own religion. The world was full of hidden connections, she realized. She just had to be open to them. And she felt truly blessed. She hadn't wasted her time in coming. She'd learned something after all.

The abbot stopped chanting. She looked up. He smiled and nodded.

The young monk escorted her back to the compound gate. She turned to thank him, and he hesitated for a moment. "Madame..." He paused again, emotions fighting to take control of his passive face. "Madame, there is something I feel I must tell you."

He shifted his weight and rubbed one bare foot against the other. Anjali smiled her encouragement.

"The woman who was found in the Mekong had bruises around her neck. Under her scarf, where it was caught in the tree root."

Anjali's stomach turned over. She didn't know what to make of this new information. Had someone strangled Sophia? If so, only a man would have that strength. On the other hand, Jackie was an unusually large woman…

Before she could speak, the monk whirled away, scurried over to the novices and joined the chanting. His haste was exactly opposite the placid exterior that Buddhists cultivated. Anjali knew better than to follow. She was suffocating in frustration, but she'd heard all she was going to hear.

She climbed into the Deux Chevaux, closed her eyes and sat quietly. She needed to think carefully. Jumping to conclusions was her weakness, but now, of all times, she mustn't succumb to that reflex. Those bruises could have been caused by Sophia's scarf catching on the tree and strangling her after she went into the river.

Need to pull back a bit, she told herself. Get some perspective. She'd learned long ago that her subconscious often showed her insights if she only gave it a chance. Her stomach began to calm, and she remembered that she'd planned to go to the market. The day's events had totally wiped out the fact that the larder was bare. Well, not really. Onhta did most of the shopping, but Anjali often picked up a few things when she felt like it. Welcoming the distraction, she started the car and headed for Talat Sao, the Morning Market.

Despite its name, Talat Sao was open all day. But it was best to go in the morning, when one was likely to find the freshest produce. Hoping everything wasn't completely picked over, Anjali parked in the concrete lot, then went to the trunk for her market basket and thick-soled, rubber flip-flops. She slipped out of her everyday sandals and put on the thongs. She was going to need them around back where the food stalls wallowed in the mud.

Anjali followed the concrete sidewalk around the white stucco walls of the new building. The Japanese had recently rebuilt Talat Sao after a fire had destroyed the old one. There'd been plans to erect another structure to house the food-sellers also, but it had never materialized. So all the foodstuffs were sold in makeshift stalls.

She rounded the corner and surveyed the squishy mud only inches below the displays of meat, fruit, and vegetables. The smell of rotting food rose from the ground where sellers had tossed spoiled items.

Good thing we grow our own salad, Anjali thought, remembering the old traveler's adage, "If you can cook it or peel it, you can eat it." That certainly wasn't true of the market's lettuce, which was probably swimming with parasites.

Her way was blocked by a man hawking live chickens strung from a pole by their tied-together legs. A prospective buyer pinched the birds' thighs until she found one to her liking. The chosen bird was unstrung from the pole and transferred to the purchaser's hand. Off it went, upside down, bound for neck-wringing, plucking and the pot.

Anjali slogged past stalls of salted and dried fish, the smell seeming to permeate everything. Next came the stench of the meat section, unidentifiable hunks suspended haphazardly, flies having a field day. It was nearly overpowering, especially to a vegetarian.

Lots easier to eat vege in India, she reflected. One problem in Laos was finding the variety of beans and lentils necessary to ensure proper protein in the diet. Another problem was the diplomatic life. It could be difficult refusing an ambassador's prized and praised main course, even if he should know better. But still, Laos was a relatively easy post in that regard. The vegetables were lush and varied, and she could eat eggs and imported milk products for protein.

A smile lightened Anjali's face when she arrived at the fruit and vegetable area. The produce was heaped in piles of red, yellow, orange and green. Their saturated colors glowed in the bright sunlight. Each seller called out to buy her wares—"the best in Vientiane!" The sharp tang of fresh cilantro and cistrusy lemon grass contrasted with the dusty smell of mounded rice. Giant flat baskets held either the long-grain variety for the platters of fluffy rice which accompanied virtually all Lao meals or the short-grain for the traditional sticky rice.

A young man passed by, pulled up his sleeve and displayed cheap watches with famous logos. Anjali shook her head and wagged a forefinger to show she wasn't interested. He gave her a bright smile and went on to the next mark.

She felt at home in Talat Sao. Some Europeans and Americans would only buy food at the few, small quasi-Western shops in Vientiane, where they could get imported, frozen meat and vegetables, as well as tinned goods. They were uncomfortable in the Morning Market. It was too strange to them. They were put off by the monsoon mud and dry-season dust. They were afraid of getting spoiled meat or contaminated vegetables. But for Anjali, Talat Sao was a scene out of her childhood. She loved the sights and sounds, especially now, when she didn't want to think about the bruises on Sophia's neck.

She got some bananas for breakfast and a pineapple for dessert, as well as eggs and the extremely long, thin green beans of Southeast Asia. Then she spied some wavy mushrooms, each about six inches across, and bought one to flavor the beans.

The sellers dumped Anjali's purchases directly into her wicker basket. Only small items like rice or peanuts were packaged after a sale at Talat Sao. Even those were usually just wrapped up in a cone of newspaper twisted on the spot. Most sellers had tissue-thin plastic bags for those who didn't bring their own carryalls. The plastic bags were always tearing, and Anjali had resolved long ago to bring her own basket.

She decided to wander back to the car through the new building. She entered the wide doorway and was in another world. The harsh light of florescent tubes distorted normal colors. Red bikes turned maroon. Yellow fabrics became pea-green. Everyone looked ghastly, despite the warm tones of their Asian skin.

The Japanese design for Talat Sao had been very orderly, but the Lao had built their stalls in a typically haphazard fashion. The labyrinth of aisles was a twisting web of cul-de-sacs ready to capture the inattentive wanderer.

This late in the day, there were few shoppers in the giant hall. Anjali meandered through narrow lanes between stalls of TV's, radios and giant portable cassette players, past aisles of Lao handicrafts and cheap, Western-style clothes imported from Thailand and Vietnam.

As she passed a cross-aisle, something in the corner of her eye made her turn. But when she got a full view of the corridor, all she saw were horizontal bamboo poles hung with the white silk scarves that Lao wore draped across one shoulder for religious ceremonies. The scarves were swaying as if something had disturbed them.

Anjali stopped to look at some silver earrings. Her niece's birthday was coming, and she loved intricate, dangling styles. But these were of very poor quality. Better to try Jackie's shop, Anjali decided and looked up.

Across the way, she thought she saw a face peering at her for a moment, but it disappeared as soon as she raised her head. The whole thing happened so quickly, she couldn't be sure if the face was Lao or *farang*.

She was beginning to feel uneasy and decided to give up her wandering. She turned down an aisle of refrigerators and headed for the door to the parking lot. The tall appliances were like the hedges of a maze. Anjali lost her bearings and wasn't sure which way to go. She turned left into a narrow side-aisle, but it was a blind alley of empty stalls. She felt trapped.

Anjali hurried to retrace her steps, turned the corner and literally ran into Cyril. Engulfed by the smell of his sweat, she looked up at his lanky frame.

She felt so small.

"Heh heh." Cyril's laugh was strangled, nervous. "I ah...I thought I saw someone following you. Wondered if you needed protection." His face looked wan in the florescent light.

Anjali didn't know whether to believe him or not. Had someone been following her? Or had it been Cyril? Quite a coincidence to see him twice in one day, especially when he'd normally be in his office. She felt distinctly uncomfortable.

She looked down the wide aisle and was relieved to see some Lao shoppers watching the two *farang*. She smiled and slipped to Cyril's other side, so she would remain in their sight. Anjali began to walk toward the shoppers, and Cyril kept pace. "This is the second time today we've been in the same spot," she said.

Cyril's eyebrows rose, and his chin went up a fraction.

"I saw you driving away from the temple just as I was arriving."

"Oh, that," he said. "Embassy business. Had to interview the abbot and monks who saw Sophia's body *in situ* as it were." His strangled heh-heh sounded again.

"Why were you there?" he asked too casually.

They turned down the central aisle. There were more shoppers here, and Anjali began to feel at ease. She saw the main entrance at the end of the corridor. Outside, sunlight bounced off the parked cars.

She looked up at Cyril and answered his question, "Why, doing what you asked me to, investigating how Sophia drowned."

His strained face tried to smile. "Oh, Anjali, I am glad." He paused. "I hope the abbot was more forthcoming with you than he was with me. Gave me a lot of religious gibberish for why he couldn't—wouldn't really—answer my questions." Cyril looked at Anjali expectantly.

Anjali looked at Cyril's long hands. Could the bruises around Sophia's neck have been caused by those fingers? Caution sprang up like a winged angel to warn her against telling all she knew. "The Abbot said the same thing to me. I think he genuinely believes we should let Sophia's spirit rest."

"Abbot one, expats zero." Cyril's voice seemed carefully flat, as if to betray nothing.

They were at the door. Anjali put out her hand to shake Cyril's, a clear sign of parting.

He took her small hand tightly in his skeletal grasp. Anjali tried not to wince as his face brightened. "Still lots of other leads, I'm sure. Follow the trail of the women's jealousy, that's the ticket." He started off with a long stride. "Must be getting back to the Embassy. Been gone too long as it is."

Anjali watched him go. If he'd come to Talat Sao to shop, why were his hands empty?

Unease accompanied Anjali back to her car. Had it been Cyril following her or someone else? Why was he behaving so oddly? What did he really want from her?

She opened the door on the passenger side and put her purchases on the seat. The creak of a car door nearby lead her to turn and see who it was. The car next to hers was the usual white Toyota sedan. Virtually every expatriate institution in Vientiane used them as official cars.

A Western man was bending over inside the back seat, his hands busy with plastic bags from the market. One of them had ripped, and he was trying to tie a knot in it. The man stood up. Anjali's eyes widened. It was Philip.

His russet beard parted in a smile when he saw her. He came around the car to take her hand. "Anjali, I'm glad to run into you. I want to apologize for my rudeness last night. Really inexcusable."

Once again Anjali found herself looking down at a man's hands. This time they were enormous, large-knuckled hams. Yes, she thought, Philip's hands could easily have choked the life from Sophia. She must talk with him, but how to ensure her safety if he was a murderer? My house, she decided. That would be safe with all the staff around.

And a social occasion would disarm him. Talat Sao had taught her a lesson about getting caught alone, even with someone she thought was a friend.

She pulled herself together and responded to his apology. "That's all right, Philip. It's a difficult time for all of us. Sophia's death has brought back a lot of sad memories."

Philip nodded, looking everywhere but into her eyes.

Anjali remembered his wife and children were in the States. "Have you heard from Frieda? Everything okay back home?"

"Everything's fine, thanks. They're living with her sister until I return next month."

"That's good. At least she's not alone."

"No, she's not alone."

"But you are." Anjali smiled to soften her observation. "Why don't you come to supper? KB's away, and I could do with some company."

He seemed surprised. "Kind of you, but not tonight. I have to spend the evening on the project accounts now that Frieda's not here to do them."

They talked back and forth until they coordinated their schedules and settled on Monday.

"We'll have a light meal on the veranda," Anjali said. So the nightwatchman could see. And Onhta would be in the kitchen. "How does that sound?"

"Sounds pretty good." Philip hesitated, as if he might say more. Then he shook his head and crossed his arms over his barrel chest. He seemed to be holding his breath, like he was keeping something bottled up inside.

"Six o'clock okay?" Anjali knew that Americans usually ate early, even in the tropics. She normally dined at eight, or even nine when it was really hot, but she wanted Philip to feel at ease, so she chose a time that might suit him.

Philip looked relieved that the conversation hadn't gone further. "See you then." He got in his car, gave Anjali a wave and drove off.

It seemed to Anjali he was ready to explode with whatever he was holding in. She had to find a way to encourage him to let that out, a way that was comfortable for him and safe for her.

That evening, after supper, Anjali sat out on the screened veranda to systematize her investigation. She smiled with contentment. She'd put away her organizational skills after what happened in Hanoi, but tonight they were going back to work. It was no good relying on chance. She had to start making things happen.

The night air was warm and humid, but the ceiling fan created a comfortable breeze. The house was fully air-conditioned with excellent, quiet installations in each room, but Anjali preferred fresh air and nature's sounds.

She opened the tablet of paper she'd brought from her desk. Traveller jumped on her lap and bumped the tablet with his head. Anjali was usually charmed when he sought attention, but tonight she was perturbed. She needed to concentrate. She settled for leaving him on her lap and balancing the tablet awkwardly above his back.

She decided to note everything she'd learned, even opinions she might be tempted to discount. And write all the questions that arose, questions for which she needed answers. First, she considered each of the possible ways Sophia could have drowned. The official verdict was accident, but almost everyone found that hard to believe. Moira was pushing for suicide, saying Sophia was depressed and had no one to turn to. But that was just her opinion. Cyril believed she had to have been murdered, and the young monk had reported bruises on her neck.

All right, Anjali thought, if Sophia had been murdered, who were the suspects? Reluctantly, she started to write the names and motives. It felt like betrayal to suspect her friends and neighbors, yet she had to admit it was also stimulating. She wasn't sure she liked the person she was becoming, but she had to continue. She owed it to Sophia. And to all the expatriate wives. And to herself. In her usual methodical way, she listed the suspects in alphabetical order.

Cyril seemed overly eager for her to investigate. He repeatedly tried to get her to focus on jealous women. Was he promoting an investigation to mask his own motive? What? Had he been sneaking around Talat Sao, following her? Even intimidating her?

Jackie and Sophia had had a falling-out over the tearoom connected with Jackie's craft shop. But what, exactly, had happened? Financial loss? That could be motive for a business woman operating on a narrow margin.

Jean-Claude had been mentioned at the reception. He'd displayed a hair-trigger temper more than once. He was said to be interested in the conquest, a love-em-and-leave-em type. Did they have an affair? Had Sophia's charm got to him? Was he a jealous lover? Upset that she was leaving Laos? Leaving him?

Karen and Sophia were always in conflict, disagreeing over everything. It was easy to see the disaffection between them. Was it just their personalities, or was there more to it? Had something happened to make Karen so mad she'd kill her nemesis? What?

Philip had uncharacteristically negative feelings about Sophia. Strong feelings. Moira reported Frieda refusing to go to Sophia's house. Why? What had Sophia done to her?

Tom and Sophia were not ideal mates. So different, it was hard to imagine how they'd got together in the first place. He belittled her, and she hen-pecked him. In public. If Sophia had had an affair with Jean-Claude, did Tom find out? Would he have reacted with rage?

Anjali reached down to massage Traveller's ears and thought about her tendency to jump to conclusions. "Quantum leaper," KB called her. She smiled. Her quantum leaps were usually right on target. Even if she did have to go back and find the logic so others could follow.

Traveller's raspy purr grew louder and louder. Anjali looked down at a cat in hopeless ecstasy and realized she couldn't let her feelings about triumphant leaps get the better of her. Sometimes her leaps were wrong, even very wrong. She couldn't afford to let that happen here. If a quantum leap led her to the murderer, she had to be sure that the facts would lead the authorities to the same conclusion.

Outside, a small creature squawked as it was caught by something larger. Traveller's ears flicked toward the sound, and his whole body went on alert.

Chasing after suspects could be dangerous, Anjali conceded, remembering how she'd felt in Talat Sao. She'd need to be careful about her safety. On the other hand, she couldn't very well get people to open up if she brought someone else along.

She realized she'd already hit on a strategy. The normal way for people to get together in Vientiane was over a meal, even just tea or coffee. That almost defined expatriate life here, at least as far as the women were concerned—a round of social events to fill the days and enliven the evenings.

She'd already invited Philip over, and she'd got Catherine to issue an invitation to her house. In fact, if Anjali thought about it, the reverse-invitation was probably best. People would feel more relaxed on their own ground or at a place of their own choosing. If they were comfortable, they'd be more likely to be forthcoming. And in expatriate Vientiane, with all its servants, she'd never be alone.

Traveller began to dance on her lap, his weight forward, his feet beating a silent tattoo. Anjali wasn't paying attention. She was still thinking through her scheme. KB was out of town, so there was a logic to her wanting company. That shouldn't be suspicious. She leaned back, pleased at her progress in developing a strategy.

The cat bounded from her lap onto the veranda ledge, ears cocked, tail twitching, a warning growl in his throat. Only the screen kept him from leaping into the garden.

Anjali got up and looked over his back, out into the night. She could see Vong, the watchman, moving around the perimeter of the compound. Vientiane was the safest post she'd ever lived in. There was petty thievery from time to time—a good reason to have someone like Vong visibly present during the dark hours. But there'd never been any crimes against people, at least not against expatriates. No one she knew had ever been harmed.

Anjali felt a chill. Would that change? Was she putting herself in danger?

Something rustled in the tall shrubbery outside. Vong struck with his club, then plunged into the leafy branches. He emerged with a writhing silhouette dangling from one hand. A rat.

Anjali put her strategy into action the next morning. She needed earrings for her niece's birthday. What better excuse to visit Jackie's shop? She timed it to coincide with Jackie's mid-morning break. She'd been invited to join her for coffee before. She was hoping to be invited again.

Anjali parked in front of the French colonial building Jackie had leased on Nam Phou Square. Heat shot off the pavement, and Anjali quickly stepped under the portico. Light from the Square's fountain bounced through the columns.

She opened the heavy wooden door, and Dari, the Lao manager, came forward. A young woman of quiet dignity, she always dressed in *pa-sin* and wore her hair in the traditional ingenue's bun high on the side of her head. Dari bowed slightly with a gracious *nop*. Her soft, breathy voice was also traditional for Lao women. "Zha-kee is busy now." She gestured toward the interior balcony where Jackie had her office. "May I help you, Mrs. Rao?"

Anjali looked around the shop with appreciation. It said a lot about Jackie—her artistic flair, her business acumen, her knowledge of Lao handicrafts. No other shop in Vientiane had such high-quality goods so artfully displayed. Bolts of hand-loomed silk cascaded over furniture of giant bamboo. Tall parasols of mulberry paper rose from ceramic pots filled with sand. Blue-and-white batik looped through the rafters.

Jackie Baxter had come from Australia in the mid-eighties with a UNDP project in small-enterprise development. By her own admission, she'd fallen in love with the Lao and their handicrafts. When the project was over, she'd stayed on, battling official disinterest and overbearing bureaucracy to start her own business.

Anjali went over to a glass case of jewelry, fancy buttons, frog closures and belts woven of thin wire. All were handcrafted of nearly pure silver, their intricate designs a testament to the skill and patience of the fingers that had made them. She asked to look at earrings and stretched out taking a decision, hoping to see Jackie.

Dari patiently held up pair after pair, discussing the artisan who had made each one and the significance of the traditional designs. Most of the earrings were from villages far up-country and carried to the capital by Jackie herself.

Finally Anjali heard Jackie descending the stairs. Anjali pointed out the earrings she'd selected some time before, and Dari was wrapping them up when Jackie appeared. A large, handsome woman in her late thirties, Jackie had a delicacy about her movements.

She was decidedly feminine, Anjali thought, for all her size. And careful how she dressed. She always wore something simple with one, or maybe two, accessories from her shop. Such a contrast to Sophia. Jackie's image was artistic but not contrived, exactly like the woman herself.

Today, Jackie was wearing a simple beige dress made of old, soft hemp with a heavy silver necklace that must have come from one of the hill tribes. "Anjali, how glad I am to see you. You're just the excuse I need for finishing off that chocolate cake upstairs. Come on, say you'll do the dirty deed with me. I know you're as big a chocoholic as I am."

Anjali laughed. "How can I refuse? You know my weakness." Diet next week, she promised her conscience.

Climbing the stairs to Jackie's apartment over the shop, Anjali admonished herself to be careful. She had to sneak up on the topic of Sophia's death. She followed Jackie to the kitchen alcove, separated from the main room by a low wall.

Jackie filled an electric kettle and plugged it in. "Did you hear what happened in Champassak? A couple of my artisans came up from there yesterday. Someone's been poaching at Wat Phou."

"I heard that also but they won't get much. Those carvings are too big to move and too unique to sell."

Jackie cut the cake into two large pieces and put them on plates. "What if I told you they found a special cache—small things, including a gold statue?"

Anjali's face showed her surprised.

"That's what my guys say." Jackie spooned coffee grounds into a *café filtre* pot. "And they say there's a Thai smuggling ring involved."

"If that's true, it's serious," Anjali said. "Those rings have moved major items before. They've got overseas contacts and the resources to bribe a saint."

Jackie poured boiling water into the pot and put everything on a woven-reed tray. She motioned with her head toward the living area. "That's probably the best part of the story. My guys say the ring's bribed somebody important in Vientiane."

Anjali took a seat in one of the rattan chairs. "Do they know who?"

"Not a clue." Jackie put the tray down on a coffee table made from a metal drum and turned on the ceiling fan. "It's all gossip at this point." She handed Anjali her cake. "Speaking of which, what do you think happened to Sophia? Was it really an accident?"

For a moment, Anjali was caught off-guard. Surely it wasn't always going to be this easy to get the ball rolling.

"Difficult to say." She knew Jackie and Sophia had fallen out, but she needed details to judge if it was cause for murder. "What do you think?"

Jackie poured the coffee into mugs from the local kiln, their earth-tones gleaming in the light reflected from the square. "I think somebody pushed her into the Mekong. I know people are saying I could've killed her. God knows, she made me mad enough. But I'm not the only one with a motive."

Anjali wasn't going to let Jackie off that easily. "Weren't you partners in the shop?"

"No," Jackie said with more firmness than seemed necessary. "Sophia was never a partner in the gallery. She came along well after I'd established *From Laos, By Hand.* Sophia tried to get involved, but that's a long story."

Anjali smiled encouragement and took a bite of cake. Jackie may have thrown the hook in the water, she realized, but it was up to her to reel the Australian in. Slowly and carefully.

"I'm the one who took all the risk. Here and with the overseas markets," Jackie said. "Long before Sophia ever came on the scene."

She left her cake untouched and lit a cigarette. A passing breeze pulled the smoke out the open window. "I'm the one who fought to get travel permits so I could go up-country and find the old folks who knew how to make these things. And set up training programs so they could teach the young people. Organized it so the Lao could work out of their homes, so their traditional lifestyles wouldn't be destroyed."

"You've really made a success of it," Anjali said. And meant it. Jackie's vision, her hard years of work had paid off. For everyone.

Jackie relaxed a bit and stubbed out her cigarette without finishing it.

Anjali sipped her coffee. It was as rich as Jackie's cake. She must have brought both the chocolate and the coffee in from abroad. "What made you decide to open a…" Anjali consciously used Jackie's word "…gallery here?"

"I wanted to test the items' appeal before marketing them overseas. Nam Phou is the prefect location."

Now that she mentioned the Square, Anjali's attention was caught by its sounds coming through the window—the ubiquitous br-r-r-ring of bicycle bells, the screech of automobile brakes for yet another near-miss collision, the rev of motor scooters by young men seeking attention. Nam Phou was the closest thing Vientiane had to a town center.

"In no time at all, we were swamped with shoppers," Jackie said. "I plowed the income back into the business. Mostly to the artisans for materials, training and profit-sharing. We were doing okay, but there wasn't much money to spare, and we still had a long way to go."

Dari had come up the stairs and waited quietly for Jackie to finish speaking. Jackie went over to the shop manager, and they conferred in low tones. Anjali was struck by how their postures showed that Jackie treated Dari as a colleague and not as an underling. Dari went back downstairs, and Jackie continued her story.

"I soon realized I couldn't be in two places as once, so I hired Dari to manage local sales and paid for her English lessons. So we were off to a pretty good start. Even made some sales to upscale boutiques in London and Sydney."

"How did Sophia become involved?" Ugh, Anjali thought, not very subtle.

But big, bluff Jackie didn't seem to notice her directness. "Sophia was one of our earliest supporters once we got the gallery going. She bought a lot of things, especially hostess gifts for her travels. Then one day, she came by with a proposal."

Mimicking Sophia's overly cultured voice, Jackie said, "Why not have a tearoom, too?"

Jackie returned to her own persona. "On first hearing, the idea didn't exactly grab me."

The Aussie mimicked Sophia's next gambit. It was uncanny. The dead woman seemed to be in the room. Sophia's voice said, "I used to be a caterer, you know. I believe you ate some of my food at the last reception. Not too shabby, I think?"

Anjali had seen Jackie do this before, seemingly recite whole scenes from memory, playing all the parts. She was awfully good at it. Her recollections often tallied with Anjali's. But it wasn't the verisimilitude that was important to Jackie. She seemed to need these replays to make sense of life.

Some people turn events over in their minds, Anjali realized, Jackie acts them out.

Jackie became herself again. "Sophia had a full proposal for staff, food, tables and chairs, hand-lettered menus on our handmade paper—the works. Including a budget." Jackie shook her blond bob, green eyes wide with remembrance of her amazement. "I thanked Sophia for her proposal and said I'd think it over."

Anjali was feeling frustrated and tried to move things along. "So what persuaded you?"

"She came by several times to push her 'little idea' as she called it, and I could see that it had merit. I wouldn't have to take on any extra burdens. It would provide something that Vientiane needed, and it would be good marketing for the gallery."

"Sounds like a good idea for both of you." Anjali recalled her conversation with Moira about Sophia needing a healthy arena for her talents. A tearoom would have been just the thing.

Jackie said, "Sophia was here everyday from dawn 'til dark. She started pushing us to do all kinds of things—upgrading our displays, publicity to hotels and tour groups, gently aggressive salesmanship."

Anjali wondered how that had gone over with Dari. It was against Lao culture to be assertive, let alone aggressive. She started to ask but realized the question might get them off on another tangent. So she said, "Then how did things fall apart?"

"Wait, I'm coming to that." Jackie fired up another cigarette and took several quick puffs. "She nearly put me out of business."

Some might kill for that, Anjali allowed.

"I'd been up-country with the artisans," Jackie continued. "When I got back to Vientiane, I was exhausted. My whole body ached." She stretched her lower back as if she could still feel the pain. "Riding on rough roads, hunched up in small boats, hiking up mountain trails with a heavy pack. But it was worth it. Everyone was so proud of their work and their income."

Anjali could envision tall, athletic Jackie hiking with her laden backpack. She looked at the Aussie's hands. Strong and sinewy.

And she'd witnessed the pride Jackie spoke of when she accompanied KB to successful projects. It was wonderful what a sense of accomplishment could do for people who'd lost hope.

Then it swept over her, how much she missed KB. She needed to talk with him about what she was discovering. If only he didn't feel such a need to supervise everything directly. For a moment, she was lost in worry that things might not be going well with KB's visit to the troubled project.

Jackie's voice brought Anjali back from her own concerns. "Dari told me all about it. A buyer for a Swedish boutique had come by. Sophia showed him our pieces as if it was her business and took his order, promising delivery for the Christmas season. Then she boxed everything up and tried to ship it out. Without the proper documentation." Jackie's drag on her cigarette was like sucking in oxygen.

"Oh, no. You could've lost your export license."

"Dari tried to explain that we couldn't do rush orders, that the paperwork might take weeks. But Sophia had made a promise to the Swede, and by God, she was going to keep it. She carried the shipment to the freight terminal at the airport and tried to charm her way through."

Just like Sophia, Anjali thought, she'd always counted on her charm to get her way. When that didn't work, she'd blow up and try to intimidate people.

"Customs confiscated the entire shipment," Jackie continued. "Tore up everything looking for drugs or contraband. Sophia told them *From Laos, By Hand* was my enterprise, and she wasn't an employee. So Customs came by and told Dari they expected to see me immediately upon my return. They weren't gentle about it, either. But they let Sophia go."

"And when you got back?" Anjali prompted.

"I raced out there with all my hard-won documents to prove everything was modern manufacture. Not national treasures, not contraband. They were very suspicious. Why was a *farang* woman who wasn't even an employee trying to ship stuff out of the country? Why didn't she have the proper paperwork? It went on and on. They were shouting, threatening to close me down and kick me out."

"You must have been terrified," Anjali said. And furious with Sophia. Furious enough to kill?

Jackie smiled and an audible huff slipped between her lips. "That's too mild a word for it. I finally had the good sense to suggest they call the Minister. We'd developed a good working relationship, and I hoped he'd vouch for me."

Her cigarette had burned down while she was talking. She glanced at the short butt and stubbed it out. "His name was like a magic wand. When they realized I knew him, they calmed down and let me off with a severe reprimand. I was left with the feeling that they'd be watching me from then on. Just one more incident, and I'd be out of here."

Jackie grimaced. "All those years of work, learning how to do business here, building up trust and a good reputation—destroyed because Sophia wanted to dazzle some Swede. I'll bet he was damned good looking."

"Incredible," Anjali said, "I'd have been outraged."

"Damn it. It was my dream, my business. How dare Sophia put me in jeopardy?" Jackie's throat sounded scratchy. She went to get bottled water from the fridge. The city water supply was so contaminated that no expatriate dared drink it. Jackie poured two glasses and brought them back to the coffee table. Anjali accepted hers with a nod of thanks.

Her hostess lit another cigarette. The heavy glass ashtray was filling with butts. "At first I was just numb. I stayed up all night trying to work out how to confront Sophia. I didn't want the expat community choosing sides. By the time morning came, I knew what I was going to do. When Dari came in, I gave her the morning off. When Sophia arrived, I shut the door and hung up the 'Closed' sign."

Then Jackie began to act out the scene. Anjali could see what had occurred through her eyes. She could feel Jackie's emotions through her voice and movements. Maybe it wasn't exactly the way it happened, but it was how Jackie remembered it. And that was important.

Anjali felt like she was with the two women in the shop. Sophia was in one bamboo chair, Jackie in the other.

Sophia stiffened her back and placed one hand over the other in her lap. Her smile failed to warm her clipped British accent. "You weren't here. I know what you're going to say, but someone had to take charge while you were gone. Someone had to be responsible."

Jackie's strong Aussie voice came very, very quietly. "That's Dari's job."

Sophia's hands flew to her hips, and she raised her shoulders. "Well, she knows next to nothing about it. Really, you should send that girl for training. She simply doesn't know how to talk with potential buyers, especially for overseas sales."

Now Jackie's voice had a slight edge. "Dari's made a lot of progress. I don't expect her to be perfect in her first months on the job."

Sophia seemed to catch herself and changed her tone. Charm poured out through her smile. "I'm sorry, I didn't mean to criticize Dari. Of course she's your responsibility." She placed an expressive hand on her chest. "I was just afraid we…the gallery was going to lose a big sale."

Jackie clenched her fists, her voice full of exasperation. "You didn't save a sale for me. I don't sell to just anyone. Aside from that, we have limited production capability. You had no idea whether we could fill that order. As it happens, we can't. You took inventory allotted for London. Now we can't fill the Harrod's order because Customs impounded the goods. Dari would've taken his card and told him I'd get in touch. That's our standard procedure."

Sophia's cultured voice still held its musical charm. "I was only trying to help. How was I to know that Customs…" She held her hands up in her typical little-girl-at-a-loss gesture.

"Because Dari told you so." Jackie was barely containing her anger.

Sophia's eyebrows shot up. She opened her mouth to speak, but Jackie rode over her. "She told you about the paperwork. She told you to wait until I got back." Jackie was on a roll now and couldn't help herself. "But, oh no, you had to dash out so you could impress that Swede."

Sophia's eyes blazed. She jumped up, her slim form contorted with rage. "Who do you think you are, talking to me like that? I've got important friends in this town. I could ruin you!"

Jackie was standing now also, her ample body drawn up to its impressive height. "Don't even try it, or I'll make sure the whole story gets out. You don't want everybody to know what a fool you made of yourself at Customs, do you?"

Sophia chewed her lip. Her eyes filled with tears, but her voice was bitter. "I was only trying to help."

"And she slammed the door behind her," Jackie said to Anjali. The pain on the Aussie's face was as fresh as if the incident had happened yesterday.

Anjali took care to make her voice gentle. "What happened after that?"

"I decided to keep my mouth shut and get on with my work. Don't sink to her level. Don't talk to anyone about it, not even Dari. But now I *am* talking about it, even though I vowed not to."

"But it helps to let all that out?"

Jackie tried to smile. "I guess I just needed to get it off my chest now that she's...gone." Jackie was uncharacteristically tongue-tied in finding that last word, but she hurried on. "Sometimes I felt like I'd burst with anger over what she did to me. I was just overwhelmed."

Anjali sensed there must be more to the story than she'd heard so far. "So what did you do?"

"Kept busy." Jackie lit another cigarette to replace the one that had gone out in the ashtray. "Tried to repair or prevent the damage. I never did get the stuff out of Customs, but I managed to fill the Harrod's order by asking the artisans to work overtime." Jackie frowned. "I hated doing that. It interfered with their home life, and that's something I'm trying to preserve."

Anjali was trying to figure out how to get Jackie to talk about the night Sophia died. But she didn't want to rush it. Wait a bit longer, she decided.

Jackie puffed on her cigarette. "I closed down the tearoom before it opened and donated the furnishings to the French Embassy's new school. Took a monetary loss on the donation but got some good will in return. And I kept quiet, just like I meant to."

Through the open window came the sound of children's laughter as they splashed in the fountain, but Anjali kept her attention on Jackie. "Must have been costly, losing all you'd spent on the tearoom."

"Like I said, I got some goodwill in return for my donation.

And I needed it. Sophia was hellbent on payback. When foreign journalists came to town, looking for stories on the new Laos, Sophia used her embassy contacts to represent herself as an arts-and-crafts expert. She'd offer to guide them to the best work. She never, to my knowledge, mentioned the gallery. If foreign media came here, it was because someone else recommended us."

"You must have been livid."

Jackie hunched her shoulders. "I'm not done yet. Remember the WIVS exhibition of Southeast Asian crafts the members had collected? And the fund-raising gala to open it? Everyone in town was invited. Except me. I'm pretty sure it wasn't an oversight. Just another way for Sophia to show how much it cost to cross her. I went when the exhibit was open to the general public. It was really good, lots of interesting pieces. Got some ideas for new products."

"So how'd you handle all Sophia's spite?"

"After fifteen years of professional life, I've learned never to let 'em see you hurt. I didn't keep my mouth shut because I'm noble. It was just good for business. After a while, people started coming to me with their own Sophia stories, and I realized I wasn't alone. I had company in my misery."

"And that helped?" Anjali said as thunder grumbled in the distance.

"Yeah, but it was poor comfort. Sophia was getting away with it. She was a menace to anyone who crossed her." Jackie massaged her shoulders, as if to relieve tension or pain. "There was a while there when every bit of gossip was balm to my soul. Particularly the speculation about Jean-Claude. The lofty Sophia falling to temptation."

"Any truth to those rumors?"

Jackie shrugged. "Her husband was away from home a lot. Hollywood handsome, but a real bore. He may have been good in the sack, but what would you talk about after?"

Anjali thought about her own husband. KB was also away often, but she always felt his encouragement. Tom only supported Sophia in the small things. "Did Sophia have an affair or not?" she asked.

Thunder sounded closer as Jackie continued, "Sophia was always huddled up with Jean-Claude at receptions. Or racing him around in that little sports car she bought from a departing bachelor. But always out in the open. No one saw them sneak across the river to Nong Khai for a quickie. If they were lovers, she was very discreet. No one knew. But everyone guessed."

The nearing thunder drove Jackie's Siamese cat out from under the couch and onto her mistress's lap. Like many Southeast Asian felines, it had a short tail kinked at the end, probably some sort of genetic mutation. The cat closed its eyes and purred as Jackie rubbed under its chin.

Anjali was interested in a possible affair, but she was here to focus on Jackie. "Aren't we getting awfully far from your experiences with Sophia?"

"Yes and no. I'm talking about how I came to realize that she was seriously hurting other people too. I kept wondering if anybody was going to stop her." Jackie pulled a face. "You know how I saw her? A butterfly and a bully. She flitted like a butterfly from one thing to another. Never developed any real expertise. She had her little WIVS fund-raisers so she could feel good about herself. But she was a bully to almost everyone who worked on those projects."

Rain hit the pavement outside like bullets. Anjali could hear the children's excited screams and running feet.

"Look what happened with the *Voice* and the Folkloric," Jackie continued. "Karen tried to treat Sophia as a professional, but Sophia didn't know how to treat others as equals. I supplied all the props for the Folkloric. I'll always believe Sophia sabotaged that production out of sheer spite. The strong she wounded. The weak, she almost destroyed."

"You're one of the strong ones," Anjali said.

"I heard Sophia was feeling unappreciated toward the end." A hint of triumph crossed Jackie's face. "Not many women came to her goodbye party. Of course she was unappreciated. As ye sow, so shall ye reap."

"So who hated her enough to kill her?"

Jackie looked startled for a moment, then recovered. "Lot of people putting their money on Jean-Claude." Jackie smirked. "Infamous lady-killer. And such perverted tastes, if gossip can be believed. Maybe he really was a lady-killer. Maybe they had a lovers' quarrel, and he pushed her in the river. Or a wild night on the banks of the Mekong. They got carried away at the height of their ecstasy, and she fell in." Jackie rolled her eyes. "Sorry, I'm just adding to the gossip."

Anjali spoke as softly as she could. "Gossip says you could have done it."

Jackie was like a soufflé jostled as it came out of the oven. Her face fell, and her breath escaped with a poof. Her reaction disturbed the cat, and it ran off into a back room. "I hated her enough. But I didn't do it. Bad for business, murder."

The monsoon had let up, but Anjali drove home from Jackie's through streets awash with water. Men were taking their shoes and socks off, rolling up their pant-legs to cross the street. It was easier for the women. They stepped out of their sandals and waded in, *pa-sins* wet to the knees.

Anjali thought about what she'd learned. Maybe Jackie had a motive for killing Sophia, but all that had happened weeks ago. Anjali couldn't picture big, blunt Jackie biding her time. Lashing out in anger, yes. Plotting for weeks on end, no.

Suppose Moira were partly right. Sophia was depressed after the party and went down to the Mekong to nurse her wounds. Someone happened along, saw her there and took advantage of the dark riverbank. But who? Once again, Anjali realized she needed more facts.

The meeting with Jackie had been fairly easy, she reflected. Dari downstairs so she felt safe, Jackie in a talkative mood. They wouldn't all be that easy.

Then a thought struck her so hard her foot hit the brake. The wheels sent up a wave of water that splashed every pedestrian within six feet. The bike-riders behind swerved around the car and kept going. No scowl crossed a face, no fist was raised at her bad driving.

It *had* been easy, Anjali reflected, too easy. She remembered how, when her brothers were caught in mischief, they'd told half-truths to escape retribution.

Just when Anjali got to her front door, the monsoon returned in earnest. She entered, thankful to have made it before the heavy rain struck again. She took her niece's gift to the study and wrapped it, mulling over Jackie's words and behavior.

As she finished tying the ribbon, the phone rang. It was KB. Anjali could barely hear him. His tinny voice came through the sound of crackling paper, the monsoon's effect on poorly insulated wires She fondly pictured his face, still lean and handsome as his black hair silvered and his cheekbones became more prominent.

When they were first married, he'd had an athlete's slim body, firm from years of playing cricket. Now, a newly emerging tummy was beginning to push against his belt. Thoughts of KB reminded Anjali how much she owed him. If she'd married a different man, she'd have been a different woman.

Not long after their marriage, KB received his first posting with UNDP. When he told her they were going to Botswana, she forced herself to put on a bright face. Botswana seemed like the end of the earth to her. Too far from home and family, from all she loved. So different from Bombay. A desert country. No culture. No concerts. No poetry readings. No galleries. A desert of sand and a desert for the soul.

Once there, she resolved to be the model UNDP wife. She dutifully attended all the dinner parties and tried to be gracious, even when her hostess was not. She learned to run a household despite the challenges of shortages and shoddy goods. She studied the language and soon discovered she was never going to be a linguist. In her spare time, she tried to emulate Mummy-ji's example and become a gardener, but all her efforts turned curly and brown.

One evening, Anjali was bemoaning her lack of a green thumb to KB.

"Why not try the International Women's Club?" he suggested.

Anjali felt dumbfounded. What did the Women's Club have to do with gardening?

KB smiled sympathetically. "They have gardening programs now and then. We've heard Mrs. Wainwright talk about them."

Anjali's face fell even further. Mrs. Wainwright was condescending and racist.

KB read her face. "You wouldn't have to spend all your time with Mrs. Wainwright and her crowd. You might meet someone new. Besides…" His eyes twinkled. "I think you might discover you've got some hidden talents."

Years later, Anjali was still grateful to KB for suggesting she become active in the community. He'd been right on both counts. She'd met Suneeta, and she'd found she had a talent for organization.

Anjali raised her voice so KB could hear her over the static. "Oh, my darling, I do miss you. What's happening up there? How's the project going?"

"Not well, I'm afraid. I'm going to have to stay a day longer to straighten things out."

"Oh dear." Anjali felt let down. She longed to talk with KB about what she'd learned. Being together was better than talking over the phone anywhere, but especially in Laos.

"I know," he said. "I feel terrible about this. But it's only one extra day. We've got to pull this one out of the fire. Then all the projects will be on an even keel. We can stop worrying."

Anjali chided herself for being so selfish about just one day.

They shouted over the static about the project's problems—transport difficulties, bureaucratic hassles, who wasn't coming through as promised.

Finally KB asked, "What have you been doing, Anju?"

"Trying to find out how Sophia died."

"What?" he snapped. "She drowned, that's how she died."

"How do you know?"

"The office told me all about it during the daily radio contact. She drowned. That's the end of it."

"Well, not really," Anjali tried to mollify KB. "There's more to it than that. How'd she drown? Was it really an accident?"

"Anjali," KB's voice sounded overly patient, and she knew his mood toward her had changed when he used her full name. "That's the official verdict," he said. "What are you trying to do? Open a can of worms?"

"No, of course not. It's just…" Anjali was lost for words, thinking about her resolve to keep a low profile in Vientiane. "…we're all wondering if that's what really happened."

KB's voice was sharp again. "What do you mean?"

"Some people say suicide. Some say murder."

"Good God, Anjali, you're too bright to go for all that gossip. This isn't like you."

Anjali realized she'd got off on the wrong foot. "I'm not saying it wasn't an accident. I'm just saying we don't really know for sure."

Static drowned out KB's response, so she hurried on. "It doesn't feel right that someone so talented, so energetic could just be gone like that."

"Why not? The gods are capricious."

Yes, they are, she thought, remembering Hanoi.

"I'm putting this badly, but I feel like knowing how Sophia died will tell me something about how I should be living." She didn't want to say how much she needed a meaningful project, didn't want to make him feel guilty.

KB's voice had an edge. "And if you find out she was murdered?"

"Well…"

"Anjali, have you stopped to think that if Sophia were murdered— and I don't believe it for a moment—but if she were murdered, you might be in danger?"

"I'm being careful. I won't be alone with anybody who might be a suspect."

"Anjali, listen to yourself. This is crazy. What's happened to you?"

The line went dead. Anjali didn't try to redial and continue the conversation. In the monsoon and with the dilapidated system then in place, they were lucky to have had as many words as they did. Besides, she felt wounded. In all their years together, in all the projects she'd organized to benefit the communities where they'd lived, KB had always supported her. Now, he couldn't even understand what she was talking about.

Anjali got up from her desk and paced around the study. She felt confined, so she walked down the hall, through the living room and out onto the porch.

The garden was a sea of islands with the spirit house on one, the swing on the another. It looked very pretty, even in the pouring rain.

She felt swept away by emotion. *What's the matter with KB? What's the matter with me? What's the matter with us?*

After lunch, the phone rang again. It was Cyril with the news that the Embassy had expedited Tom's departure and that he'd left on the morning plane.

"No reason to hold him here," Cyril said, "and lots of reasons for him to go. The verdict's been announced. It's officially an accident. His tour was basically finished, and now that he's answered all the authorities' questions, why should he stay on in that house filled with memories of Sophia? I couldn't do it."

Anjali was dismayed. "But Cyril, I don't understand. If you think Sophia was murdered, Tom would be a prime suspect. How could you send him off so easily?"

"Well...er...it wasn't me, Anjali. It was the Embassy. The Canadian Government and the Lao Government want to put this thing to rest."

Anjali was incredulous. "And you didn't speak up about your suspicions?"

"How could I? It was a done deal."

No wonder Cyril had never got anywhere in the foreign service, Anjali thought. *No stomach for doing the right thing. Just going along to get along.*

"Besides," Cyril continued, "it couldn't have been Tom. They were too close. Even if I didn't like him, I have to admit he loved her. And he was up-country at the time."

Poor Sophia, Anjali thought. *Her own Embassy didn't care how* she'd drowned. If it had been Tom who'd died, would things have been different?

Cyril was rattling on. "It was one of the women. That's who you should be going after."

Anjali's tone betrayed her exasperation. "You don't know that. We don't even know if it was murder."

Cyril's voice quavered. "It was murder. I just know it."

"As far as I'm concerned," Anjali said, "I'm trying to find out how Sophia ended up in the Mekong. Maybe it was murder. Maybe suicide. Maybe accident."

"It was murder," Cyril said stubbornly.

Now Anjali felt really angry. "Look, Cyril, here's how I see it. You're not the only one who cares what happened to Sophia. We're all wondering about it, especially the wives. If this strong, vibrant creature could meet a violent, premature death, what does that say about the vulnerability of all *farang* women?"

She could hear Cyril's voice coming through gritted teeth. "All right, have it your way. Just find out what happened." But he couldn't resist a parting shot. "It'll be murder, you'll see." His voice became triumphant. "And it'll be one of those *farang* women you're so concerned about who did it."

Cyril's phone clicked in her ear. Anjali put down the receiver and stared at the antiquated black instrument.

Wheels within wheels, she thought. Jackie telling half-truths. Cyril talking out of both sides of his mouth. Everyone playing a game. And KB afraid she'd get hurt.

That evening, Anjali looked out the car window as Thongsy drove through muggy streets and wished she didn't have to go to Burt's.

She was tired of a lifetime of dinner parties, tired of evenings where she unofficially represented UNDP.

They passed a bamboo kiosk lit by the usual forty-watt bulb hanging from a cord. The dim light silhouetted a Lao man buying two cigarettes from the vendor. He leaned forward to light one from the vendor's match, and the bulb revealed pure pleasure on his face.

Anjali knew KB depended on her to help at these functions, even when he could attend. In the early days, she'd put herself in neutral during the shoptalk and gossip. But she soon realized what was said might be significant. KB often asked what she thought about an evening's conversation. Tonight, with KB up-country, she knew it was important that she be his eyes and ears. But KB hadn't been very understanding about her needs, and things felt out-of-balance.

Thongsy slowed as traffic increased in the commercial heart of town. A family-laden moped pulled alongside. The young Lao mother perched lightly on the rear, legs to one side, holding onto nothing but the toddler in her arms. Anjali smiled and waved at the child. It waved back, and Anjali was surprised to find tears pricking her eyes. She hadn't realized her emotions were so near the surface.

Thongsy turned into the street leading to Burt's compound. Anjali sighed. Burt was the leader of the foreign investment community in Vientiane, and UNDP was promoting private-sector growth in Laos. She bowed her head and submitted to duty.

The gates opened, and Thongsy drove through. Burt's company had built a shirt factory and a house for the managing director within the same compound. They were separated by a wall and a garden, so Burt just walked from one side of the compound to the other to go to work. That sort of arrangement wasn't unusual. The city had no zoning, so most neighborhoods were mixed. A mansion might be next to a slum, a hotel or a sweatshop.

Thongsy opened her door, and Anjali stepped out onto the concrete drive. She breathed in deeply and held it in for a moment. Then she let it out slowly, feeling her dissatisfaction fade.

Tonight was different, she reflected. She wasn't here just for UNDP. She was also here to learn about Sophia. The trick would be to get people to open up.

Burt threw open the door and enveloped Anjali's hand in a two-fisted embrace. "Anjali! Always welcome here. You know Wilhelmina and Tsing." His hail-fellow-well-met persona matched his big, athletic frame. She followed his loud tropical shirt and gray buzz-cut into the living room.

Anjali smiled as the young couple rose to greet her. Wilhelmina had worked closely with Sophia. What might she know?

Anjali had a lot of respect for Wilhelmina. The thirty-year-old economist's fate had been like that of many professional wives. She'd come to Laos as a dependent spouse with Tsing, a computer specialist on a World Bank project. It had taken half a year before she'd found a job. Rather than sit idle, Wilhelmina had turned her considerable talents to helping WIVS make their fund-raising and -disbursement more efficient.

The bell rang, and Burt opened the door to greet Larry and Vicki. Anjali remembered Vicki from Sophia's goodbye party, but they'd never had a chance to get acquainted. Larry had been advising the government on privatization of public industries for several months, but Vicki had only recently arrived from America. Such an arrangement was so typical that it was called "Pack, pay and follow." Although he was in his forties, this was Larry's first post overseas. He normally was an academic. Must be a big change from what they're used to, Anjali mused.

"Hi, Larry!" Burt winked in Vicki's direction. "Introduce us to the lovely lady you've brought *this* time."

The American ignored the older Australian's jibe. "Anjali, you've met Vicki. Sure is great to be together again."

Burt broke in. "Right, who's drinking what? Your usual gin-and-tonic, Anjali?"

She accepted her tall glass with thanks. Burt distributed white wine to the other women and beer to the men. He waved vaguely for everyone to help themselves from a plate of the ubiquitous puffy chips flavored with dried shrimp.

Slim pickings for hors d'oeuvres, Anjali observed. Maybe dinner would be better.

Burt poured himself a generous scotch and settled on an obviously imported sofa. A company house, Anjali recognized, no woman's touch to soften it. The whole room had that institutionally furnished look—a coordinated suite of beige furniture with matching coffee and side tables, pictures selected from a catalog, no personal knick-knacks, no Lao crafts.

"How's the project, Tsing?" Burt asked. With that, the men were off on the usual shop-talk, and the women were left to listen or converse among themselves. Even Wilhelmina was excluded although she now worked on a project to attract foreign investment.

After a while, Burt remembered the rest of his guests. "Hear the latest to-do at the Club?"

Anjali tried to think of a way to work Sophia into the conversation. She and KB didn't go to the expatriates' club often enough for her to remember if Sophia had been active or not.

"That's the place for you, Larry," Burt was saying. "Nothing like a good game of squash after work to get the kinks out."

"I'm afraid I don't play."

A hint of tension between Larry and Burt, Anjali realized. But why? She took a shrimp puff and paid more attention to the two men.

Burt brushed a hand across his thinning pate. "Yanks almost never do. Never mind, swim some laps in the pool. Be like us Aussies. Daily exercise, that's the ticket for survival here."

Anjali could see she wasn't going to get a word in edgewise and let her mind wander to how hard Sophia had worked to enhance these evenings. You had to give her credit for that. Sophia had tried to do a lot of things right, even if she'd failed.

Then Anjali heard Burt say, "The squash players hit the ceiling. As far as they were concerned, it had always been a squash court, and that was that. Let the aerobic jumping jacks and the yoga pretzels cavort somewhere else."

"Speaking of the latest gossip," Larry said, "who's the bigwig involved in smuggling stuff out of Champassak?"

Burt pursed his lips. Upset with Larry, Anjali wondered, or upset at losing the limelight?

Wilhelmina dove at the topic. "I heard it was someone in the Foreign Affairs Ministry."

Not for the first time, Anjali noted the young woman's accent. Her father was Dutch, and that was her first language, but her mother was Indonesian. Wilhelmina spoke English, but rather formally and with a Dutch accent. Yet her voice was softer than a European's.

Tsing said, "It must be a diplomat. With pouch privileges. Then he could get it out of the country without an inspection."

"Nah," Larry said. "A diplomat wouldn't dare. It's somebody in the private sector." He looked over at his older host. "Sending the stuff out in a shipment of cheap T-shirts or whatever."

Burt snubbed the bait. "I vote for Jean-Claude. In charge of import-export at the French Embassy. Knows everyone who matters." The cook caught his eye. "Shall we go into dinner?"

Anjali rose with renewed resolve to bring up Sophia's death.

What had she been thinking, Anjali wondered, about the main course being better than the hors d'oeuvres? Burt was always trying to recreate Australian food. She looked aghast at the tough roast beef, mealy potatoes and boiled beans.

The cook set a Lao dish of stir-fried vegetables before her. Anjali smiled her appreciation at Burt's thoughtfulness and felt a bit guilty watching her fellow guests saw away at the beef.

Burt poured the wine. "One thing you can say about the Club. It's a boon to the ladies. Vientiane can be a real wife-killer."

Anjali grabbed at the opening. "Are you talking about recent events?"

"No, I'm talking in general. Most of the wives have two responses to life here—frantic activity or total withdrawal."

Vicki stopped sawing for a moment. "Why do you say that?"

"If you do not fill your days, they can really drag," Wilhelmina said. "Too much of that, and you start to feel depressed."

Vicki persisted. "I'm overwhelmed with things to do."

The air conditioner kicked into high, and Burt raised his voice to be heard. "You're setting up your household, but what will you do when that's done?" He went on to catalog the problems plaguing foreign wives in Vientiane.

Anjali saw Wilhelmina's and Vicki's eyes glazing over. She was disappointed no one had followed her lure to talk about Sophia's death. She'd probably been too subtle, but how could she bring up the topic without being too obvious?

"All this is wearing to the ladies," Burt summed up. "Some women thrive here…"

Anjali's ears pricked. Here was a chance to mention Sophia.

He continued, "Jackie, because she has a proper job to do. Moira, because she really got involved with the language and the culture. Wilhelmina…"

"Because I'm half-Asian," she interrupted, "and think this is a better place to raise children than a lot of other places we have lived. Including Australia."

Anjali was surprised that the normally gracious Wilhelmina would take a dig at Burt's home country. Then she remembered it was Wilhelmina's country also. She and Tsing had been born in Asia, but they were Australian citizens now.

Burt's skin was too thick for Wilhelmina's arrow. "Depends a lot on what type of woman you are. Some women shrink and fade. Some get tough. Some take one look and go home. My own lady wife stuck it for two months. Then she moved to Bangkok and granted me conjugal rights on monthly visits."

Vicki's head swung around in obvious amazement. Anjali frowned, trying to figure out how to bring Sophia's death into the conversation.

Burt smiled at Vicki. "I joke about it, but it was probably best for both of us. Laos is no place for her, and I can concentrate on work without worrying if she's going to make it or not."

Larry started to speak, but Burt cut him off. "Look, I love my wife, and I like having her around. But I'm not going to ask her to sacrifice if she feels miserable here. She's got a good job and a nice little apartment in Bangkok."

Larry sat there, silenced and glowering. His short-sleeved white shirt was starting to show perspiration marks, despite Burt's roaring a.c.

Vicki looked at Burt. "You've reinforced my decision to chair the WIVS Bazaar. Sophia…" She paused and blinked rapidly. Anjali exhaled a surreptitious sigh of relief as Vicki continued, "…Sophia asked me and said Wilhelmina would be glad to help.

Wilhelmina's eyebrows shot up before she could control them. It looked to Anjali like Sophia hadn't said anything to Wilhelmina about it.

"You didn't tell me you were taking on the Bazaar," Larry said. There was a slight edge to his voice, but Anjali couldn't discern exactly what it was.

Vicki answered with some asperity. "There hasn't been time to tell you, what with your twelve-hour days and all my moving hassles."

"Sophia asked you to head up the committee?" Anjali prompted. She had to keep the focus on the dead woman.

"Now there was a woman who had no idea how to live here," Burt said.

Anjali smiled to herself. This ploy was working.

Vicki gasped. "How can you say that? Look at all she did for the community. Where would we be without WIVS?"

"WIVS helps a lot of women," Burt conceded. "Gives 'em a sense of accomplishment. But there's another side to that story, and I wouldn't be honest if I didn't spell it out. WIVS is a bunch of bored housewives who don't really want to get involved with the Lao, playing Lady Bountiful and squabbling amongst themselves. Am I right, Wilhelmina?"

Wilhelmina pushed her lumpy potatoes around her plate. "Only partly. True, the members are almost exclusively housewives. But a lot of the women are qualified to work. Yet they cannot find a job. And it is almost impossible to become truly involved with the Lao. The government will not allow us to do real volunteer work. They do not want to risk being embarrassed by the success of some expatriate wives."

"That's no excuse for all the squabbling," Burt said as the cook began clearing the table.

Wilhelmina sat back from her half-eaten dinner. "You are right, Burt. There are some disagreements within WIVS." Her Dutch accent made the acronym sound a bit like 'VIVS.' "But look at what you said about the row at the Club. There is always tension when two or three are gathered together."

Yes, Anjali thought, but was Cyril right? Did one of the WIVS squabbles end in murder?

Burt's cook appeared with dishes of vanilla ice cream flown up from Bangkok.

Burt persevered. "My God, the WIVS ladies're disorganized. They manage to get a tremendous amount done, but in the midst of chaos. Someone'll call and beg you to give over your Saturday afternoon to set up tables for a fund-raiser. You show up at the appointed hour, and everyone's scurrying around. No plan, no one in charge, everyone in charge. You ask what to do, and one of 'em will say, 'Put the tables over there.' You set up half the tables, then another lady says, 'No, no.

Put 'em over *there*.' By the time you've moved the friggin' tables back and forth all afternoon, you don't care whether you attend that night or not. Am I right, guys?"

Larry scooped up a spoonful of melting ice cream. "Not when Wilhelmina's in charge. But I've moved my share of tables for WIVS, that's for sure."

Vicki's voice was a bit testy. "I didn't know that."

"I had to keep busy while I was alone," came Larry's defensive reply. Vicki did not appear mollified.

"Look, Vicki," Burt said. "Do yourself a favor. Keep your WIVS Bazaar in perspective. Go ahead, organize a good one. I'll do whatever I can to help. But don't start thinking WIVS is the most important thing in Vientiane, the way Sophia did."

"I don't think you're being fair to her," Vicki said. "She was one of the most helpful, least egotistical persons I've ever known."

Wilhelmina's spoon stopped halfway to her mouth. "Sophia had many sides, Vicki. Perhaps you knew her such a short time that you only saw one."

Anjali remembered Wilhelmina hadn't been at Sophia's goodbye party. Why not? Some conflict there? Could she be a suspect?

"Wilhelmina's got a point," Larry said. "I remember the night we met. A dinner party during my first week here. She had the most extraordinary upper-class British accent, so I said, 'You don't sound Canadian.' Just to make conversation."

"Bet she loved that," Burt said, the irony clear in his voice.

Larry ignored Burt. "Sophia got all stiff and said, 'How do you think Canadians are supposed to sound?' Okay, I might have been more sensitive, but everybody has to get used to prying questions here. I get them all the time. How much money do you make? How come you don't you have any children?"

"Why isn't your wife here?" Burt chimed in. "That's almost as good as when did you stop beating her."

Larry grabbed the conversation back. "I stammered about my own mother being English and wondering if she also had an English parent. Or had she gone to school in England? That got her off her high horse, but I couldn't see why she was so quick to take offense."

"You never told me that story," Vicki said.

Increasing stress in that voice, Anjali thought. "There are so many stories about Sophia," she said. "And so many rumors about her death. It's hard to know what to believe."

Burt responded, "I think she was murdered."

"Why on earth would anyone want to kill Sophia?" Vicki countered.

Tsing spoke up. "She stepped on a lot of toes, hurt a lot of people's feelings."

Burt slurped the last of his ice cream. "Look at the Vientiane Follies. Sophia talked me into dancing in the all-male ballet. Don't mind making a fool of myself in public, so I went to the rehearsals and sat in the back with my mates. Drank a few beers. Had a few laughs when the others made fools of themselves. Those rehearsals were filled with catfights, and Sophia was at the center of most of 'em. You were there, Wilhelmina. What'd you think?"

"I will not go into the details, but she made it clear that the Follies were more important than anything else we had to do. If you did not go along with that, she could be extremely unpleasant."

Was that why Wilhelmina didn't come to Sophia's goodbye party? Anjali wondered. Sophia abusive because work came first?

Burt got up to lead everyone into the living room for coffee. "Come on, let's play detective. Suppose it was murder. Who killed Sophia and why? It's like that game, Miss Crimson with the slipper in the bathroom or whatever it is."

Burt encouraged everyone to help themselves from the carafe and cups on the coffee table. The bitter aroma circled the room. Anjali noticed Vicki and Larry had moved to separate chairs. Before dinner they'd been side-by-side on the couch.

"Got a list of suspects for you," Burt said. "Jackie, Karen, Cyril, Jean-Claude and Tom."

Anjali burned her tongue. "Why Cyril? I haven't heard his name mentioned before."

"Sophia used to do an absolutely devastating imitation of him," Burt said. "Had it down pat, mannerisms and all. Someone told Cyril, and he was speechless with humiliation."

Larry poured coffee into his cup. "Oh, come on. That wimp? Cyril hasn't got the guts. Besides, that's not motive for murder."

No, it wasn't, Anjali agreed. But Cyril was no Milquetoast. Look how tenaciously he was pushing her to investigate. Something else going on, but what?

Larry leaned back. "Why would you include Jackie, of all people?"

His host passed the powdered creamer and sugar. "Sophia really screwed her on a business deal. Jackie lives near the spot where Sophia's car was found, and she often roams the streets at night when she can't sleep."

That was something new, Anjali realized, Jackie roaming the streets at night. But how did Burt know?

"Motive *and* opportunity," Larry said.

Wilhelmina sat up straight. "That is a good example of how gossips run away with facts. Jackie has too much good sense and too much to lose. She did not murder Sophia. No one did."

Burt raised a hand like a traffic cop. "Hold on, Wilhelmina. You're jumping the gun. We haven't reviewed all the suspects yet."

Wilhelmina's face held just the hint of a scowl. Most un-Asian, Anjali observed. Wilhelmina had strong feelings on this topic.

Burt continued, "Jean-Claude's a suspect because of a lovers' quarrel and Tom, because he found out about Jean-Claude. What about our lover-boy?"

"The French keep pretty much to themselves," Tsing said. "Does anyone know Jean-Claude?"

When Tsing's question was answered by the sound of coffee-sips, Burt spoke up. "Okay, leave Jean-Claude to the side for the moment. Let's look at Tom. The spouse is always the first suspect in a murder case."

Anjali was piqued that Cyril hadn't done more to keep Tom in-country and held her tongue. Now that the group had latched onto the topic, maybe all she had to do was watch and listen. She could see lines of tension being drawn among the people in the room.

Larry clearly couldn't wait to speak first. "Tom's the exact opposite of Sophia. Likes to play the country boy. Always away on his rural water projects. I used to wonder if he spent so much time in the field just to get away from her."

Vicki folded her arms across her chest. "I don't think you're being fair to either one of them. And this is a nasty little game."

Larry finished his coffee. "Look, Vicki, you didn't see them together as much as I did. They were always bickering in public. After a couple drinks, they'd start in on each other. I was embarrassed more than once."

Tsing said, "I hear what you're saying, Larry, but I see it differently. His mud-spattered-hydrologist is as much an affectation as Sophia's pose. I've heard him say scathing things about the Lao. Tom and Sophia were both playing neocolonial roles."

"That is the way I also saw them," Wilhelmina said.

There it was again, Anjali noted, another hint of things not right between Wilhelmina and Sophia.

Tsing leaned forward. "But it was more complicated than that. More than once, I saw their eyes meet. He'd smile at her, a very special, knowing sort of smile. And just for a moment, you'd see the human heart of her. I think he truly loved her. With all her faults and idiosyncrasies. She'd have been lost without him. He was the port in the storm of her life."

Larry said, "I heard Tom was playing around." Vicki sucked in her lower lip and turned to face the wall, but Larry didn't seem to notice. "Dancing too close with another man's wife. Strange car parked in his driveway when Sophia was gone. That sort of thing."

"But that's gossip about how he played around," Burt said. "If Tom's a suspect, it's because Sophia was having an affair with Jean-Claude. I don't know about the Frenchman, but I do know about Tom. A man's man. Keeps himself fit, a real sportsman."

Burt glanced at the sideboard and looked embarrassed. He went over, picked up a plate of chocolates and brought them back to the coffee table, talking all the while. "Tom's done a great job out in the bush with a bunch of villagers. Gave 'em the right kind of technical assistance. Nothing too fancy, just appropriate to their needs and abilities."

He rambled on. Anjali could see Larry squirming with the need to take the floor again. Vicki grabbed a surreptitious look at her watch. Wilhelmina began passing around the chocolates. Anjali took two.

Burt finished, "If I'd been Sophia's husband, I'd have killed her long ago."

Larry looked startled. Vicki's eyes flew up to the ceiling. Wilhelmina and Tsing remained tactfully impassive.

"Why?" Anjali asked. Had that been a Freudian slip? Burt was alone in Vientiane for weeks, his wife down in Bangkok. Had he had an affair with Sophia? And it went wrong?

"She was a helluva flirt," Burt said. "Anything in pants but especially the diplomats and more especially Jean-Claude."

"Me too," Larry broke in. "Despite that awkward first meeting."

Vicki turned to look at Larry with raised eyebrows and open mouth. He drew in his head like a turtle that had just got burned.

Burt went on as if Larry hadn't said a word. "Had to be hard to live with a woman like Sophia. Not hard to kill her, though. A walk in the moonlight, an over-balanced embrace, and all your troubles would disappear."

Anjali gazed at Burt. Was he describing theory or reality?

Larry was almost snarling with emotion. "Are you saying Tom did it or not?"

"Tom couldn't have done it," Burt said. "The night she died, he was up-country for his final inspection trip. People say he could've come down and back that night, but I don't believe it. She got to him, sure, but not enough to kill her. He's just too regular a guy."

Larry couldn't hold in his triumph. "Then why did his Embassy hustle him out of the country this morning?"

Burt held out his hands, palms up, as if to state the obvious. "Compassion for his loss. And he was at the end of his project anyway."

Vicki spoke up, petulant and defiant. "If it has to be murder, why not a robber? Lots of people are saying that."

Wilhelmina said, "The Embassy Security Chief told me Sophia's purse was found in her car. She still had her jewelry on. This is just another example of gossip running away with facts."

"So nobody killed Sophia," Vicki said.

Larry ignored Vicki's statement. This evening was so typical of what happened to the wives, Anjali reflected. No one cared what they thought. Even Sophia. Those who admired her found her entertaining, but they didn't care whether she had an idea in her head or not.

"Sophia was always wearing ethnic costumes," Larry was saying. "A kid puts on outfits to explore being a cowboy or a doctor or a space man. Part of growing up. But Sophia was still playing dress-up in her forties."

"Okay, back to the main question," Burt said. "Who murdered Sophia? Ready to vote?"

"This isn't a game," Tsing gently admonished. "It's life. A woman's been drowned, and we don't know why or how. Or who, if that's relevant."

"Yes, but it's a fascinating way to spend an evening, isn't it?" Burt countered.

Anjali looked around the room. No one else seemed to agree with their host. But she'd picked up a lot of clues. Then guilt swept over her. Just like a snoopy old woman, she thought. Did she really want to be like this?

Burt was prattling on. "I think she was murdered. Don't know who did it, but I'd stake my life it wasn't Tom."

"I'll agree with you there," Tsing said, obviously trying to be conciliatory to his host.

"It was not murder," Wilhelmina said firmly, and Vicki emphatically nodded her assent.

"It has been ruled an accident," Wilhelmina continued. "We have to accept that." She stood up. "Time to go home. Tsing is taking the boys to Buddha Park tomorrow morning."

Anjali realized that his excursion would give her an opportunity to meet with Wilhelmina. The woman clearly had a more complicated relationship with Sophia than she'd appreciated. While everyone was busy with goodbyes and belongings, she invited Wilhelmina for brunch.

"I must stay home because Mother always calls on Sundays. But why don't we have brunch at my house?"

Anjali accepted with pleasure. Through the open door, she saw Larry try to take Vicki's arm as they went down the steps. Vicki shrugged him off and went on ahead. Anjali shook Burt's proffered hand and tried to see beneath the blustery facade. Could Sophia have had affairs with both Burt and Larry? Was that the reason for tonight's sparring between the two men?

Anjali asked Thongy to drive home by the river. When they got near the spot where Sophia's car had been found after she died, Anjali told the chauffeur to pull over. She got out and walked along the road, humid air settling around her like a wet velvet cloak.

Dark clouds covered much of the sky. The cloying scent of jasmine engulfed her. She passed through alternating deep shadow and a streetlamp's dim light. As near as she could reckon, she arrived at the spot where the women had sat at dawn and Sophia had left her car at midnight.

Anjali moved into the narrow park between road and river. She couldn't see it because of the shrubbery, but she knew she wasn't far from the Lane Xang Hotel. She could hear the faint voices of departing dinner guests calling farewell across the parking lot. She shivered. During the day, the park was full of laughing children, and it had been glorious that morning when they'd watched the dawn. But now it seemed dark, damp and far from the Vientiane she knew.

She walked past the empty swings and looked down into the water, her mind restless. Had Sophia been alone after her goodbye party, full of anger and pain? Had she been with someone? Who? Why was she here, in this particular place?

Anjali tried to feel Sophia's presence, but she couldn't. Impossible to put herself in Sophia's shoes. Foolish to try. She turned to go back to the car. Tom's driver stepped out of the shadows.

Anjali started. She looked past him for Thongy, but she couldn't see the car. She hadn't realized she'd walked such a distance.

Tom's driver inched forward. Sweaty shoulders hunched above the straps of an undervest worn without a shirt. His posture was supplicating and menacing at the same time. "Madame should not be here. Dangerous place."

She was determined to keep calm. "Yes, dangerous for Sophia. I know."

"No, Madame, you not know. Dangerous for you. My friends tell. They work house servants. They hear. You go talk many *farang*. You talk 'bout Mme. Sophia. This dangerous. You no talk anymore. Dangerous."

He came nearer, his arms and hands now fully extended. Anjali backed up.

She thought about KB's warning. Was this how Sophia had died? And now she was going to die too? Anjali felt panic starting to rise. She reminded herself that the Lao were a gentle people. It didn't help.

Her heel slipped into a muddy hole. The man was almost close enough to touch her.

They both jumped when the car lights came on. Anjali looked down the road. Thongsy was speeding toward them. She realized she'd been holding her breath and let it escape.

Tom's driver whirled in his rubber flip-flops and ran off down one of the narrow alleys in the labyrinth of old Vientiane.

Thongsy bounded out of the car. "Madame, are you all right? I saw the man. It is not safe for you to be alone here."

"No, Thongsy," she said, "maybe it isn't safe now."

Thongsy drove home through dark streets while Anjali slouched in the back, thinking about what she'd said. Not safe on the riverbank at night. Maybe not safe continuing to ask questions, especially with everyone's servants listening and gossiping.

She looked up to see Thongsy watching her in the mirror. His eyes immediately darted back to the road.

Anjali sat up straight. She wasn't some Westerner to be cowed by tattling servants. She'd had servants all her life. She felt more alive than she had for a long time. She wasn't just Sita; she was Devi too. She didn't care if Tom's driver said it was dangerous. She didn't even care about KB's warning. He wasn't here, and she was. She had to do what she thought was right.

As soon as she got home, Anjali went to her desk. She took out the tablet with her notes about suspects and motives. Pondering what she'd learned at tonight's party, she added two more names to the list, Burt and Larry. Twenty years separated the two men. And they were very different. Their shirts said a lot about them, Burt's red-and-purple tropical print, Larry's plain white one. Yet somehow they felt in competition. Just the young lion taking on the old lion, or something else?

Sexual jealousy? Had Sophia been involved in multiple love

triangles, or was she just a flirt? Even so, more than one woman had died of flirting. Sexual jealousy, sexual frustration, sexual anything was a powerful motivator. She'd seen it in so many posts.

Anjali gazed at her plump reflection in the night-black window and remembered the Somali women, so slim and feminine. And a young KB's eyes gazing off into the distance, "They're so alluring…"

But when he'd seen her face, he'd taken it in both his hands and said, "Oh, Anju, I'm not saying this very well, but I'm trying to be honest. Yes, I'm tempted. All the men are. But when I think of you," he'd smiled down at her pregnant tummy, "and our baby, I know I could never risk losing you, even if my wildest fantasies came true."

The handsome face of a Sri Lankan diplomat flitted across Anjali's memory. She sighed, recalling his attentions years ago in Nairobi. She'd been tempted also, she conceded. One couldn't live this long and not find someone tempting. But yielding to temptation, that was something else.

She considered Tom's driver. Could he have learned of Sophia's philandering and killed her out of some misguided idea to protect Tom's honor? She'd heard of such things happening in faraway villages. She added his name to the list and reviewed the new names. Not a lot to go on. Even less for Wilhelmina. Best wait until after their brunch before deeming her a suspect.

Enough for now, she decided. After midnight. Time for bed.

A queasiness in Anjali's stomach drifted into her consciousness, but she didn't want to wake up. It was still dark outside. She rolled over onto her back and pulled her knees up. That usually helped.

The nausea grew into cramps, and Anjali had to admit she was in for it. "Probably that ice cream," she muttered. "Melted on the way up from Bangkok and refrozen." It'd happened before. Both cramps and queasiness boomed in a rising crescendo until Anjali was fleeing to the bathroom and relief.

After a while, she ran cold water on a washcloth and wiped her face. She looked at the Imodium on the cabinet shelf but decided against it, at least for now. Better to let food poisoning take its course for twenty-four hours, she knew, than to trap it inside to flourish. Best just to replace liquids and electrolytes.

Then she remembered that KB had taken the last of the powdered electrolyte packets with him up-country. Pepsi, she thought with resignation. She hated the fizzy, sweet drink, but she knew it was a decent source of what she needed.

Things seemed to have calmed down, so she padded out to the kitchen and opened the fridge. She always kept a few bottles for guests. Feeling a bit weak, she poured a glass and sat down at the kitchen table to sip slowly.

To distract herself, she turned her attention to Sophia's death. What if Vicki and Wilhelmina were right and it wasn't murder?

She acknowledged that suicide was just the sort of flamboyant gesture one might expect from the dead woman. Sophia always did whatever she made up her mind to, even when it hurt. If she couldn't be a winner, she played with all her might for the sympathy vote.

Anjali recalled an incident not long after they'd arrived in Vientiane. WIVS was planning to initiate an annual "Woman of the Year" award to the member who'd done the most for the organization's projects. The whole thing had been Sophia's idea, and the general assumption had been that she'd get the first award. But the Nominating Committee had also named several other women.

Looking back, Anjali thought the Committee had known it was unlikely for any of these women to win the award, yet their efforts could be recognized through the nominations. But it hadn't been that simple. When it was all over, the gossips told the tale.

Sophia had sat through the Committee meeting with tight jaws, gone home, thought it over and withdrawn her name from nomination. Sophia's claque had seen it as noble. It was clear, they said, that Sophia would have won, so she'd withdrawn in order to give others a chance. But many had seen it differently. Sophia had perceived the nomination of others as a slap in the face. If she couldn't be the sole nominee for the first award, she'd be the martyr.

Although Anjali hadn't given the idea much credence, she now conceded that Sophia might have taken the ultimate path to martyrdom that night by the Mekong. Something might have so upset her that the only way to win was to die. Her final act could have been the ultimate effort to say, "I'll show them. Then they'll be sorry."

Traveller arrived, blinking solemnly in the unaccustomed light. Anjali reached down to scratch behind his ears and wondered if she were going too far with this quest. Sophia's death could have been an accident. A stroll along the Mekong after her goodbye party, a patch of slick mud, a crumbling embankment, a fall and no one to see or help.

Anjali finished the Pepsi. She'd learned too much to accept the official verdict. Sophia had caused so much hurt in so many quarters, been hurt herself so much, that accident would have been a cruel irony.

She put the empty glass down and stared out the window at dark clouds gathering to cover the stars. Maybe she just didn't want Sophia's life to have ended like that.

The nausea and cramps were gone. Only weakness remained. It looked like this siege wasn't going to be as bad as some she'd sustained. "Let's go back to bed," she told Traveller, and he led the way. She soon drifted off, the rain on the tile roof lulling her to sleep.

Anjali woke the next morning at nine-thirty, her head full of wool but her stomach back to normal. Thank goodness this was Onhta's day off; otherwise, she'd be fretting at Anjali getting up so late.

Outside, a hot sun lifted fierce humidity from the rain-soaked ground. Too late for yoga, Anjali showered, put on a vintage *shalvar kemiz* and draped its long, scarf-like *dupatta* across her neck. Then she downed a glass of mineral water, climbed into the Deux Chevaux and sped toward Chao Anou, the street of the bakers.

When she rounded the corner into Chao Anou, she had to slow down. The whole street was alive. Hawkers trundled bikes hung with cheap plastic toys in bright colors, shouting their wares. Anjali watched giggling children chase each other around the columns of shop porticos and wished she had that much energy this morning. Under the shade of the extended roofs, decrepit iron tables hosted the buzz of breakfasters, while rib-striped dogs fought for scraps in a street strewn with refuse.

Anjali parked in front of the Happy Oven Bakery. She looked at the shop's new sign with its elaborate curlicues and smiled. The name was probably a translation from the Lao. Increasingly, Vientiane shops had English names. It drove the French wild.

She raced inside for sweet rolls and croissants. Suneeta was there, buying tea cakes. She was dressed, as always, in an eye-catching sari and gold jewelry. Anjali couldn't help feeling a bit dowdy.

They exchanged a warm embrace. "How's the reception coming?" Anjali asked.

"Very nicely, thank you. We're looking forward to seeing you both there."

Anjali's brow crinkled. "I don't know if KB will be back in time."

Suneeta's voice showed her concern. "Nothing wrong, I hope? KB's not sick? Not an accident?"

"No, no, nothing like that. He keeps postponing his return because of problems with the project."

Suneeta chuckled. "Just the usual delays then." She looked into Anjali's face. "But you miss him, don't you?"

Anjali nodded and gave her order to the woman behind the counter. She wanted to change the subject. This was neither the time nor the place to discuss KB. "Wilhelmina's invited me to brunch. Thought I'd bring along some pastries."

"I'm so glad she got that job," Suneeta said, "but it's a shame she's getting paid so little because she's a local hire. Project managers are always happy to take advantage."

Anjali opened the door, and they walked out into the cacophony of Chao Anou on a Sunday morning.

"Speaking of mutual acquaintances," Suneeta said, "what's wrong with Karen?"

Anjali stopped and looked up at Suneeta. "I haven't seen her. Why?"

"I saw her just now, down by the river. Even from a distance, I could see she was upset. She turned away as soon as she saw me, so I didn't like to interfere."

The street noises dimmed as Anjali focused her attention on Suneeta. "Where, exactly?"

"That narrow playground near the hotel. She was all alone. And crying."

"How extraordinary," Anjali said and kissed Suneeta on the cheek. "Must run, or I'll be late for brunch."

Anjali felt guilty as she headed for the playground. She'd wanted to get away to look for Karen. That was no way to treat her best friend. She'd better phone Suneeta later.

She shifted her attention to the riverside park. That spot again. Why was it so important to everyone? She drove slowly down the length of the narrow green. All she could see were Lao children playing and their mothers chatting. No *farang*. No Karen.

Anjali chastised herself. What had she expected? Karen was long gone. And what would she have done if she had seen the woman? Anjali glanced down at her watch. If she didn't get to Wilhelmina's, she'd be late.

She pulled away from the curb and wondered what was going on. Karen couldn't be grieving for Sophia. Those two were far from being friends. They were more like opposing avatars, each standing for a different direction, a different purpose to life. It had been like fire and tinder to see them together, each lighting small explosions of temperament in the other.

Anjali's memory dredged up a conversation at a dinner party they'd all attended not so long ago. Sophia had been holding forth on what was wrong with expatriate women who didn't join WIVS.

"They're lazy and self-centered," Sophia said with satisfaction.

"Maybe they have other interests," Karen countered.

Candlelight bounced off Karen's glasses and gleamed on Sophia's auburn curls.

Sophia smirked. "Something self-centered, no doubt."

Karen smiled and inclined her head. "Something creative, perhaps, like photography or weaving."

"They should leave the weaving to the Lao, then. They've been doing it for centuries." Sophia looked around the table for agreement. All eyes suddenly turned to forks and food. No one wanted drawn into the altercation.

"And the photography?" asked Karen, her voice carefully polite.

"Leave that to the professionals. Who wants to see someone's snapshots of boy-monks?"

"I do. And they're not snapshots."

Arriving at Wilhelmina's house, Anjali could still feel the tension of that evening. Like so many times when Sophia and Karen had been thrown together, they'd disagreed on every topic raised. It had never flared into a real fight; they were both too well-bred for that. But one could feel the conflict in the air between them, like electricity before a storm.

The stress of Anjali's memories melted as she looked at Wilhelmina's garden. Orchids and ferns cascaded from the damp shade of tall trees. Heliconias ran riot with their strange red-and-yellow flowers that weren't truly flowers at all. Frangipani scented the air, and multicolored crotons lined the path to Wilhelmina's colonial bungalow. The house must have stood there for decades.

Wilhelmina came out on the bougainvillea-draped porch. "So kind of you to bring pastries." Anjali handed over her white sack and followed Wilhelmina to the kitchen. "Coffee or tea?" asked her hostess.

"Tea, please. With milk and lots of sugar. I didn't sleep well last night, and I need the energy."

Wilhelmina placed the pastries on a typical Southeast Asian plate of stylized blue flowers on a white background. "I hope you were not kept awake by Burt's attempt to solve the mystery of Sophia's death." She began putting everything on a black-lacquered tray.

The formal phrasing of Wilhelmina's English again caught Anjali's ear. Maybe she was just translating from the Dutch. Hard to speak fluently when English was your third or fourth language. So different from her own family. They'd all spoken English before they'd learned Hindi. Anjali wondered if she sounded off-putting herself, the way Sophia had.

Wilhelmina led the way to the verandah as Anjali responded, "I was mulling over what I heard at the party. But I've also been thinking a lot about Sophia on my own."

Her young hostess poured the tea and passed the milk and sugar. "I have heard the servants' gossip about how you are trying to find out what happened."

Anjali put two heaping spoons of sugar in her tea. "It started with a request from a friend. I wasn't keen to take it on. But now, as I learn more, I feel I have to find out how she drowned."

Wilhelmina's brow wrinkled. "Why do you need to know?"

"To see justice done." Anjali took a deep drink of the sweet tea. A conversation with Wilhelmina was like talking to two people, she thought. Sometimes she talked like her Dutch father and sometimes like her Indonesian mother.

Wilhelmina said, "How can justice be done? If the case is reopened, it will also open old wounds. It will hurt everyone and help no one. The official verdict means harmony will be restored. Please do not destroy that."

Her mother talking, Anjali thought, social harmony more important than justice.

"The case would be reopened only if necessary," Anjali said. "It depends. If Sophia was murdered…"

Wilhelmina interrupted, "She was not murdered. It was an accident. You will ruin your reputation and hurt KB also. You are the most respected woman in Vientiane."

Dutch side now, Anjali thought, and Wilhelmina obviously meant expatriate women. Lots of Lao women were more respected, some of them former princesses, some of them members of the new regime.

"That's exactly why I can do it," Anjali said. "Why I must do it. I can't respect myself if I don't." She finished her tea and felt some energy returning.

Both women sat stiffly in their chairs. Anjali decided to leave it alone for a while. Maybe Wilhelmina was using both sides of her ethnic heritage to hide something. If so, that was like using both barrels of a shotgun to hit a target. She couldn't miss. Anjali would have to come at her own target from all sides. But never directly.

Her hostess also seemed to sense she'd gone too far. She poured more tea. Her graceful hands were the color of ancient ivory against the dark blue pot. Anjali offered Wilhelmina the plate of pastries. They each took one. Wilhelmina sipped her tea. Black, Anjali noticed, with neither milk nor sugar.

Just get the conversation going, she thought. Then she could work her way back to Sophia. "You said last night that you've found Vientiane more congenial than lots of posts."

Wilhelmina's face relaxed. "Yes, I have." She broke off a bite-size piece of croissant. "Vientiane seems only slightly different from where I was born. And having household help is such a boon after having no one in Australia."

"This house was not ready when we arrived," she continued, "so we rented a temporary one. It was too small, and the garden was tiny, so the children could not really play. The electricity was always faltering. The stove did not work, and the air conditioners needed constant repairs. The staff suffered also, but they seemed to see it as just part of sharing our lives."

Anjali's mind returned to Somalia and weeks spent in a hotel room full of packing cases. Sophia's death made Anjali need to make sense of how she'd lived. She kept seeing how all the wives went through similar things.

Wilhelmina said, "When the time came for us to leave the first house, the staff wanted to host a *baci* for us. I am sure you have been to one?"

"Many times. It's a beautiful ceremony." Anjali recalled Sophia disparaging the *baci* as an adulteration of Buddhism. But it felt right to Anjali, marking life's transitions with a ceremony of blessing.

"The baci was held in our new house the evening we arrived," Wilhelmina said. "The family of Tsing's secretary, Sisomphane, donated their *khan*."

Anjali could easily picture the silver urn filled with flowers and tall, narrow candles, the celebrants gathered around. She reached for a second sweet roll and assuaged her guilt remembering Daddy-ji's advice for sustaining energy—if you can't sleep, eat.

Wilhelmina continued. "Sisomphane's father conducted the ceremony. The spouses and children of our extended Lao family were all there. Sisomphane arranged the long, white cords out from the *khan*, one to Tsing, one to me, the rest to those kneeling on the mats in a circle."

Anjali could see it, thin cords carrying blessings from the *khan* to each participant's hands clasped in prayer. The leader would have chanted Buddhist sutras and asked the honorees to hold an egg, a cooked chicken and fruit as symbols of the blessings of life.

She'd heard translations of the blessings which were quite poetic. Should you fall into fire, may you not burn. Should you fall into water, may you not drown. Should you fall into mud, may you not be soiled.

Anjali had a vision of Sophia floating in the Mekong, her

beautiful silk dress muddy from the riverbank. She blinked her eyes to clear the image and concentrated on Wilhelmina's *baci*.

The leader would have taken short cords from the *khan* and tied them to the honoree's wrists to bind the blessings. Then everyone else would have taken more such cords and done the same, whispering their own blessings to Tsing and Wilhelmina.

"By the end of the *baci*," Wilhelmina said, "our wrists were covered in cords. And they also had cords from us in token of our blessings for them. From the moment that Sisomphane's father began to chant until the last cord was tied, my cheeks were wet. I was overwhelmed by how our Lao staff had made our lives their lives."

Anjali thought about Tom's driver. "How protective would a staff member be, I wonder. If the relationship were really strong, would he commit a crime? What if he thought his employer's honor had been seriously damaged?"

Wilhelmina's face and voice were filled with concern for her guest. "Anjali, you are obsessed with Sophia. I do not believe that one of her staff would have harmed her. They were devoted to her."

Wilhelmina passed the fruit plate, and Anjali realized she was doing it to ease the sting of her remark. Anjali took a slice of papaya and a wedge of lime to squeeze over it. "Yes, but what about Tom's staff? Would his driver not tell the authorities if Tom came back that night and met Sophia by the riverbank? Would the driver do something himself?"

"How can you say such things?" Wilhelmina seemed to struggle to maintain her demeanor. "Think about the *baci*. The Lao are kind and gentle."

That's what Anjali had always thought, but now she wasn't so sure. She resolved to talk with Tom's driver. Best not to mention that, though. "You were typically kind to Vicki last night. Burt was giving her such a hard time."

Wilhelmina relaxed once more. "We have all experienced those first-weeks blues. Unsolicited advice, too much to do, so many challenges."

Anjali nodded and smiled. "I think it will help Vicki to work on the Christmas Bazaar, even though WIVS events can be stressful."

Wilhelmina regarded Anjali as though she were assessing whether to take her words on face value. She seemed to come to a decision. "It helped me when I was Chair. It gave me a sense of accomplishment when I could not find a job."

Wilhelmina's Bazaar had been a grand success, Anjali remembered. All the expats came to buy cakes, jams and jellies, potted plants, hand-printed note cards and used books. Wilhelmina had also talked the embassies into preparing and selling their ethnic dishes—shashlik from the Russians, sushi from the Japanese, satay from the Malaysians. Anjali and Suneeta had made samosas for hours.

A light breeze began to stir the leaves outside the veranda.

"Sophia was much in evidence at the Bazaar," Anjali said.

"She was enormously helpful. She shared her culinary talents with the Cooking Group and her artistic talents with the Print Group."

"But Sophia could drive people too hard. Did she make any of the women mad?"

Wilhelmina looked at Anjali with a hint of exasperation. "You are not trying to get back to that topic are you?"

Anjali took herself to task. Wilhelmina was half-Indonesian. It had been too soon to bring Sophia's squabbles back into the conversation.

Her hostess shook her head. "I want to remember the good things now. Sophia was always ready to lend a hand when I first arrived."

And the bad things, Anjali wondered, how could they get to that? "Why don't we go for a walk in the garden?" she suggested. "It's cooler now, with that nice breeze."

Wilhelmina's pleasure was evident. "We've made several improvements now that the rains have started again." She opened the screen door and led her guest into the garden.

Anjali could recognize many of the trees and plants—mango, guava, coconut, banana, ginger, jasmine, gardenia. She looked down at some plants she hadn't seen before. "Those are lilies aren't they? The big white ones and the little pink ones?"

Wilhelmina laughed. "We use the names the children gave them. It would spoil their magic to apply horticultural terms. We call the pink one 'the rain flower,' because it blooms in the monsoon. And the white one with tendrils is 'the fairy flower,' because the blossoms look like fairies dancing in the shade."

"The whole compound is splendid," Anjali said. "Your gardener must be a wonder."

"I could not do it without him. You can see how old this house is. The garden was just as old. The previous tenant was house-proud but not garden-proud. So we set to work to awaken the sleeping princess. That is how I thought of it. I do not know how I would have dealt with the stress without this garden. It has been my source of serenity and strength."

"Sophia's garden was incredible," Anjali said. "I wonder if she also felt such stress. Maybe that would explain why she lost her temper so easily."

Wilhelmina looked like her two cultures were warring deep inside. Conflicting emotions crossed her face. Finally, the Dutch side seemed to win. "I have often wondered the same thing. Sophia could not accept it when I got a job and reduced my WIVS participation. She was hurt and angry. She came here and lectured—no, scolded—me about how selfish I was. She was very, very personal in her attack. She treated me like a naughty child from an inferior race."

"She wanted to hurt you as much as you'd hurt her," Anjali said.

Wilhelmina tilted her head slightly to one side. "Perhaps." She looked off into the distance. "I *was* hurt. But then I realized that was just the way Sophia was. I am not a child. I am proud of my heritage. We WIVS women are the same. We are adults, and adults learn from such experiences. We grow, and we move on."

She turned her delicate face toward her guest. "Anjali, no one murdered Sophia. Sometimes she made us angry, but it was never worth killing over."

Anjali threw up her hands in mock surrender. "Okay, okay, you've convinced me. Nobody in WIVS had anything to do with Sophia's death."

Wilhelmina spoke firmly, perhaps more forcefully than her Indonesian mother would have liked. "It was an accident."

But one word rang in Anjali's mind like a bell. Maybe.

So that was why Wilhelmina wasn't at Sophia's goodbye party, Anjali thought as she drove home. Like a good Indonesian, she was avoiding more conflict. But what about her Dutch side?

Anjali's deliberations shifted to the tension she'd observed between Larry and Burt. On impulse, she turned the car toward the vacant lot where the Americans played softball every Sunday afternoon.

She didn't know whether it was all the sugar she'd consumed at Wilhelmina's brunch or her new sense of purpose in life, but she was once again fully energized.

She drove slowly by the lot in hopes of seeing whether Larry had come to the game. There were too many white Toyotas to be sure if one of them was his. Two men were pulling cases of beer out of the back of one of them. Oh dear, she thought, all Americans look alike—baseball caps and blue jeans.

Then one of them looked up, and she saw with pleasure that it was Larry. She drove down to the end of the line, parked her little Deux Chevaux and hurried to catch up with the men.

She was halfway to the field's entrance when she realized she'd forgotten to lock the car. Turning back, she saw the string of Toyota roofs like a white caterpillar with her own car the black-and-wine head. She rushed down the line, locked the car and scurried back through the entrance to the field.

"Steerike three!" shouted a deep voice, and a group of men and women jumped up to change places with the players on the field. The vacant lot was a milling mass, and Anjali couldn't recognize anyone, let alone Larry.

She stood on the sidelines uncertain about how to find him. Would he be playing, she wondered, or watching? He didn't seem like the athletic type when she considered the exchange with Burt over sports at the Club.

Gradually, the two teams sorted themselves out, and Anjali could see a crowd of spectators drinking beer in the shade of some scrubby trees. She'd last seen Larry carrying two beer cases, so she headed toward the drinkers. Sweat trickled down their shouting faces.

"Easy out!"

"OK, baby, OK. Let's go!"

"Show 'em, slugger!"

She'd never understood this game, she thought, remembering other times and other places where she'd watched softball. She knew it was supposed to be descended from cricket, but she'd never payed much attention. So what should she say about why she was there?

"Hi, Anjali," said a familiar voice. "What brings you here?" It was Larry. He'd come up behind her while she was trying to figure out what to do.

She smiled up at him. "Oh, the house gets lonely with KB away. Thought I'd come see what the Americans were doing." Sounds pretty lame, she rued.

"Great!" said Larry. "Let me buy you a beer."

They started through the crowd of overheated bodies.

"How about a Pepsi instead?" She knew the Americans would never have lemon squash.

"Ball two!" shouted the deep voice, and half the crowd groaned.

Larry led her over to the cooler, gave a dollar to one of the blond women in charge and handed Anjali a bottle of Pepsi with a straw.

After hurrying to and fro in the hot sun, she was terribly thirsty and took a deep sip. The Pepsi was barely cool, but at least it was wet. She heard the bat hit the ball and looked out at the field. A woman was running along a muddy track between two bases. Anjali knew enough to be sure that was what they were called.

Then she looked around at the spectators. "Vicki here?" she asked.

"Ah…no. She's got a headache." Larry shifted from one foot to the other. "Thought I'd come out for some air and give her a little peace." He gulped his Lao beer.

"That's too bad," Anjali said, recalling the increasing strain between husband and wife as Burt's party wore on.

"Batter up!" cried the deep voice, and the crowd started chattering again.

"Some game last night, huh?" Larry said.

"You mean Who Killed Sophia?"

"Yeah. Just like Burt to pull something like that."

"I'm not sure I understand."

Larry resettled his cap on his head. "You know he really had a thing for her."

"No, I didn't." Anjali took another sip, pleased at how the conversation was going.

"Yeah. Always trying to get Sophia over in a corner. Horniest guy in Vientiane." Larry's neck and ears turned red. "Sorry, Anjali. Didn't mean to be so crude. What I mean is, that's what happens when you don't have your wife around."

Anjali looked into Larry's face and wondered if he were speaking from experience.

Larry seemed desperate to change the subject. "What do you make of this smuggling thing down in Champassak? Could it be linked to Sophia's death?"

"How so?"

"Sophia was really into arts and crafts. Had lots of contacts. Maybe she found out what happened, and they killed her."

"The smugglers, you mean?"

"No," Larry explained, his patience showing, "the big cheese here who's helping the smugglers get the stuff out."

"Ball four. Take your base."

Part of Anjali's mind was distracted by the deep voice. What did that mean—pick up the base and run with it? So much running in softball.

But the main part of her attention was focused on Larry. "Who do you have in mind?"

Larry shrugged. "Dunno. Could be Burt. Like I said last night, it'd be easy to smuggle the stuff out with a factory shipment. Just grease a few palms here and there."

He had her full attention now. Anjali turned her body toward him. "So you're saying Burt could have killed her."

"Crack!" went the bat.

Larry grinned down at Anjali. "Yeah, guess I am."

"Home run!" screamed the crowd.

Anjali left the game early when she realized she wasn't going to get more out of Larry. She wondered if what he'd said was a smokescreen or what he really thought. Or perhaps he'd just been trying to get Burt in trouble. One thing for certain, she decided, it paid to be more proactive. She had to set up more meetings.

She pulled into her compound and left the car in the shade of the overhanging roof. House and garden were empty. Sunday was the usual servants' day off. Only Vong, the night watchman, would be there later, when darkness fell.

Anjali went inside, took a pitcher of lemonade out of the fridge and a glass from the cupboard, then went to her study. She already had a Monday dinner arranged with Philip. That left at least one more victim and Sophia's best friend. And Tom's driver, but she hadn't a clue how to organize a talk with him. Maybe Thongsy could help set something up for Tuesday.

Traveller jumped up on her desk and began to bat an eraser around. Anjali sighed. Traveller had a way of begging for attention when she had least time to give it. She looked for the small ball he usually played with, spied it under a chair and rolled it out the door. Traveller was off the desk and down the hall in a flash.

Her study restored to tranquility, Anjali called Karen and invited her to a picnic at Buddha Park on Wednesday. Then she phoned Catherine to confirm morning tea the day after.

She finished her second glass of lemonade and realized she was suddenly exhausted. It was hot and muggy. The air was heavy against her skin. Where's the rain? she wondered. So refreshing, the monsoon.

She went out into the hall, found Traveller and carried him to the bedroom. The two of them had a long nap curled together beneath the whirling ceiling fan. They slept until dusk. Anjali got up, muzzy with sleep and sultry air. She fed Traveller some of the ground-meat-and-rice mix that Ohnta cooked because there was no commercial pet food in Vientiane. Then Anjali fixed herself a simple dinner and went back to bed.

Something woke her—the cat jumping on the bed, mice scurrying between the walls, a sound outside the window. She lay awake, eyes searching the darkness. Then something darker stood out against the shadows of the night. Across the room, someone's head and shoulders were silhouetted against the window. She reached for the flashlight kept on the bedside table because of frequent blackouts. Slowly, silently, she turned it toward the window and pushed the button.

The silhouette became a man, eyes narrowed against the sudden light, hands gripping the bars that protected her. He turned and ran, but not before Anjali saw it was Tom's driver.

Her heart beating wildly, she jumped out of bed, grabbed a robe and ran to the window. Traveller followed and leaped up on the sill, twitching his tail with irritation.

"Vong! Vong!" Anjali shouted.

The night watchman came running, wiping sleep from his eyes. "Madame! *Qu'esque ce passe?*"

She told Vong about the intruder, and his face sank with shame. He turned his own, more powerful beam down on the ground. Anjali watched its progress from the safety of her barred window. Vong walked along, following footprints that lead away from the house and to the wall. She saw several smudges on the whitewashed concrete where the driver's muddy feet had scrabbled for purchase in a desperate effort to get over.

There was no point in pursuing him. It was too easy for Tom's driver to lose himself in the shadows of the dense foliage on the other side. And no point in calling the police. Whenever the few petty crimes or fender-benders occurred in the expat community, everyone found the police to be ineffectual.

Vong came back to the window, apologizing profusely in his broken French. He'd been worn out by an elaborate family funeral for his uncle and fallen asleep at his post. Anjali assured him she understood and resolved to get a second night watchman until all this was over. They could divide the night into two shorter shifts and patrol the grounds.

With painstaking care, Vong placed a chair below the bedroom window and sat up alertly facing the compound wall.

Anjali went back to bed, turned on her side, and pulled the pillows into a nest. She felt enervated and yet on edge.

She knew she'd be awake the rest of the night and wished for KB—not to protect but to comfort. Traveller wound himself into the crook of her knees, and the sound of his purring soothed. Anjali found her eyes closing.

It was raining when she awoke, a soft, gentle rain, comforting to body and soul. Yoga loosened Anjali's joints and sent her spirits flying.

After a light breakfast of fruit, tea and a mini-baguette, she talked with Onhta about supper for Philip that evening. The cook went off to the market, and Anjali was left alone with her memories of the previous night. What had Tom's driver wanted? To talk? Or something more?

Daddy-ji had taught all his children to face their fears. And Mummy-ji had been proud of Anjali when she did. She went outside to speak with Thongsy. "What is the name of Tom Powell's driver?"

"Kham-pun, Madame."

Did Thongsy know where Kham-pun lived, Anjali asked. He did. Then they would go there tomorrow and talk with him.

"But Madame…" Thongsy started to say.

Anjali gave him a kindly shake of her head and went back inside. She recalled Wilhelmina's *baci*. The Lao were such gentle people. Surely Kham-pun only wanted to tell her something. She was determined to give him the chance.

Ohnta brought back vegetables for an intricately flavored luncheon salad and the makings of an omelet for supper. Over lunch, Anjali began to feel apprehensive about Philip's visit. How much would he volunteer? How much should she pry? He didn't seem like the type to be a murderer, but mild-mannered men had killed before.

She rebuked herself—she didn't even know if it was murder. And if it wasn't, what right did she have to probe Philip's wounds? What a quandary, damned if she did and damned if she didn't. Either Philip was a murderer, or he wasn't. She had to find out.

Anjali felt irritable, irritated with herself. This search for how Sophia had drowned was making her feel useful again, but what else was it doing to her? She wasn't sure she wanted to be the kind of person who discovered what had happened.

Out of respect for his religion, Anjali didn't offer Philip alcohol, nor did she take any herself. Ohnta brought juice and a cold appetizer—large, transparent rice noodles wrapped around marinated vegetables. She set them on the veranda's dining table and withdrew.

Philip appeared ill-at-ease, squirming in his chair, crossing and uncrossing his legs. His emotions seemed dammed up, ready to burst.

Anjali had thought very carefully about how to approach the topic of Frieda and Sophia. It would never work to be direct. "Everything going okay with the transition?"

"Yeah. The new team's really sharp. I'll probably be able to leave at the end of the month." He tasted Onhta's noodle-rolls and smiled his appreciation.

"Remind me, where's home?" She knew it was in the States, but which one she couldn't remember.

"Indiana. It'll be wonderful to see the family again."

"How's Frieda?"

Philip folded his arms across his chest. "Greatly improved. I wouldn't be here otherwise. She was in awful bad shape, you know." He took up his fork and stabbed a bite of roll.

Anjali looked into his eyes, wanting him to see how she felt. "I didn't know. I'm sorry."

"I'm sorry too," he said in a carefully modulated voice.

His fork clattered on the plate, and his face collapsed with anguish. "It should never have happened. It was all because of Sophia."

Anjali felt torn, pleased that her strategy had worked so easily but guilty over Philip's pain. "Do you want to talk about it? Sometimes talking helps."

He smiled ruefully. "That's one of a preacher's jobs, helping the troubled talk it out." He was literally hugging himself.

They sat quietly for a while, as if on the edge of something they weren't sure of.

Finally, Philip spoke. "I need to make a confession, but I can't tell the church hierarchy."

Anjali's heart leaped. She glanced at Vong making his rounds and disciplined herself not to jump to conclusions.

Philip looked at her for a moment, then seemed to make up his mind. "I trust you, Anjali. I know you'll keep my secrets."

Anjali tried to appear non-committal.

He gazed off into the distance, his eyes unfocussed, seeing nothing before him. Finally, he spoke. "I hated Sophia for what she did to Frieda."

Anjali kept quiet, not wanting to interfere with the flow of his confession.

Philip tilted his head back, eyes on the ceiling. "I came to Laos to witness my faith. I wanted to counteract the trauma of the CIA's Secret War." His head came upright, mouth turned down, eyes bitter. "A dirty little war. Military pilots wearing civilian clothes dropping two million tons of bombs. For nothing. The Pathet Lao took Vientiane anyway, and thousands of innocent Lao were killed or maimed."

Anjali was off balance. How'd they get from Sophia to bomb-disposal? And how to get Philip back on the right topic?

He continued, "Now, twenty years later, people are still injured or killed by those bombs. Many of them weren't even born when the bombs were dropped."

Philip finished his noodle-rolls in two big bites. Onhta peeked around the kitchen door to see if they were ready for the next course. Anjali gave a slight nod, and Onhta brought out a beautifully prepared omelet on a bed of fluffy white rice. The platter was garnished with cherry tomatoes and thin carrot strips fashioned into flowers with cilantro leaves.

The cook set the platter before Philip. He piled food on his plate and set to work.

He seemed more relaxed, so Anjali helped herself to some omelet and headed back toward her own topic. "And while you were saving lives, Frieda was preserving traditional architecture. You were both making important contributions to Laos."

Philip nodded. "Frieda wanted to help save Vientiane's heritage before it vanished in the name of progress."

Now they were back on the subject of Frieda, Anjali could soon turn the conversation to Sophia. "Frieda knew how to work within Lao culture and outside official circles. She didn't try to make a big splash. That's why she was successful."

Philip went on to talk more about Frieda's efforts to preserve Lao architecture, and Anjali bided her time. She passed Philip the omelet and rice. He took generous second helpings of each. A sure sign that a man was comfortable, she thought. Or that he wasn't eating very well while living alone. Or both.

When he was finished, Onhta came out to clear the main course and set a tart fruit-and-vegetable salad before them.

Philip mounded salad on his plate. "Frieda felt at home in Laos, full of peace."

Now, Anjali decided. "And Sophia destroyed that peace."

Philip put down his fork, his mouth grim, his huge fists on the table. His narrowed eyes stared at Anjali.

She held his gaze, not daring to say more. Her entire body was tense. She tried calming down with the reminder that Onhta was in the kitchen and Vong outside. Then she realized Philip was warring within himself.

He straightened his shoulders and gave a slight nod. "Yes."

Anjali made her body relax slowly so as not to disturb Philip's story.

"Sophia stopped by the house not long after we arrived. Frieda told me about her visit. Apparently Sophia was very pleasant, if a bit aggressive."

Philip detailed Sophia's usual approach to newcomers, ending with a plea for Frieda to join WIVS. "But Frieda isn't a joiner," Anjali said.

"Being around other people just sucks the energy out of her."

That was something of a surprise. Anjali had known that Frieda was shy, but this seemed to go beyond shyness.

Philip went on, "Besides, she didn't have much time to spare. She was setting up house, raising four children, studying Lao and serving as bookkeeper for the project."

Anjali nodded to encourage him to continue.

"Later on," he said, "when I met Sophia, I realized there may have been other reasons. We're plain people. We don't believe in show. Sophia was flamboyant and artificial in my eyes, and I imagine in Frieda's eyes also."

"How did Sophia take it when Frieda declined her invitation?"

"Frieda didn't say much, but sometimes her silence is more eloquent than someone else's impassioned speech. Sophia never invited her again. Frieda might have been able to go now and then to a WIVS program, but she's not one to push in where she doesn't feel welcome."

Anjali recalled Moira's foiled attempt to take Frieda to a Koffeeklatch. But that was much later. What had happened?

Onhta appeared to clear the table, and Anjali suggested they move over to the rattan armchairs. Onhta brought homemade papaya sherbet and a large, decorative thermos to the coffee table. The thermos had a push-top so Anjali could serve hot tea for hours, if need be.

Philip dipped into his sherbet, eyes sparkling with pleasure.

Anjali smiled. How could a man who loved desserts as much as she did be a murderer? She frowned at herself—that was totally silly. She poured them each a cup of tea. "So that first meeting was awkward but not really upsetting?"

"The real problems started when we joined the chorus."

Anjali had heard rumors of conflict in the expat chorus, but no details. She let Philip see the interest in her face.

"The chorus was a second family for Frieda and me. We sang our hearts out, and we had a lot of fun doing it."

He paused, emotions playing over his face—pain, sadness, anger. He put his hands on the arms of the chair as if to rise, then fell back.

Anjai waited.

Philip's voice was strained. "Every time there was a decision to be taken, Sophia made trouble. Always in opposition to June. You know her, don't you?"

Anjali nodded. June had taught music at a community college back home. Coming out to Laos with her agronomist-husband, she'd founded the chorus and done a splendid job.

Philip's throat seemed constricted. He kept swallowing. "Frieda's shy, but she has a strong sense of justice. She tried to head off those confrontations before they blew up, but Sophia would round on her and say something nasty."

Philip stopped talking abruptly. He rubbed his russet beard and gazed into the distance. "I've left something out. I wanted to tell the story without mentioning it, but it won't make sense if I don't."

Anjali didn't know whether to be anxious or relieved. Relieved, she decided. She had to know what had happened.

Outside, the night creatures were singing their evening raga. Philip listened for a moment to the frog chorus, took a sip of his tea and returned to his story.

"Everyone has within them a pain that can be summoned at another's touch. Sophia seemed to know instinctively where to probe. Frieda's twin sister committed suicide. They were incredibly close, and Frieda never got over it. Her loss made it easier to hurt her."

Anjali felt as if layers were being lifted from someone she'd thought she'd known.

Philip continued, "The weekly chorus meetings were a chance for Frieda to soar on the wings of her voice above her grief, to be lost in the joy of music, if only for a few hours."

"And Sophia ruined that chance to soar," Anjali said.

Contempt tinged Philip's voice. "She smashed Frieda's joy over and over. Whenever she came to June's rescue, Sophia would snarl, 'Are you your sister's keeper?'"

Anjali shuddered. Such a talent for malice.

"The final reckoning came during the Vientiane Follies," he said.

"I was surprised to see Frieda at the rehearsals. It didn't seem like her sort of event."

"Neither one of us would have got involved, but Sophia asked the chorus if they'd sing a few songs, and they agreed. So we went along with the decision. After all, we thought, it can't be too great a burden to sing at a WIVS fundraiser."

After what they'd experienced at Sophia's hands, Anjali mused, why did they ask for more? Did their pacifist religion blind them to the truth? Or cause them to keep trying when there was no hope? Or teach them it was noble to suffer?

Philip stared at his empty cup. He seemed tired now, no energy in voice or body. He was just reciting. Anjali poured more tea and wondered if this lack of emotion was a way of protecting himself from pain.

"From the start, it was conflict piled on conflict," he said. "Sophia wanted to dictate what the chorus would sing so it would fit her concept of the Follies. One of the songs was downright risqué. A lot of the chorus members were from the religion-based NGOs and wanted it dropped from the program. We won that round."

"And the other conflicts?"

The tension came back into Philip's voice and body. Anjali could feel the pressure building. "There was no doubt that the two best voices in the chorus belonged to Sophia and Frieda," he said. "Sophia wrote a duet and asked Frieda in front of the whole chorus if she wouldn't..." he held up his fingers and made the charades sign for quotation, "'…let bygones be bygones and sing this little tune.' Despite her misgivings, Frieda said yes."

"Oh dear," Anjali couldn't help interjecting.

Philip was sitting bolt upright, feet flat on the floor, hands braced on the armrests. "Sophia's little tune had some double entendres that weren't very subtle. Frieda asked to change those lyrics, and Sophia blasted her in front of the entire chorus."

He grimaced. "Then Sophia wanted to wear short costumes to show off her figure. Frieda's gained a lot of weight after four pregnancies. She'd look ridiculous in a mini-skirt. More important, her sense of propriety would never allow her to be so bare on stage. At one of the rehearsals, Sophia called Frieda a prude and asked how she managed to have so many children."

"That must have happened after I'd gone," Anjali said. "I usually just did my bit and left. If I'd been there, I'd have said something."

Philip's smile was fleeting. "I know you would've." Anger filled his voice. "What Sophia did at the dress rehearsal was far worse. It was downright evil."

Philip wasn't acting out the scene the way Jackie had, but his description of the dress rehearsal was so vivid that Anjali felt she was experiencing it through his eyes.

It was hot in the school auditorium where the Follies rehearsed. From his stance against the left wall, Philip could see the seats down front filled with performers, their makeup shiny with sweat. Everyone seemed a little hysterical, reacting too fast and laughing too loud.

The Three Little Maids from Laos had sung. Anjali Rao had recited her poem and gone home. The Nam Ngum Lake Corps de Ballet had flitted across the stage and into the wings. Now all that remained before the finale was Frieda and Sophia's duet. He'd been standing there, waiting ever since the chorus had sung, praying all would go well this time.

One of the Three Little Maids started for the cooler of drinks at the back of the hall, but she was stopped by another Little Maid whose accent marked her as Deep South, USA. "If Ah was you, Ah wouldn't go back theah." She gestured toward the raucous, red-faced men in tutus. "They're all drunk as skunks. Besides…" Irony spilled from her crimsoned lips, "…ya don't wanna miss Sophia's duet, do ya?"

"Guess I'll go for a cigarette instead," the first Maid responded and headed outside.

Sophia appeared center stage, her long legs cascading from a purple micro-mini. Catcalls and wolf whistles echoed from the Corps de Ballet. Sophia smiled, put one hand on a cocked hip and posed with the other over her head like a chorus girl.

Then she looked down at the performers and put both hands on her waist. "Why is everyone sitting down there?" Irritation conquered her smile. "You're supposed to be lining up for the finale when we start our duet." She clapped her hands. "Chop-chop. Let's go."

The performers began to get up, more than one raising eyes to heaven and grimacing. They looked sideways at one another, and some giggled. Philip stayed where he was, masked by the moving crowd. He wanted to see the duet.

Sophia shaded her eyes and surveyed the auditorium. "I really came out here to look for Frieda. You're not hiding her back there, are you, boys?"

"Not bloody likely," a male voice called back.

Frieda stepped out from the wings, head down, shoulders hunched.

Sophia whirled. "Here she is at last!" She began to applaud, and her minions joined in. It was hard to tell whether there was true appreciation in that applause or mockery.

Frieda shuffled over to join Sophia, her knees pushing against the bottom of her skirt. It was an exact match of Sophia's except for length.

Sophia bent her graceful neck down to look in Frieda's face. "Are you ready, Frieda?" She said it loud enough that everyone could hear her condescension.

A few people shambling toward the stage door looked over with tightened eyes.

Sophia glided to the piano and nodded graciously at the pianist. The opening bars sounded, and Sophia swanned back to center stage.

"Oh, I'm just wild about Laos, and Laos is wild about me," the two women began to sing. "The heavenly blisses of these misses…" they gestured at themselves, "…easy for all to see."

Philip felt his chest constrict. Was that another double entendre they'd missed?

Sophia was cavorting around Frieda. They'd tried it earlier with both of them doing a vaudeville routine, but Frieda wasn't comfortable with a buck-and-wing. So now it was Frieda's role to stand there and sing as if nothing was going on while Sophia pranced.

"The food's just like chocolate candy, and just like honey from the bee…" Sophia stood behind Frieda, waving her arms up and down like beating wings.

Only the tutu-clad men were left in the line moving toward the stage door. They were grinning at Sophia's antics.

"Oh, I'm just wild about Laos, and it's just…"

Sophia glanced over at the grinning men and stooped down as the duet went into its big finish. Philip saw two of Sophia's minions look at each other in surprise. Some new stage business? he wondered. The minions hurried to line up the performers backstage.

"…wild about, cannot do without, simply wild about me!"

With the last line, Sophia jumped up with Frieda's hem in her hand. She didn't lift it very high, but it was high enough. The men could see Frieda's sagging thighs and pouchy knees.

"Take it off! Take it all off!" shouted the last man, disappearing through the stage door.

For a moment, Frieda looked like she didn't understand what had happened. Then her face blanched. She ran off the stage and out the door to the car park.

"She sobbed all the way home," Philip finished the story, swallowing hard and blinking back his own tears.

Anjali was furious. Why hadn't she stayed? She'd known Sophia was stressed that night, primed to do something wrong. "But why didn't the story get out? I never heard a thing."

"Almost no one saw it. They were busy in the wings when it happened. The men—when they sobered up—were embarrassed about their part in it." Philip gulped the last of his tea.

Anjali wondered what had possessed Sophia. Her revenges usually took more subtle forms. Was this another sign she was overwrought?

Outside, the evening raga ended abruptly. There was a moment of silence, then the skies poured down rain like a silver curtain. Why couldn't such a curtain could fall in life, Anjali thought, silencing evil and nurturing good? The night creatures were harmless, but Sophia wasn't. Someone should have done something. Perhaps someone did. She looked at Philip.

He slumped down in his chair, his voice increasingly sadder as he went on. "The Follies took away all Frieda's pleasure in singing. She stopped participating in the Chorus. She lost interest in Lao architecture and language lessons. She stayed home. The only people she saw were those who cared enough to come—June, Moira, Karen. She developed chronic stomach trouble, but when we went to the clinic, they couldn't find a pathological cause. She found it hard to get up in the morning, and she needed a nap in the afternoon."

Anjali studied Philip. She'd never seen such naked pain on a person's face. Was all this reason enough to kill Sophia? Not for the Philip she knew. But did she really know him?

He continued, "She spent more and more time with the Bible, often just staring at it on her lap. When night fell, she sat alone in the dark."

He wagged his head left and right. "Then she started to cry. For no reason. 'What's wrong?' I'd ask. 'How can I help?' 'I don't know,' she'd say, 'I don't know what's wrong.' And there was terror in her voice."

The penny dropped, and Anjali saw the contrast. Frieda wasn't just shy. She was as depressive as Sophia was manic. What kind of people are we? Anjali asked herself. Why didn't any of us see how depressed Frieda was? Too busy contemplating our own navels?

He put a fist to his heart and closed his eyes. "I'd been so engaged in destroying bombs that I hadn't paid attention to Frieda. She couldn't cope, so she just withdrew." He opened his eyes and looked squarely into Anjali's. "And I, the savior of the Lao, was looking the other way."

Anjali felt her own pain well up. Not Philip, she prayed, not a murderer.

He pulled back from his dark vision with obvious effort. "We flew down to Bangkok as soon as I could arrange it. June and Jim welcomed our kids into their brood for as long as it took. Frieda saw a psychiatrist, and he recommended counseling and medication. I consulted with our Mission Board, and the whole family returned to Indiana. At first, Frieda was admitted to the psychiatric ward. Finally, with the prayers of our congregation, she came home to Bloomington."

Philip looked at Anjali with haunted eyes. "I stayed on as long as I could before coming back here. I never heard Frieda sing again. Not in the church choir. Not in the shower. Never."

Anjali's hand came up to cover her mouth. She couldn't bear it.

Philip looked down at his clenched fists. "I hated Sophia enough to kill her. I am weak. I am prey to temptation. But I did not yield to my desire."

He needed to confess, Anjali reminded herself. "But you feel guilty because you wished her dead?"

He blinked his eyes rapidly. "Frieda's better now, and I put that terrible wish behind me."

Philip wasn't yet truly comfortable, Anjali realized. She could feel the tension emanating from his voice. As gently as she possibly could, she said, "But that's not all, is it Philip?"

He turned to Anjali, his face full of agony. "I am a minister. 'Forgive us our trespasses, as we forgive those who trespass against us.' But I cannot find in my heart the charity to forgive Sophia for what she did to my Frieda."

He gritted his teeth and turned away. "God help me, I still hate her, even though she's dead. Where there is no contrition, there can be no forgiveness."

His tears brimmed over, streaking his face and wetting his beard. He made no sound, no sob, no ragged breath. He sat sunk in his misery.

Anjali felt self-loathing come to bury her. He hadn't done it. But she'd pushed too far. She was a useless old woman, leading him to pain and then powerless to help. She was a fool who asked too many questions.

Then Anjali realized there was something she could do. She placed her hand on his forearm, careful to make a gesture of friendship and no more. She let him feel the empathy in her touch. She didn't look at him. She didn't want either of them embarrassed by the intimacy of that moment. They sat quietly in the dim lamplight, listening to the rain.

"Thanks, Anjali," Philip said after a while. Then he got up and drove off into the silver curtain.

Watching him pull away, Anjali realized she'd never felt such a failure in her life.

Exhausted, she went out to the kitchen to tell Onhta she was free to go. It was well past the cook's normal departure time. Anjali felt guilty at having asked her to stay until Philip left.

Onhta was passing the time by cleaning rice for the next day. She stood by the sink, swirling the rice round and round in a thin aluminum pan from the market. The pot was half-filled with water, and the swirling motion caused the dirt and debris to rise to the top.

Anjali waited quietly for Onhta to finish. The cook reached into the pot with a delicate forefinger and thumb to extract a blackened kernel. Then she drained the rice in a colander and covered it to keep it clean until she returned to boil it the next day.

"Thank you, Onhta," Anjali said and turned to go.

"Madame, may I speak?"

Anjali turned back and smiled. "But of course." As always, they were speaking French, the one language they had in common. She felt physically and emotionally worn down by the evening's conversation, but she knew Onhta would never have asked to speak under the circumstances unless it was important.

"You are tired, Madame. Please sit." Onhta pulled out a kitchen chair.

Anjali gestured for the Onhta to sit too, but the cook hesitated. She didn't wish to act above her station, Anjali realized and thought of a good reason from Onhta's point of view. "If you sit, I will be better able to hear you."

The cook looked uncomfortable, but Anjali smiled and gestured again. Onhta took the other chair and carefully tucked her *pa-sin* under her legs. "Madame, I do not wish to give offense, but the men have asked me to talk with you."

Anjali knew she meant the men of the household—Vong, Thongsy and Kongkeo.

"We had a meeting while you were eating your lunch." Onhta looked a bit sheepish at this admission that they hadn't been working, but Anjali smiled encouragement. "The men told me about what happened here last night."

Anjali was touched by their concern. "Please don't worry. I know the man only wanted to talk."

"Forgive me, Madame, but the Lao have black hearts."

"I'm sorry?" Anjali wasn't sure she understood.

"It is a saying. It means we are smiling and gentle on the outside, but inside, we never forgive an injury. Even if it takes years, a Lao will remember and have revenge."

"But I have not injured that man."

"How do you know? Perhaps you caused some injury without meaning to."

Anjali shook her head. "I can think of nothing. I hardly know him."

"Madame," Onhta said, "I do not wish to intrude. It is for you to decide. But we talked a long time, and we all resolved that I should tell you that the Lao have black hearts."

"Thank you, Onhta," Anjali said with as much solemnity as she could muster. "I am deeply touched by your concern." She used the plural form of "your" so Onhta would know she meant the concern of everyone. "I will think carefully about what you have said."

Anjali rose to her feet. It was a signal Onhta could not ignore. The cook rose also, gave a respectful *nop* and left.

Anjali lay listening to the soothing sounds of morning—birds singing outside her window, Onhta moving around the kitchen, the muffled drum from the nearby temple. It was past time to get up, but Anjali's whirling mind kept her pinned in bed. So many things to think about. Like Onhta's warning last night about the Lao having black hearts.

She found it hard to accept that warning. All her evidence was to the contrary—street accidents amicably resolved, *bacis* generously conducted for foreigners whenever a Lao thought they needed one, the quiet thoughtfulness of the house and UNDP staff. There had to be a benign reason for the driver's appearance at her midnight window.

Traveller climbed up on her stomach and began to purr. Anjali stroked his neck and considered why no one, not even Philip, had stood up for Frieda against Sophia. She'd seen it happen in posts all over the world—someone badly misbehaves, and no one tries to stop them. The other expatriates think it's more important to keep the peace, so they try to avoid the offender. Failing that, they smile on the outside and seethe on the inside.

It often made matters worse if one tried to challenge the Sophias of this world, Anjali mused. Then sides must be chosen, and the small expat community is split. After a while, people begin to resent the person who initiated the split, even if that person was right.

When Jackie and Karen had challenged Sophia, they'd ended up being seen as part of the problem. And poor Frieda—she'd dared to stand up to Sophia and been nearly destroyed while everyone looked the other way. All three women had suffered increasing isolation in an already claustrophobic environment.

Enticing smells drifted through the house from the kitchen. Best get up, she told herself.

After breakfast, Anjali tried to call the French Embassy to make an appointment to see Jean-Claude, but she couldn't get through. The ancient phone lines of the old colonial structure were always shorting out in the monsoon. She decided to go by later in the day and see if she could get in to talk with him.

Anjali put down the phone, and it rang under her hand. It was Philip. Hearing his voice brought back the feeling of being weighed down by failure when he'd left the night before.

He thanked her for dinner, then said, "I feel lightened, Anjali. I'm grateful."

She felt like a burden had been lifted from her own body. "And your call has lightened me. I thought I'd failed you."

"Oh, no, Anjali. I'm truly thankful for your patience and concern. You helped a great deal."

They talked a bit more, and he rang off. Anjali felt a surge of joy. She'd helped Philip after all. And learned something in the process.

She went out to find Thongsy so they could go talk with Tom's driver. The chauffeur was polishing the official car. When he saw her, he looked a bit guilty.

That was odd, Anjali thought. The Lao almost never showed emotion. And what did he have to feel guilty about? Then she remembered the staff talking yesterday when they should have been working.

"To Kham-pun's house," she said.

"Oh, Madame, we may not be able to find him."

Anjali couldn't figure out what was going on. That was a strong statement for a Lao, and especially for Thongsy. He clearly didn't want to go. Probably more of this black heart business, she decided. Well, she wasn't having any.

"Nevertheless, we will try," she said and settled into the back seat.

Thongsy piloted them through downtown Vientiane's crowded streets, his stiff back radiating disapproval. How hard it was to read the Lao, Anjali mused. One had to pay attention to the littlest things.

Eventually, they came to the circle surrounding the monumental arch of Anousavari. Anjali looked up at the bizarre blend of L'Arc de Triomphe topped with Southeast Asian domes and recalled climbing up inside with KB to view the city not long after they'd arrived. Most of Vientiane was no more than three stories, and they could see across the rice fields to the horizon.

KB's shirt was wet with perspiration after the climb. "Did you hear the rumor about how Anousavari came to be built?"

Anjali was out of breath and thinking about how she had to lose weight. She just shook her head.

KB smiled down at her and used his folded newspaper to fan her flushed face. "They say that during the war, the Americans gave the Royal Lao Government cement to repave the airport runway so U.S. military planes could land more safely. The Lao diverted the cement to construct Anousavari, because they wanted Vientiane to have an arch that rivaled the one in Paris."

Anjali looked at him in amazement. "Is that true?"

"Who knows? It's a great story, but it's always hard to know what to believe here." He turned toward the stairway and held out his hand. "Ready for a cold drink, my darling?"

Thongsy weaved through the usual crush of mopeds and bikes with a scattering of cars in the traffic circle. The space around the monument was so broad, at least a hundred yards, that even in the rush hour, it could seem nearly empty. Yet the Lao always surged together near the arch, and it was tricky maneuvering through the press of disparate vehicles.

Just after the circle, Thongsy turned off the wide boulevard leading toward the distant hills and drove through ever-narrowing streets until they were in a completely Lao neighborhood. This was the first time Anjali had been in this part of Vientiane, and she gazed at her surroundings with interest. No cars passed, only bikes and a few mopeds. Most people were on foot. She was conscious of being the only *farang*.

She could easily see through the flimsy fences of bamboo and wire. No concrete walls here, she observed, no ornamental gardens. Instead, bare earth sported tufts of uncut grass with a few papaya and banana trees. Unfettered chickens and ducks scratched in the dirt. Men dressed in shorts and undervests tended small vegetable plots with hoes and rakes. Their bent backs lent a bucolic air to the city.

Most houses had a few flowers potted up in old tin cans. The Lao really did care about beauty, Anjali reflected. She looked at the men tending their vegetables. It was just more important for them to use the limited land to feed themselves than to grow ornamentals.

The houses were built in the traditional fashion, the ground floor open, often with a large wooden loom beneath so the weaver could take advantage of shade and breeze. A lot of Lao women still wove the cloth for their *pa-sins*, as their ancestors had done for centuries. The houses were built of wood, often with walls woven of palm or banana leaves, so that air could flow not only through open doors and windows, but literally through the walls. Wide eaves protected those walls from the monsoon.

Thongsy shifted down to first gear and coaxed the car through the puddles in the unpaved roads. Good thing they weren't in the middle of a heavy rain, Anjali thought. It'd be hard-going in a car.

Finally Thongsy pulled up in front of a house on cement pillars. Kham-pun's family had some money, then. Poor houses had wooden supports.

"Madame, are you sure you want to go in? Perhaps no one is home."

Anjali sighed. What was the matter with him?

Without replying, she got out of the car and walked toward the staircase under the house. She could hear Thongsy following. His steps seemed reluctant.

She passed a loom, threads dangling where cloth had recently been cut away. It was much darker here, and a smell of dampness and slaughtered chickens rose up from the beaten earth. Over in the far corner, a thick log had been upended for a chopping block. A hatchet was stuck in the top, and a few rusty feathers fluttered on the ground.

Suddenly, two scowling men came down the stairs and barred the way. Neither of them was Tom's driver.

Anjali turned to Thongsy in time to see his eyes widen.

"Thongsy," she said, "please explain that we are looking for Kham-pun."

The chauffeur made a stiff *nop* to the men and translated her words. The men did not return his gesture. They spoke sharply.

"They are his brothers, Madame. They say he is not here."

"Please ask when he will return, so that we may talk with him."

Anjali watched Thongsy translate and the men respond. The brothers seemed uncharacteristically offensive for Lao, and Thongsy appeared more and more uncomfortable.

"They say he has gone back to their village, Madame. They do not know when he will return."

This sort of thing was common, Anjali knew. Many Lao families lived partly in town and partly in the ancestral village, traveling back and forth for work, celebrations, funerals and fresh farm produce. In this way, the extended family spread out and shared its resources. Those who had work in town brought cash into the family, while others produced vegetables and meat for themselves and the town-dwellers.

Kham-pun's brothers advanced and spoke more harshly. The odor of their acrid sweat engulfed Anjali. She was disconcerted by the display of anger on their faces.

Thongsy backed away, and his voice trembled slightly. "Madame, I think we should leave now. These men say they cannot help us. They say we should return to our own homes."

Anjali's stomach began to cramp. She made an effort not to look at the hatchet over in the corner. She didn't want to remind the brothers of its presence. Using every ounce of will and a lifetime of yoga, she summoned up a calm demeanor. Then she made a *nop*, said "*Kawb jai*" and turned to go.

Her "thank you" was not well-received. The two brothers

followed Anjali and Thongsy to the car and started shouting. Their cries brought the neighbors running from their gardens. The car was suddenly surrounded by the sharp teeth of rakes and hoes raised in threatening hands. Anjali's stomach took another twist.

Thongsy pushed the buttons that automatically rolled up the windows and locked the doors. Anjali was frightened. This couldn't be happening.

She looked out the window. A mouth with a missing tooth was shouting against the glass. Onhta was right, she realized, the Lao do have black hearts.

Thongsy got the car going and began to make his way through the crowd. Just moving made Anjali feel better. Thank God he was driving carefully. The last thing they needed was to hit someone.

It was impossible to turn the car around, and Anjali wondered if Thongsy knew another way out of the neighborhood. The crowd had parted, but they were following the car. Thongsy couldn't speed up on the narrow, rutted road.

Anjali felt apprehensive and looked back through the rear window. A man with a scar distorting his chin had started running after the car. He was carrying a sickle lifted against the sky. The rest of the crowd was right behind him.

Thongsy wrenched the wheel to the left and pulled into an even narrower alley.

What was he doing? Anjali fretted. She looked through the windscreen. The alley was a dead end. The crowd could catch them. She put a hand to her cramping stomach.

The chauffeur accelerated past houses on pillars like giant jail bars. The car rocketed from side to side on the ruts.

We'll get a puncture, she worried.

Thongsy was heading straight for the fence at the end of the alley.

Does he expect me to jump out and run? Anjali thought wildly. She looked back and saw the crowd round the corner.

Thongsy wrenched the wheel again, and they were in a narrow track between two houses. Branches beat against the windscreen. The track narrowed.

We're not going to make it, Anjali despaired. And KB doesn't even know where I am.

She bent forward and tried to look through the windscreen. The track was widening again. Anjali's stomach relaxed a notch. Up ahead, she could see Anousavari rising above the rooftops.

The next moment, their car shot out into the nearly empty circle. Anjali never thought she'd be so happy to see that preposterous monument and it's wide-open spaces.

Thongsy slowed and said, "Where to now, Madame?" Neither voice nor body betrayed the emotion he must have been feeling.

"Il Ristorante," Anjali replied. She felt the need to celebrate.

Alberto welcomed Anjali with his usual brio and led her toward the small table in an alcove that she preferred when eating alone. They passed a table of WIVS members, all of them friends of Sophia. Anjali greeted each by name, but their responses were cool.

The restauranteur left Anjali with a menu and a bottle of mineral water. She decided on pasta with baby peas and a mixed salad, then looked up for a waiter. Instead, she saw the nearer WIVS members twisted around to look at her while their friend on the other side of the table spoke in a sibilant whisper. When they saw Anjali look their way, they all turned back abruptly. But the whispering continued.

So the gossip had begun, Anjali realized and wondered what rumors they were passing around. Was she out to bring Sophia's killer to justice? Or to ruin her reputation by digging up sordid stories? How tiresome this was. Anjali smiled at the one woman who was still staring as Pasquale arrived to take her order.

Jackie had once called Pasquale "easy on the eyes." She was right, Anjali thought. Pasquale certainly was attractive. Not just in looks, but in personality. Alberto was round and bombastic, while Pasquale was slight and flirtatious. But not in any way that was off-putting. He seemed genuinely to like women and showed his appreciation. Even to overweight Indian grandmothers.

His thoughtful consideration eased Anjali's tension over the morning's events. But after he left, she got a bit shaky remembering what had happened at Kham-pun's house. She didn't want to feed the WIVS gossip, so she kept her trembling hands in her lap and tried to look normal. But inside she was reliving the menacing brothers and their threatening neighbors.

What had made them so angry? What had Kham-pun told them? Anjali didn't see how she could ever find out, because she'd never get a *laissez-passer* to go to his village, and under the circumstances, she certainly wasn't returning to his family's house in Vientiane. Frustration conquered her nerves, and she raised a hand to straighten a wayward fork.

Pasquale arrived with her pasta and a complimentary glass of wine. "You look like you could use one, signora. Is everything okay?"

She smiled. "Yes, thanks, everything's just fine." Not really, she thought, but there was no point in discussing it with anyone except KB.

Pasquale glanced at the WIVS table. "Signora, I have heard rumors. They say you are investigating Sophia's murder. Is this true?"

"Not really. How Sophia died is a job for the police. But of course we're all talking about it. We all wonder what happened."

One of her brother Ashok's taunts came back to haunt her. "Liar, liar, pants on fire." But her lies seemed to satisfy the restauranteur.

"Be careful, signora," Pasquale said. His words brought back memories of the morning, and he seemed to sense Anjali's distress. He hesitated as if mulling over whether to speak or not. Then he made up his mind. "Don't let the gossips hurt you. You are too fine a person to be destroyed by this chitty-chat."

Pasquale's use of one of his pet phrases made Anjali smile. Seemingly encouraged by her improved demeanor, he added.

"Everyone is looking after you. Even Signor Cyril. Only yesterday he was asking about the lunch you had last month with the Indian Ambassador."

Anjali had no idea what he was talking about. Then she remembered having lunch with Raj while Suneeta was in India and KB was up-country.

"I told him not to worry," Pasquale continued. "The Ambassador always takes good care of you." He bestowed his pearliest grin and turned back to the kitchen.

That was odd, Anjali thought. What did it matter to Cyril whom she had lunch with?

She concentrated on the pasta to take her mind off the gossip. When she was finished, Alberto set a bowl of mixed salad before her. Il Ristorante was one of the few places where Anjali would eat salad. She knew they grew their own under rigorously safe standards. She looked up to thank him and saw, all over the room, quick glances her way, then heads pulled together for a whispered conversation.

Oh, this is really too much, she thought. She'd come to celebrate her deliverance from the mob, and instead she was the center of attention. What had she got herself into?

Alberto mentioned he'd made fresh tiramisu, one of Anjali's favorite desserts. But she was anxious to leave the suddenly stifling environment and refused even a coffee. She finished the salad, paid the bill and walked out into Nam Phou Square fifteen minutes before Thongsy was due.

Heat and humidity crashed against her skin. This is so unlike you, Anjali lectured herself, get a grip!

She walked over to look in the windows of Jackie's gallery. There were some beautiful new metal bowls and a striking length of silk.

Too heavy for a sari, but it would make exquisite pillow covers.

Behind her, she heard laughter and turned to see the WIVS members climbing into a car. The last one smirked at Anjali across the car's roof before she got in.

Anjali felt a kinship with Sophia and all her victims, weighed down by words.

Thongsy drove up just then, early as usual. Anjali smiled. Really, he was the most thoughtful and conscientious man. She'd never known him to be late, and he contrived to be early as much as possible. She sank into the comfort of her seat and asked Thongsy to drive to the French Embassy.

Waves of heat baked her soles as Anjali crossed the Embassy's unshaded parking lot. She looked up, wishing for a cooling shower. Once inside the colonial building, she was instantly refreshed. Its thick walls and high ceilings, louvered shutters and wide verandas trapped the slightest breeze. Anjali asked the receptionist to let Jean-Claude know she was there.

"I'm sorry, Madame, but Monsieur Martin is up-country until Monday."

Frustrated once again, Anjali made an appointment for Monday afternoon. She went back out to the parking lot, where Burt was just exiting his car.

"Anjali! Good to see you, as always. But what brings you to the French Embassy? Thinking of changing your citizenship?" he said with a wink.

She smiled in return. "No, thinking of talking with Jean-Claude."

"Hot on the trail, are you? Bet they turned you down. His Excellency hustled Jean-Clalude's tail up to Oudamsai until all this blows over. Didn't want the French lover involved in the official investigation, I'll wager."

"I don't know anything about that…" Anjali shrugged, annoyed that Burt seemed to have heard the gossip about her investigation. And taken it for granted. "…but I have an appointment to see him Monday."

Then she remembered what Larry had said at the ballgame about Burt and Sophia. But Burt started up the Embassy steps before she could work out how to raise the subject.

"Well, good luck to you," he said. "It's about time someone took that heartbreaker down a peg. More than one Lao lady in trouble, or so I've heard." He vanished into the shade of the reception hall.

Larry was accusing Burt, and Burt was accusing Jean-Claude, she thought. Would Jean-Claude accuse Larry?

If Jean-Claude had done half the things the gossips accused him of, Anjali reflected, he'd never have had time to sleep. But what if Sophia had found out her lover had got one or more Lao women pregnant? She'd have been enraged. Might she have threatened to make it public? Gossip was one thing, but true exposure could ruin Jean-Claude's career. Would he have killed Sophia to keep his shenanigans secret?

Getting carried away again, Anjali admonished herself. Just keep digging until you find the facts. She started toward the car. Thongsy jumped up from where he'd been squatting in the shade of a mango tree with the Embassy drivers.

What was she going to do about Burt? Anjali wondered. She really needed to know about his relationship with Sophia, but she hadn't a clue about how to bring it up. As far as that was concerned, Larry's interest in the minute details of Sophia's life was niggling at her.

Everyone seemed in such a rush to tell her things. Jackie, Larry, Burt. But just because someone said something didn't make it true. Not even Philip's confession, she reluctantly concluded.

Thongsy opened the car door, and she got in the backseat. More and more frustration. No chance to talk with Kham-pun. The unexplained menace of his brothers and neighbors. The gossip at Il Ristorante. Jean-Claude sent to Oudomsai.

What a wasted day, she thought. Then her spirits brightened. Picnic with Karen tomorrow, then tea with Catherine the next day. Jean-Claude on Monday. Burt still to tackle. Larry, too. She wasn't down yet. Sooner or later, she'd fathom who was telling the truth.

Anjali entered her door and plopped down in a chair. Onhta arrived with a cold lemonade and the news that Cyril had called. Oh, bother that man, Anjali thought.

She carried her lemonade into the bedroom and changed into a faded, old *shalvar kemiz*. Then she called Cyril's office only to be told that he'd just left for Champassak on Embassy business. He'd be gone for two days, his secretary said.

Anjali polished off her cold drink. At least she wouldn't have to deal with Cyril for a while.

She got another glass of lemonade, sauntered to the veranda and began a list of things for the picnic with Karen. She'd got as far as hard-boiled eggs and a sweet, when Kongkeo opened the gates to admit a familiar car. It was Suneeta.

Anjali hurried outside to welcome her friend, admiring her new cotton sari of dark olive banded with red and gold. In addition to Suneeta's usual armload of thin gold bangles, she was wearing cascades of small golden balls dangling from her ears.

When Anjali got a closer look, she realized that Suneeta's beautiful face was full of worry. Conscious of her own gardener and Suneeta's driver, Anjali put off asking what was wrong until they were inside and alone.

She led Suneeta into the living room and turned on the high-tech air conditioner. It sighed as it started, then made hardly a sound. Onhta brought more lemonade and fruit without being asked. Suneeta sat on the overstuffed couch, fiddling with the end of her sari until Onhta returned to the kitchen and shut the door.

"Oh, Anjali, I don't know what to do," Suneeta moaned.

"What is it, Suneeta? What's the matter?"

"That dreadful Pam asked me to lunch so she could tell me Raj was having an affair. Said she'd hesitated to say anything, but then decided I ought to know."

Anjali recalled Pam fawning over Sophia at her goodbye party. "I don't believe it. Consider the source."

Suneeta shook her head emphatically. "No, I don't believe it, either. But you know what this kind of gossip can do. And we've got this big reception coming up. Raj can't afford something like this right now."

Anjali remembered the events at Il Ristorante and felt a stirring of apprehension. "Did Pam say with whom Raj is supposed to be having this affair?"

Suneeta's voice filled with scorn. "I didn't ask. Didn't want to give her the satisfaction."

Anjali laid a hand on her friend's arm. "The best thing you can do is act like nothing's happened. Go to the reception and make sure everyone sees how happy you both are together."

"Should I tell Raj? I don't want him to worry. But I don't want him to be ambushed by gossip."

Anjali considered both alternatives for a moment. All in all, she decided, it was best for Raj to know and said so.

The two women talked over anti-gossip strategy for a while, drinking their lemonade and nibbling at the fruit. Suneeta gradually relaxed and was even laughing by the time she left.

But Anjali was preoccupied with memories from Il Ristorante. Cyril had been asking Pasquale about her lunch with Raj, and the WIVS members had been whispering.

Minutes later, Anjali sat at her desk, chin propped on hands, thinking about what Suneeta had told her. Why wasn't KB here? They might need to nip this gossip in the bud.

The phone jangled and gave her hope. Maybe it was KB. They could talk after all.

"Hello?" Anticipation rose in her chest.

It wasn't KB, but his secretary. Anjali's hopes sank.

The roads were washed out, and KB wouldn't be home until at least Friday. His secretary relayed his apologies for not calling Anjali directly, but he was in a village with no phone and had contacted the office by radio. Anjali thanked her and rang off.

Now she was truly depressed. Everything seemed to be going wrong. Just when she really needed to talk with KB, to seek his counsel and comfort, his return was delayed again. She'd spent a lot of her life like this, needing her husband and having him far away, up-country on some project. Always a worthy project, but that only made her feel worse—selfish and not as independent as she wanted to be.

Then another worry took hold. Maybe she should drop this investigation into Sophia's death and go back to keeping a low profile. The double-barreled gossip about her being a snoop and having an affair with Raj could deal a one-two punch to KB's career, even if he did make a success of things here in Vientiane. She'd seen men brought down by their wives' behavior.

The first time was in Nairobi. KB was thrilled to be working in UNDP's most important African post. But after the delights of living in Paris for a year, Anjali had been reluctant to return to the sub-Sahara. That mood had changed when she was drafted to chair a refugee relief committee.

The committee had been particularly successful, but one unexpected result of their efforts was a love affair between two of its members, the wife of the American Ambassador and a young French NGO worker as married as she was. At first, they'd been discreet, but as their infatuation ran rampant, they became so careless it seemed they wanted to be caught. Finally, they were.

His family had gone down to Malindi for a beach vacation. She talked her husband into renting a cottage not far away. The lovers would meet in a bush clearing just off the beach. One night, her cries were so enthusiastic that they alarmed a night watchman at a nearby house. His employers were away. He had no one to consult, so he did what he thought was best and called the police. The two were hauled off to the station for indecent behavior in a public place.

They were later released into the custody of their own institutions. The NGO worker got sent home immediately, and it wasn't long before the Ambassador found himself back in Washington with a desk job.

But a wife didn't have to get caught in *flagrante delicto* to hurt her husband's career. If she lacked social finesse or drank too much or talked too often about things she shouldn't, her husband would find his longed-for promotions and postings stymied.

It wasn't fair, Anjali mused, but that's the way it was. She hadn't really done anything, but a successful Res Rep's wife had to be above reproach. She felt thwarted, unsure what to do.

"Oh, *merde*," she thought and laughed aloud when a word she'd heard on Parisian streets came unbidden to her lips. She'd been carefully taught by all the women in her family never to swear or to say dirty words.

"*Merde!*" she shouted, "*Merde!*" And instantly felt better.

Onlhta came running. "Madame, are you all right?"

Anjali felt chagrined. "Yes, Onhta, thank you. I'm just a little frustrated by today's events."

"I know, Madame. Thongsy told me."

Anjali realized Onhta only knew about the morning's frustration. "I should have listened to him. He said we wouldn't find Kham-pun at home."

"That is because he knew so in advance, Madame."

Anjali was taken aback. "I'm sorry…what do you mean…he knew so in advance?"

Onhta looked guilty, as if she'd spoken without thinking.

Or perhaps it was conflicting loyalties, Anjali thought. To whom did Onhta owe more loyalty, to her mistress or her co-worker?

Onhta held her head down. "He went with the rest of our men to Kham-pun's house yesterday evening."

"He what? Who went?"

Onhta raised her head but didn't look Anjali in the eye. "Thongsy, Kongkeo and Vong. They went to talk to Kham-pun and found him alone at home. They warned him to stop bothering you. They were worried about black hearts."

Anjali was stunned. She didn't know what to think. The Lao men of her household had wanted to protect her, so they'd seen to Tom's driver themselves. On the one hand, they'd thwarted her investigation. On the other, they'd wanted to help.

She recalled Thongsy's efforts to warn her away from Kham-pun's house, both before they'd left and after they'd arrived. She should have paid attention. A Lao driver wouldn't directly confront his mistress, but Thongsy had tried his best to keep her from going.

Onhta was watching Anjali closely out of the corner of her eye.

Anjali decided that, everything considered, she was deeply touched by the men's devotion. "Onhta, where is Thongsy?"

"He has gone home, Madame. It is after his working hours."

So it was, she realized. "Please tell him…and Vong and Kongkeo, that I am very grateful for their kind efforts. They have surely made merit by their wish to help a foolish old woman."

Onhta smiled shyly. "My brother went also, Madame. We decided it was not fitting that I should go."

"Please thank your brother also."

Onhta bowed with a *nop* and started to leave. Then she stopped. "Madame?"

Anjali nodded her assent to hear more.

"You are not a foolish old woman."

Despite her attempt at self-control, Anjali's eyes were teary. "Thank you, Onhta. Thank you very much."

Then she turned back to her desk so that neither of them would be embarrassed.

Anjali was still trying to decide about keeping a low profile the next morning when the phone rang.

KB, she thought and flew to pick up the receiver.

"Anjali? Cyril here. I tried to call you yesterday, but you weren't in."

Anjali's heart plummeted. "I thought you were in Champassak."

"I am. Isn't the connection amazing?" He cleared his throat. "And thank goodness for that. I heard something disturbing at the Myanmar reception the other night."

Anjali felt irritated. She didn't need Cyril and his disturbances this morning. She pictured his skeletal hand gripping the receiver far away.

"And what was that?" she asked warily, shifting position.

"I'm afraid the gossips are at work again, Anjali."

I know, she thought, just get on with it. She braced herself to hear about her lunch with Raj at Il Ristorante.

"They were talking about KB," Cyril said.

"KB?" Anjali felt lost, off-track.

"I don't know how to say this gently, so I'll just go on, shall I?"

"What is it, Cyril," she said through clenched teeth.

"They're suspicious about KB staying up-country for so long."

"I don't understand. It's none of their business."

Cyril's voice sounded too forceful. "Well, they've made it their business. They're saying his prolonged absence has something to do with Sophia's death."

"But that's preposterous!" She didn't know whether to be angry or worried. Or both.

"Of course it is," he agreed. "Have you discovered anything that might clear his name?"

"For God's sake, Cyril, there's nothing to clear."

"You'd better find out what did happen," Cyril persisted, "for KB's sake."

Anjali drove to Karen's house with renewed commitment. Cyril's call had chased away any inclination to keep a low profile. She knew KB wasn't involved in Sophia's death. Now she had to prove it.

She picked up Karen, and they rode several miles downriver to the decrepit gates of Buddha Park. It wasn't a great spot for a picnic but it was one of the few places outside Vientiane where foreigners could go without a travel permit.

Anjali pulled the Deux Chevaux into a rutted space beside the road. The two women got out their picnic things and headed for the tumbledown entrance with its strands of sagging wire. Tall weeds scraped against their knees, and singing insects rose up from the scent of warm grasses disturbed by their sandaled feet.

As she entered, Anjali looked to the right to see one of her favorite park structures, a colossal concrete head featuring an open mouth lined with square red teeth.

She recalled a previous visit and the laughter of Lao children crawling through those grinning lips to arrive at a three-tiered depiction of earth with hell below and heaven above. Then their laughter had burst from the top of the head. They'd climbed through a tiny opening to look across the grounds to the Mekong.

But now their laughter was only memory's echo. The park was deserted. The two women passed a giant reclining Buddha, somewhat misshapen and elongated, but nevertheless recognizable as the Enlightened One.

The giant statue was why foreigners called Wat Xieng Khwan "Buddha Park." A Lao artist with an ecumenical Asian vision had filled several acres of field with fantastic cement figures. When the Pathet Lao won the war, he'd fled to Thailand, leaving behind his sculpture garden of pop religion to slowly decompose.

Here and there above high grass rose statues with iron bars sticking out where arms used to be, crumbling steps up to stupas and glittering colored glass embedded in eroding concrete. Demons challenged mythical creatures with wings and spiral headdresses. Despite the aura of decay, Lao still came to worship, as evinced by burnt joss sticks and fruit-offerings.

A surreal setting for eliciting secrets, Anjali reflected.

She and Karen walked on until they came to a pavilion by the river, an ordinary rural affair with packed-earth floor and corrugated roof held up by bark-stripped logs, all sides open. Inside were a few hand-hewn wooden tables and benches, along with a smiling girl dispensing soft drinks from an iced cooler and her younger brother selling coconuts and bananas.

Anjali bought two coconuts. The boy expertly lopped off the ends with a machete and inserted straws so they could drink the tangy liquid inside.

The two women moved a bit downriver, spread a palm-leaf mat and settled down to their picnic. Anjali looked up to make sure they were still in sight of the Lao girl and her brother.

Karen leaned back, relaxed, against a tree. Long ago, Anjali's nursemaid had taught her to sit on mat or cushion without need of such support. She sat comfortably erect, looking at Karen's profile against the surging Mekong.

At first glance, the American seemed very ordinary—forty or so, medium build, medium coloring, her long, light brown hair held in a clasp behind her neck. An attractive, but not a pretty, face. With glasses. But anyone who had spent time with Karen knew she had extraordinary charisma. There was a vital force emanating from her that made her a natural, even a compelling, leader.

Anjali thought about how charisma can be a dangerous thing, a temptation to both leader and followers, and wondered where Karen's charisma had led her during her stay in Vientiane.

They sat in the shade, refreshed by the river breeze, lunching and chatting. From time to time, ominously overloaded boats went by, powered by noisy engines trailing blue smoke.

They'd finished the coconuts and were drinking wine from plastic glasses when suddenly, without preamble, Karen said, "Rumor's out that you're tracking Sophia's killer."

"I wouldn't go that far," Anjali replied. "But I would like to know what happened. The town's full of gossip, but what are the facts?"

"Yeah, *full* of gossip," Karen said with bitterness. "I wanted to kill her. I even had the chance." She turned to face the other woman square in the eye. "But I didn't. There's a fact for you, Anjali. I didn't kill Sophia."

Maybe a fact, maybe not, Anjali thought. "Can you talk about it?"

Karen pulled her legs back under her body. "Why do you want to know?"

Anjali realized she didn't need to talk about KB, just what would make sense to Karen. "It's somewhat complicated. It's not only to do with Sophia. It's to do with me. And you. All the wives who follow their men from country to country."

Karen reached for a hard-boiled egg. "And you think if you discover why Sophia drowned, you'll decipher how we can make sense of constantly reinventing who we are?"

"Something like that."

Karen concentrated on peeling her egg, carefully putting bits of shell to one side and cutting the egg into fourths. Anjali kept silent, waiting to see what would happen. The orderly task seemed to help Karen think things through.

"I can't figure it out either," she said. "Beats me how to be a dependent spouse and still feel good about yourself."

Anjali nodded to show she appreciated Karen's point.

Karen's lips pushed out from the pressure behind them. "When I came out to Laos, I was already wounded. So it was easy to hurt me."

"I'm not sure I understand," Anjali said.

"Four deaths in the family in less than a year, burned out on my job, national president of my professional society, saddled with a do-nothing board and a big deficit. So when Ben was offered the public health job here, I said, 'Let's go!' I was totally stressed out."

Anjali cut the chocolate cake she'd bought at the bakery. "You needed a vacation."

"I thought of it as a sabbatical. Thought I'd take time off and get everything back in perspective. Planned to write a book on what I'd learned from twenty years in the field."

"About journalism?" Anjali asked, thinking how Karen had improved the *Vientiane Voice*.

Karen took her plate of cake. "About how journalism can nurture development of democracy. I was a consultant advising Third World newspapers and NGO publications. Helping them effectively cover and comment on current events."

Anjali took a bite of cake and held back her reaction to the barest tingle of her tastebuds. Made with cocoa, normal in a climate where it was difficult to keep baking chocolate. But she did miss the richness of the real thing.

"So you gave up all that to come here?" she asked.

"Yeah, already wounded and the first thing that happened was another wallop."

"Sophia?"

"No, just the way things are. I discovered I didn't count for much."

Anjali smiled in sympathy. "That must have been hard."

Karen poured herself more wine from the cooler. Anjali's wine was finished, but she had to keep her wits sharp. She switched to bottled water.

"We were at our first Vientiane social event," Karen said. "It turned out to be a three-hour diatribe against the Lao. They were lazy. They were venal. They were stupid. They were tricky. They were secretive. They didn't keep their promises. It went on and on. As soon as we could decently go, I gave Ben the high sign, and we made our exit."

"What a ghastly introduction to Vientiane," Anjali said. But not unusual, she thought, remembering Burt and Vicki. And her own experiences early in KB's career.

Karen sipped her wine. "On a personal level, it was just as bad. I was just an appendage to my husband. I'd expected it to some extent, but not to that degree. I was introduced as Ben's wife. I was asked what he did. If I ventured to voice an opinion on a topic, no one was interested. Quite a different affair from when I was heading up my own in-country team of consultants. When I had my own identity. Nicely humbling."

Their attention was momentarily caught by a small boat chugging downriver, a red motor scooter lashed upright amidship and pointed toward the prow. Behind it crouched its beaming owner, a hand laid proudly on the rear fender. For a moment, the engine faltered, and both the boatman and his passenger looked worried. Then the boatman gave the engine a swift kick, and it caught again. Anjali smiled back at the two grinning faces bobbing by.

Karen continued, "Ben and I laughed about it on the way home, but we were troubled."

"Is that why you got involved with the *Voice?*" Anlali took a long swig of water.

"You bet. When Sophia asked me to take over as editor, I jumped at it. Thought it would give me a chance to amount to something here."

"And it did."

Karen's voice was self-mocking. "Yeah, got to be a big cheese." She turned serious. "But I also made a contribution, and that's important to me. The *Voice* had been just a mimeographed newsletter. I thought we could make it into a small-town paper, and we did."

Anjali smiled. "Everyone reads it. Not just *farang*. Lao too."

A flock of birds struggled upriver against the wind.

"It took a lot to make that happen," Karen said, "especially because the government was looking over our shoulders and setting lots of conditions. But I looked on it as a development project. If we had to work with the Government Printers, we'd help them improve the quality of their printing. If we had to teach local businesses what advertising was, we'd be contributing to the growth of a market economy."

Karen drank some more wine and smiled. "One businesswoman told me we should pay *her* to advertise in our paper."

Anjali watched two birds vie for the same breadcrumb. "Sophia was on the committee?"

"Yeah. She was a pain in the ass. But talented and energetic. I reckoned I could ignore her bossiness."

"Not so easy, perhaps?"

"She wanted everything her way. That got tiresome pretty fast. As the weeks rolled on, I found I liked her less and less."

Anjali finished her water. "But you did like her in the beginning?"

Karen added more wine into her own empty glass. "I'm not sure 'like' is the right word. We had a lot in common, and I thought we might end up friends. But Sophia didn't want friendship. She wanted adulation. I finally decided she maybe had a weak ego. Whatever it was, I didn't want any more, so I started avoiding her whenever I could."

Anjali thought back over the times she'd noticed Karen doing that. "But Vientiane's a small place. The expat community even smaller. You must have been thrown together a lot."

Karen pulled up a tuft of grass and shredded it. "I remember one dinner-dance where we ended up at the same table. We'd sat down first with some friends. But they were also friendly with Sophia and Tom, so they called the Powells over to join us. Kind of spoiled the evening for me. Tom kept cracking jokes about his Lao colleagues, while she was making smart-aleck remarks about what everyone was wearing. The rest of the table was laughing uproariously, but Ben and I spent a lot of time on the dance floor just to get away."

"But your success with the *Voice* must have been a comfort?"

Karen emptied her glass in one long swallow. "It wasn't a success in the end. Higher-quality printing meant higher costs. So now the Lao who work at the Government Printers are getting in trouble with their bosses. And no one wants to be editor when I'm gone. It's too much work for a non-paying job. So I really failed. I went too far and created something that can't survive." Karen looked down. "I'm ashamed I forgot such a basic principle for any development project."

"And the Folkloric?"

Karen poured wine into Anjali's empty glass and her own. "I had this idea to showcase the revival of Lao arts. Dance, puppetry, storytelling, painting. We could encourage the artists by presenting their work in a Folkloric production. And earn some money for WIVS projects by selling tickets."

Anjali's mind jumped back to a similar endeavor in Papua New Guinea years ago. They'd worked so hard, but the first Folkloric had been the last. No one wanted to suffer such misery again. She thought of all the failed efforts of women's groups over the years and felt a deep sympathy for Karen. And Sophia. They'd been determined to make things happen in Vientiane.

"Lots of peril in Folklorics," she said.

Karen nodded. "Sophia couldn't stand it that someone else might have an idea for a project. So she set out to sabotage it."

"When Sophia first arrived, she was a big fish in a small pond, " Anjali said. "But it wasn't long before other talented women arrived. Sophia never learned how to work with women like you and Jackie. She was an accomplished amateur, but she couldn't share her pond, especially with professionals. I wonder what would have happened if the pond had been bigger, if there'd been less crowding."

Karen drank more wine. Despite how much she'd imbibed, her voice was still lucid. "Oh, she was devious. She started out enthusiastically and publicly supporting the Folkloric. But meanwhile, she was doing her damnedest to cripple my efforts."

"How so?" Anjali didn't want any wine, but she also didn't want to hurt Karen's feelings, so she pretended to sip it.

"Sophia made a big show of being the first volunteer to serve on the committee. Then she called to say someone new had come to town who had years of experience in costume design and could they come over to talk about the Folkloric. I said yes, and Sophia's new friend, Liz, gave me all the reasons why we could never bring it off. Most of her critique was predicated on her three weeks of acquaintance with the resources Vientiane lacked."

"But those sorts of people are always around, always ready to look at the gloomy side. You've got enough mettle to stand up to someone like that."

"I refused to react to Liz's gloom-and-doom. Then Sophia brought her to the next committee meeting, so she could repeat her negative take. Several committee members asked Liz to reserve judgment until she'd heard the plans for circumventing the difficulties, but her pessimism infected others."

"On the whole, though, the committee supported you?"

"Yeah, but it was a war of attrition. Nothing terribly overt, but Sophia's daily salvos slowly wore me down. She couldn't stand it when the committee decided to hold the Folkloric at the Arawan so the Lao would feel comfortable attending."

Anjali had been to events at that traditional restaurant and saw the wisdom of the choice.

Karen continued, "Sophia thought it should be at an ambassador's residence for the prestige."

Yes, Anjali recognized, Sophia would have wanted to score points in two directions. A prestigious venue for a WIVS fund-raiser and an opportunity for one of her ambassador-friends to make a diplomatic gesture.

Karen examined the dregs in her glass. "The weekend after the decision for the restaurant had been taken, Ben and I were at a reception. Ambassador Johansson came over and said he was delighted to host the Folkloric. I almost choked. Then I said I was sorry, but there'd been some mistake. We didn't want to be always calling on him. He'd given so much to WIVS already."

Nicely done, Anjali thought. Karen was quick on her political feet. So was Sophia, come to that. The two of them were well-matched.

Karen finished her wine. "The man's a diplomat, so he said all the right things to extricate us both from an embarrassing situation. I didn't inquire—and he didn't volunteer—who had asked him to host the Folkloric. But it sure sounded like something Sophia would have done. One of her favorite strategies was to present people with a *fait accompli* if she couldn't talk them into doing things her way."

Sophia was wasted in Vientiane, Anjali reflected. She'd have been a grand success in the Byzantine court.

Karen poured herself another glass of wine. Anjali's glass was mostly full, and she shook her head at Karen's offer of more. "So Sophia just wore you down, is that it?"

"Yeah." Karen gulped some wine. "But it ended in a big blowup."

"I didn't know that," Anjali said.

"No one did. I was too hurt to talk about it, and Sophia was too embarrassed." Karen grimaced. "It all started when Sophia came up with the idea to combine the Folkloric with a musical comedy review. She invited me to lunch so we could talk it over."

Karen had been writing stories all her life, Anjali reflected, as the *Voice* editor brought the scene to reality. Once again, it was like being there.

As they entered Il Ristorante, Sophia asked Pasquale for a table in the corner away from the main crowd. "So we won't be disturbed," she told Karen.

Once seated, Karen soon realized that Sophia was playing the thoughtful hostess, ensuring that Karen had everything she wanted, engaging her in small talk about people they knew in common. Why the sudden friendliness, Karen wondered, what did Sophia really want?

When their empty plates had been cleared and the espressos served, Sophia turned her famous smile on Karen. "I've been thinking about the Folkloric…"

Yeah, I'll bet you have, Karen thought and brought the demitasse to her mouth. The hot drink was comforting.

"…about how much we all want it to be a success," Sophia continued. Then she made a small face of worry. "But I'm concerned that not everyone will be interested in Lao folklore." Her voice took on a conspiratorial air. "You know how many lowbrows we have here. Those guys working on the bridge and the telecoms project. They'll never go for something like that."

Karen drew breath to speak, but Sophia dashed on, enthusiasm tumbling out. "What if we combined the Folkloric with a musical comedy review? That way, we could capture the lowbrows as well as the highbrows. Something like a Vientiane Follies, showing the humorous side of life here. You could produce the Folkloric bits, and I could produce the Follies!"

Karen sipped her coffee and wondered whether Sophia wanted just some of the limelight or all of it. "Sounds like a strange pairing to me. How can we combine a show poking fun at living in Laos with a program celebrating Lao culture?"

"You lack a little vision, that's all. Let me take care of how to blend the two."

Karen tried not to lose her temper, to find another tack. There had to be a way out of this.

"I like the idea of a musical comedy review," she said, watching Sophia smile. "Sounds like a lot of fun for everyone. But the concepts of the two shows are so different, they'll fight each other. Tell you what. You put on a separate Follies, and I'll give you my full support. Let's produce two shows and do a great job with each one."

Sophia blanched. "Not what I had in mind at all. You don't seem to understand."

"Oh, I think I understand perfectly. That's why I'm suggesting two separate shows."

Resentment conquered Sophia's beautiful face. "All right. If that's what you want, I'll have to stage it the week before the Folkloric." Her eyes filled with mocking challenge. "Then we'll see who gets the best audience."

Karen couldn't believe this was happening. Was Sophia out to hurt her and the Folkloric any way she could? Didn't she realize this would harm everyone in the end? "How's that going to help WIVS? We don't want two competing shows."

Sophia's smile was triumphant. "I've already planned a trip to New Zealand. I couldn't possibly produce a show any other time."

Karen read Sophia's expression and gave up the effort to compromise. "I see through your little game, and I'm not playing. You're not going to spike my show."

She followed Sophia's glance around the room. The increasing tension at their table was attracting attention.

Sophia gave a tight little smile. "Why don't we go for a walk down by the river, where we can discuss this with more privacy?" She signaled Pasquale, paid the check and led the way to the narrow park beside the Mekong.

Karen was determined not to be in Sophia's wake and walked alongside her. Neither woman spoke until they were well away from ears that understood English.

They passed Lao children sailing merrily back and forth in the swings, their mothers talking quietly together on a bench. A boy was hawking soft drinks from a bamboo hut. Karen was conscious of his eyes tracking them as they walked to the very edge of the riverbank.

Sophia whirled around and said, "I'm not trying to spike your show. I'm trying to save it, for God's sake. You don't have the least idea what works here."

Karen felt like she'd been punched in the stomach, but she fought back. "Then how did I manage to make a success of the *Voice?*"

Sophia stood silhouetted against the river, fists at her sides, face contorted with anger. "You think you're so much better than the rest of us, but you don't know a thing. You're no good at volunteer projects. You don't know how to work with WIVS members. And you seriously believe that everyone will rush to your highbrow show."

Karen tried to speak, but Sophia cut her off, both hands chopping downward from a pinnacle under her chin. "No. Let me finish. Stay home with your computer and let someone else run the projects." Her eyes narrowed. "Someone who knows how."

Karen looked up at Anjali. "I thought of pushing her in the river right then and there."

Anjali's heart jumped. Was this a confession, despite what Karen had said at the beginning? She held her tongue and waited.

Karen's hand flew up to her own cheek, and her voice turned husky. "Sophia couldn't have hurt me more if she'd slapped me in public."

Her eyes slipped sideways toward the Mekong. "I would've loved to see that muddy water wash the venom off her face." She shivered. "But I wasn't so hurt that I couldn't realize pushing her in could've killed her. My hands trembled to do it, but I walked away."

"That was pretty rational, under the circumstances," Anjali said.

Karen gulped down the rest of her wine. "That's me. Mind over emotion, every time." She poured herself the last glass from the bottle.

Anjali pondered two different interpretations of Sophia's behavior. Perhaps she couldn't stand to share the limelight. Or maybe she really did think the Folkloric was in trouble and wanted to save a WIVS fund-raiser the only way she knew how.

She leaned forward. "Forgive me, but I don't see how Sophia's childish spite could hurt you so much. Even if you were wounded when you arrived."

Karen's face dissolved, and her words slurred. "Because it was all true. I didn't know how to work with volunteers. I'm a professional. I don't know how to coddle and cajole bored housewives into doing what they should do. What they volunteered to do." Karen hung her head. Tears ran down her nose and salted her wine. "Listen to me. I do think I'm better than they are."

Anjali considered how Sophia had a knack for finding the weakest spot. She'd done the same thing to Frieda.

Karen wiped her wet face with shaky hands. "I tried so hard to make a go of it here, but I was the wrong person for the job. For the *Voice*. And for the Folkloric."

"So you resigned," Anjali said.

"So I quit. I've turned into a quitter. I couldn't stand the stress at home, so I quit my job and came here. Then I couldn't deal with the stress here, so I quit the Folkloric. You know what I found out about myself, Anjali?"

The older woman shook her head.

"I'm so used to winning, I can't stand losing."

Anjali felt herself fill with empathy. What had happened in Hanoi wasn't just about keeping a low profile in Vientiane. It had dealt a blow to her self-confidence, a blow from which she was only now recovering.

Karen tossed back the full glass of wine and sagged against the tree. "I didn't kill Sophia after her goodbye party. I was too sunk in self-pity to be that active. I was sitting at home, trying to figure out who I'm supposed to be."

Anjali gave her a gentle, encouraging smile. "And have you found out?"

Karen smiled in return, but her eyes were fighting back tears. "Nope, not yet, but I'm getting there. I've decided I'm a compassionate introvert. I want to make the world a better place, but working with other people takes too much out of me. I've got to find out what I can do all by myself." The corners of her mouth turned down. "Sophia was right. I should stay home and work with my computer."

Anjali dropped Karen off at her house, then drove home beside a Mekong turned to rose and gold by the coming sunset. Birds drifted here and there, following the last swarms of insects before night fell. The street-food venders were setting up, and their charcoal fires scented the air. Mothers called to children to come in from play and wash their hands.

How could a place so peaceful be so full of suffering, Anjali mused. Her thoughts turned to Sophia. In a perverse way, the dead woman had sometimes helped people by harming them.

On impulse, Anjali turned the Deux Chevaux into Sophia's old street and drove to her compound. There was a fresh breach in the wall, white stucco fallen, bricks dented, cement crumbled. Perhaps the moving truck had hit it when Tom left in such a hurry, Anjali reflected.

The iron gate had been left ajar, and she tried to slip through. The wind tangled her *dupatta* in the ornate scrolls of the rusting gate. She turned to free it, then stepped into Sophia's garden.

Inside, all was wet and dripping, as if there'd been a passing shower in town while she'd been at Buddha Park. The scent of damp earth and decaying leaves rose up to enfold her, and she could feel a slight breeze coming over the wall.

Anjali walked down a garden path of brick in a herringbone pattern. Moss was creeping from the cracks to cover the bricks, and the monsoon had sprouted weeds amid the downy green clefts. On either side lay fallen palm fronds as big as a person, each a haven for smaller leaves bunched between the stiff blades.

Only a few days since the gardener had been let go, she realized, but it didn't take long in the tropics.

There'd been a glorious stand of banana trees in one corner, Anjali remembered, but now they were sagging from weight of water and lack of care. One had toppled sideways and lay like the forgotten remains of a captivating memory. Anjali bent down to touch it. Her passing hand stirred a spider web jeweled by water drops and setting sun.

Poor Sophia, she brooded, as lost as her beautiful garden.

For a moment, she thought she heard Sophia's tinkling laugh. But it was only the wind chimes stirring in the breeze. The sound pulled Anjali to the porch.

She huddled on the steps, saddened by the decaying garden and the fading light, watching a tiny green lizard cautiously make its way up the wall.

What a wasted life, she thought. So much energy, so much to offer, but stunted by…she recalled Moira's phrase…always making do.

Something brushed the *shalvar* ballooned around her ankles, and Anjali looked down. A silver-gray cat had crept from under the porch, bedraggled and emaciated. Sophia's cat, Anjali realized, consciously abandoned or left behind through inattention. She sighed. Or maybe there'd just been no one to take it in.

Anjali reached down and scooped the cat up into her lap, drying it with the ends of her *dupatta*. She cradled it in her arms and hummed the lullaby with which she'd once comforted her boys. The cat began to purr, and Anjali found herself weeping.

When it grew too dim to see the end of the garden, Anjali rose and carried the cat to the Deux Chevaux. She made a nest of her *dupatta* on the passenger seat and set the cat inside, relieved to hear it still purring.

Then she drove home under deep shadows where trees grew over compound walls.

Anjali was surprised to find Kongkeo opening the gate long after he should have gone home. And even more surprised,when she pulled forward, to see the entire household staff in the space between the house and the outbuilding. They'd spread a grass mat in the pool of light created by the outdoor lamps and were seated around a Lao woman. It was Moira's maid, Pathoumphone.

They rose when Anjali drove up. She looked down at the gray cat asleep on her *dupatta* and decided to leave it there for the moment. Kongkeo arrived from the gate as she stepped out of the car. Five dark heads bowed politely over five pairs of hands held in respectful *nops*.

Anjali offered her own *nop* and tried not to look startled.

"Madame," Onhta said, "Patumphone is waiting for you." The cook seemed to see the questions in Anjali's head. "Patumphone is the sister of my brother's wife. She wishes to tell you something."

Vong brought the old wooden chair used by the night watchman for Anjali to sit on, but she sank down on the mat so they would all be on the same level. Her staff and Pathoumphone arranged themselves before her, feet tucked to the side so as not to display their soles and give offense.

"Yes, Pathoumphone?" Anjali said.

Pathoumphone looked at Onhta, who gave her a little nod of support. "I asked Madame Moira what to do, and she said to come see you."

Anjali wondered if Moira had been searching out secrets again. "It was good of you to come."

Pathoumphone's eyebrows crinkled upward with concern, and she glanced at Onhta again. Onhta nodded more forcefully, and Pathoumphone blurted out, "My cousin has been trying to meet you."

Anjali looked at her staff in bewilderment. "Your cousin?"

Thongsy's face was as impassive as ever. "Kham-pun, Madame. The driver of Mr. Tom."

"Kham-pun is your cousin?" Anjali said to Pathoumphone.

"Yes, Madame. He asked me to arrange a meeting," Pathoumphone looked sideways at Thongsy.

Curiosity bounced inside Anjali's head. "What about?"

The maid bowed. "Not for me to say. Kham-pun has something important to tell you."

Anjali tried mightily not to let her triumph show.

After some discussion, they agreed that Pathoumphone would bring Kham-pun the next morning at eight, before Anjali had to leave for tea with Catherine.

Anjali watched Pathoumphone speed off on her bicycle and thought about Kham-pun. His behavior had been so typical of the Lao. A culture so subtle that it was impossible to understand what they were doing and why they were doing it.

Had he been threatening or warning her that night by the Mekong? Warning, it now seemed. Why had he appeared in her bedroom window after midnight? A misguided idea about making contact before he knew about the connection via Pathoumphone and Moira?

Anjali recalled UNDP training for families about to embark on their first overseas assignment. A major point had been that one key to success in other cultures was tolerance for ambiguity. She shook her head in smiling amusement. They surely must have had Laos in mind.

She turned her thoughts to more important questions. What did Kham-pun want to tell her? Did he know how Sophia had drowned? Could it have been Tom after all? Was it really murder? Would it clear KB's name?

Time enough for all that tomorrow morning, she chided herself and turned back to the car. Onhta had already carried the picnic basket into the kitchen.

Anjali opened the car door and looked down at the sleeping cat with some trepidation. How would Traveller react to another feline in the house? She reached down and lifted the cat in her *dupatta*-nest. The cat opened one pea-green eye and gave a small mew, then settled against Anjali's bosom.

Onhta held open the screen door. Anjali carried the cat into the kitchen to find a saucer of milk-soaked rice already on the floor. Onhta smiled and nodded.

Ever thoughtful, Anjali acknowledged.

The door to the rest of the house was closed. Anjali could hear Traveller brushing against it, but the small cat was ravenous and had attention only for her supper.

When she'd finished and cleaned paws and face, the two women risked a meeting. Onhta opened the door, and Traveller sailed in, lord of the manor, plumed tail held high. The gray cat crouched in submission, and Traveller came over to sniff at her.

Anjali watched Traveller's tail, always an indicator of his mood. It was waving with interest, not lashing with anger.

The delicate-bodied cat rolled over and presented her belly. Traveller hulked over her, his intentions unclear. Anjali knelt down, her hands poised to grab him. Then he lowered his head and began to lick the silvery fur of the foundling's face.

Anjali sighed with relief and looked at Onhta. Her gentle smile was like a blessing.

Later that evening, the phone rang. This time, it was finally KB. With the welcome news that he was definitely coming home Friday afternoon.

"And what about you, my darling?" he asked. "Been keeping busy? Not still sleuthing, I hope?"

Anjali decided not to worry him with anything along that line, especially not the gossip about him and Sophia. "The most recent event is that I've adopted a cat."

"Good lord, not another one. How's Traveller taking it?"

"He seems to be in love."

"But he's fixed," KB protested.

"Fixed or not, he's in love."

KB's voice turned husky. "Me too, darling. Only two more days."

Anjali felt a deep yearning creep over her. And me a grandmother, she thought with pleasure. "I'll be waiting."

That yearning was still with her when she found the two cats curled around each other, fast asleep on the bed. Not long now, she thought and slipped into the far side so as not to disturb their yin-yang embrace.

She was up the next morning, yoga'd, showered, dressed and breakfasted by the time Kongkeo opened the gate to two bicycles.

Anjali stood beside the grass mat which Onhta and Thongsy had again arranged outside. She was bursting with inquisitiveness, but she knew how important it was to keep a calm demeanor.

Pathoumphone led Kham-pun to meet Anjali. He was dressed in black cotton slacks and a light blue shirt, freshly washed and pressed, his driver's uniform.

Who would he drive for now? Anjali wondered. How would he survive? Usually departing expats ensured that their staff had new positions, but Tom probably hadn't had time for this last courtesy.

Everyone raised their hands in a *nop*, and Anjali gestured for the two visitors to sit. Her staff went back to their chores, but she knew they were hovering near.

Kham-pun waited politely for her to proceed.

Onhta appeared from the kitchen carrying a tray with Anjali's everyday teapot and cups. The housekeeper knelt to place the tray on the mat.

"Will you take some tea?" Anjali asked. "You must be thirsty after your long ride."

Kham-pun looked at Pathoumphone. "You are very kind, Madame," Moira's maid said.

Onhta poured tea for the three of them, then withdrew to the kitchen.

Anjali sipped her tea, knowing that they would wait to raise their own cups until she had raised hers. She engaged them in small talk for a few moments. Then, when she felt the time was right, she said, "I am very glad you could come to see me. I have been wanting to talk with you."

Kham-pun looked as if he, too, were holding in a lot of emotion. "Thank you, Madame." He glanced uncertainly at Pathoumphone, and she jerked up her head as if to say, "Get on with it. Don't waste Madame's time."

His eyes darted back to Anjali. "I want talk you long time too."

Kham-pun's English wasn't very good, Anjali recognized, a sign of so many things—his generation and their education lost to war, his status as a driver for a project leader and not an ambassador, perhaps his own lack of ambition. She wondered if she would be able to understand him and smiled encouragingly.

Kham-pun ducked his head. "Madame, please forgive. Must ask, why you want know Madame Sophia?"

She checked her assumptions. "Why have I been asking questions about Sophia?"

Kham-pun nodded.

Anjali spoke slowly and simply so he could understand her English. "I need to know how she died."

"Why, Madame?"

She paused to search her heart. For KB? Yes, to clear his name. For herself? That, too, so she'd have at least some sense of accomplishment in Vientiane. But there was something more important. Because an unexplained death was an affront to life.

"Her death makes no sense," she said. "And that is not right."

Kham-pun took some time to digest this. He sipped his tea and sighed. "I carry big news long time. Not know what to do."

"Sometimes it is best to tell someone such news."

He nodded. "Lao all say you good woman. Can trust."

"Do you want me to keep a secret?" Anjali worried whether she could, depending on what he had to tell her."

"No, no. I tell you. You do right thing."

Anjali felt relieved. "I will try to do the right thing. Is it about Mr. Tom?"

Kham-pun looked dumbfounded. "Mr. Tom? No, no. He gone now. 'Bout my brother."

Now it was Anjali's turn to be dumbfounded. "Your brother?"

"Yes. He night watchman Embassy. He see things. He tell me."

"At Embassy? Which Embassy?"

"Canada. Canada Embassy."

Cyril! Anjali thought. Was that what all this had been about? Did Cyril kill Sophia and then use Anjali to create a smokescreen? Oh, clever Cyril, to ask her to investigate.

"What did your brother see?"

Kham-pun was excited now, talking louder and faster. "He see tall man carry something into Embassy. After midnight. Man very, very thin."

Cyril. Anjali felt her suspicions confirmed. But why would he kill Sophia?

"What was he carrying?"

"Small bag. Carry small bag into Embassy."

Anjali chastised herself. What had she been expecting? He wouldn't have been carrying Sophia. "Did your brother see what was in the bag?"

"Yes. He look through mailroom window. See man open bag and

put in box. Then put box in pouch. Is right? 'Pouch'? That what my brother say."

The diplomatic pouch, Anjali realized. The contents were never inspected by Customs.

"What did he take out of the bag? What did he put in the box?"

"Little silver Buddha." Kham-pun shook his head emphatically. "This wrong. Buddha belong us. Not Canada."

Pathoumphone stuck out her lower lip and bobbed her head once in vigorous agreement.

Anjali hurried into the house as Kongkeo closed the gate behind Pathoumphone and Kham-pun. She didn't have much time before she had to leave for Catherine's, and she desperately needed to think.

Had Sophia found out that Cyril was smuggling precious artifacts, and he'd killed her? Anjali had a vague memory of someone proposing that scenario before.

On the other hand, the Embassy watchman could have been lying, a disgruntled employee trying to get a superior in trouble. But if that were the case, why would the night watchman tell his brother? Why not tell someone at the Embassy?

She tried to remember when Cyril was coming back from Champassak. What had he really been doing there? Embassy business or his business?

Best to talk with Cyril first, she decided, not to accuse, but to see if the night watchman held a grudge against him.

It was still relatively early in the day. If Cyril were back, he might be at home. She went into her study and called his house. Her breath puffed out in exasperation. The line was busy.

She waited a few moments, then tried again. Still busy.

She decided to call the Embassy. The Lao operator would only say that Mr. Witherspoon was not available.

"But has he returned from Champassak?"

"I could not say, Madame. He is not available."

Blasted bureaucrats, Anjali thought. The same the world over. Keeping tight control over the tiniest gate.

She looked at her watch. Time to leave for Catherine's. She'd have to be content with stopping by Cyril's house after tea. Even if Cyril wasn't there, she felt she knew his houseman well enough to believe he'd tell her whether or not Cyril was back.

Anjali grabbed her purse and headed for the Deux Chevaux. Then a memory stopped her in her tracks. When Cyril had called yesterday, the connection had been unbelievably clear.

What if he hadn't been in Champassak after all?

"You're right, Anjali. I was Sophia's best friend. But I'm not going to share her secrets with you or anyone."

It had been nearly half an hour since Catherine had spoken those words, and Anjali was drowning in frustration. She'd tried every tack she could think of to get her hostess to change her mind. Didn't Catherine want to stop the gossip about Sophia? She didn't want to add to it. What about the travails that all dependent wives faced? Catherine spoke of "Twenty-five years of coping in deserts and jungles, in villages and bush, no hot water, no safe water, rotten meat and wormy flour, rats scampering across the floor..." But she couldn't be moved to talk about Sophia's similar experiences.

Anjali had switched to the good things about the international life, and Catherine had waxed poetic. "Masai warriors leaping impossibly high in celebration of their virility and a Pakistani bride swaying with shining eyes among the women of her family. And once, before the wars which ripped them asunder, I saw blue-eyed Afghans dancing in the snow."

But when Anjali had tried to relate this topic to Sophia, Catherine had raised her voice. "I told you I'm not going to talk about Sophia, and that's it."

Outside, the monsoon beat against the bungalow's closed

windows. Anjali watched as Catherine sat erect and poured them each another cup of tea, her light blond hair dulled by the artificial light. Catherine always struck Anjali as being a bit faded—pale skin, pale eyes, pale hair. A life in the tropics did that to some women, Anjali mused. The color seemed to have been bleached from them, leaving only a trace of the vibrancy that must have been theirs when young.

She turned her thoughts to what she knew about Catherine. Could she find a clue about how to get Sophia's best friend to talk?

Catherine and her husband, Frank, were Australian. He was managing a project to improve production of non-rice crops. She was a nurse but hadn't had much chance to practice her skills. Anjali had heard Catherine talk about how she often couldn't get a work permit because there were rules against hiring foreigners if host-country nurses were available, "never mind that those nurses didn't want to travel up-country and work under difficult conditions."

At one post, Catherine had tried to set up a well-baby clinic, donating her services, but she'd been shut down by local health officials for embarrassing them. Catherine seemed to feel that her abilities had been squandered as she moved around the world with Frank.

Anjali remembered often seeing Catherine carrying a book of poems. That was unusual in Vientiane, where most people read paperbacks from the Bangkok Airport. If they read at all.

She observed her hostess lighting a cigarette with well-manicured hands. Catherine's whole appearance was like that. Carefully coiffed hair, neatly pressed linen dress, spotless sandals. She had herself well under control.

Anjali shifted in the chair's batik cushions. Maybe she'd been going at this all wrong. She was focusing too much on Catherine. "Let me tell you one of my own stories."

Catherine put her cup down on the coffee table and leaned back against the rattan couch, her face a mask of determination.

Anjali's voice held a note of sharing among sisters. "Some years ago, when KB was deputy Res Rep in Indonesia, riots broke out all over Jakarta. There were food shortages, and dissident groups stirring up the people, playing on their ethnic hatreds, turning Muslim against Christian, Malay against Chinese. Women and children were dragged from their homes and butchered. Blood literally ran in the streets. At the height of the riots, the mob overran UNDP Headquarters. They let the Indonesian staff go, but they kept all the expats hostage, KB included. They threatened to kill one staff member every hour if their demands weren't met. But their demands were incoherent and difficult to satisfy. When the first hour had passed, they killed a young UNDP staffer and threw his body out into the street. I saw all this on television. My boys were home from boarding school. I kept trying to reassure them that their father would be all right. But deep in my heart, I didn't know if I could believe it."

Catherine's eyes had grown moist as Anjali spoke. She leaned toward her guest. "What happened? How did KB survive?"

Anjali's eyes teared, her throat froze, and for a moment she couldn't continue. She took a deep breath and let it out to calm herself.

"My children's father put his life on the line for everyone else. He began to negotiate. They'd locked the Res Rep in a closet. KB was the ranking officer. He offered to call the President of Indonesia to relay the protestors' grievances if they would let the UNDP women go. And he kept his promise. A compromise was eventually reached, and

KB came home a hero. Decorated by the Indonesian Government and commended by UNDP. But I thought the price was too high to pay. I wanted him to quit, go back to India, work in his family's business and have a safe life."

"But he didn't."

"No, I came to my senses. He wouldn't have been KB if he'd done that. He actually agreed, for the sake of our children. But I woke up one morning and told him we couldn't go. We'd stay in Jakarta, and then we'd go on to the next post too. How could I ask him to destroy himself because I was afraid?"

"I've often thought we're like pioneer women," Catherine said. "The women who follow their husbands across the world. We need the same traits."

"You're right," Anjali said softly.

"But sometimes we just don't have enough of those traits to see us through, like your time of self-doubt in Jakarta. I wonder if the pioneer women didn't either. Do we all fall down from time to time? And if we do, who will pick us up if we don't do it ourselves?"

Outside, the rain had stopped, but Anjali could see gray clouds hovering just above the treetops. She knew Catherine's question was rhetorical, so she kept silent.

Catherine continued, "In my case, I fell down when I lost my baby. My first, my son. There's always a special bond with the first, isn't there?"

"I do feel that way about Anand, but I'd never let anyone else in the family know."

"You love the others just as much, but the first is somehow more deeply a part of you. When he died, it was like a field amputation.

But medics cut off a limb to save a life. My life wasn't saved. It was destroyed."

"Oh, Catherine," Anjali said, "I never knew you lost your first. It must have been devastating." It would have been for her, had she lost Anand.

"He was so special, my Andrew. Named for my father, who had recently passed away. By the time he was five, we were living up-country in Kenya. He learned to speak Swahili before he learned English. He swam off Lamu and rode his father's shoulders in the Serengeti. He played with his African friends, mimicking their fathers' ancient board games with pebbles and dents in the dust. He was a child of two cultures, tough and healthy and strong."

Catherine brushed back a lock of hair that had strayed out of place. "It was such a little cut that took him away. Just another part of growing up. Except he didn't grow up. Inside was a virulent infection which changed a simple wound into crushing grief in twenty-four hours."

Anjali heard the confiding tone in Catherine's voice and knew it was her role now just to listen.

"He came home one afternoon with a shallow puncture in his heel. Something—a thorn?—had stabbed him through his heavy bush sandal. He wasn't even crying by the time he got back. I cleaned it up and popped on an elastoplast. His father had just left on a two-week trip. I gave the cook the evening off and made Andrew's favorite dinner."

Catherine smiled. "Just a coincidence, really, that we had his favorite foods, but I've been forever thankful for that last gift. He went to bed just like always. When he didn't come down to breakfast,

I went up to wake him. Nothing unusual. Small boys often sleep late."

Anjali nodded, thinking of her own sons.

Catherine's voice was strained, as if holding in the emotion she was reliving. "He was flushed and feverish. His breathing was shallow. His heel was red, hot, swollen. And there were red streaks moving up his leg. Blood poisoning. Everyone who lives up-country keeps a medical kit far more sophisticated than anything we'd think about back home. I took his temperature—over forty. I gave him penicillin. I ran to the radio. Dead. No way to call the Flying Doctors.

"I ran to the Land Rover and made a bed in the back. I didn't want him to hurt, you see, not my boy, not to hurt on that long trek to Nairobi. I filled the jerry cans with water and petrol. I packed food. I loaded him in the back, and I drove all day through the heat, giving him penicillin every four hours. But it wasn't enough, and my boy died in that soft bed in the back of a Land Rover in the heat of an African savanna."

Catherine could no longer control her voice. It trembled like Sophia's bedraggled cat left behind in the rain. "And I died. There was a pint of medicinal whiskey in the first aid kit of the Land Rover. I held my boy, and I drank it down. I didn't cry. I still had so much to do. I drove on into Nairobi, to the project leader's house, and carried Andrew up the walk. I don't remember much of what happened after that. I fainted when they opened the door. The doctor came to sedate me. The project leader got in touch with Frank, and he arrived the next day. At the funeral, everyone said kind words, but I was completely and absolutely numb. Nothing registered."

Anjali had seen that happen when her sister's baby died of cholera. It hadn't seemed to register on Lakshmi. Anjali had sat with her, crying, but Lakshmi couldn't cry. Not for days.

Catherine lit another cigarette, sucked in the smoke and hungrily held it. She let it out slowly. "I was dead for a long time. I sat home in a darkened room, didn't bother to dress or wash or comb my hair. I just drank. After a while, I came back to life. I wept away my anguish all through one afternoon. I dried my tears. I returned to my duties and pastimes. But I bought booze on the sly." She grimaced. "Stayed completely sober while knocking off a quart a day."

Anjali thought about how she and KB had stood together since those tough days in Hanoi. "But Frank was a comfort to you?"

"When he was home, he did his best. But I was alone while he was away on the project."

"Children can help with that loneliness. I've met your children. You must be very proud of them."

Catherine laughed, a short, regretful laugh. "Oh, Anjali, you see them now, when they're getting good marks at university. But a few years ago, I found out my kids also had substance-abuse problems. That really woke me up. I cleaned up my act, and I helped them clean up theirs. We all went for family counseling during one of our home leaves, and our love for each other pulled us through."

Anjali thought about Anand's call on her birthday. "In my darkest moments, that's what's pulled me through. My family's love."

"Oh, but there were shady times first. I was a drunk. I slept around. I made passes and passed out at diplomatic receptions. I screamed obscenities at my husband and children who were dearer to me than life itself. I threw tantrums in women's clubs. I wallowed in self-pity and thought there'd never be a day for me. I'm still an alky. I'll always be. It's a daily battle not to take a drink, especially when things get rough."

Anjali's mind rested for a moment on how she used chocolate

to help her through bad times. It wasn't as harmful, but it was still addictive.

"It's not easy doing without the booze," Catherine said, "but I like myself better. At least I can be honest with myself. I'm an alcoholic. And I'm fighting it everyday." She stubbed out her cigarette in tempo with the repetition of the last two words, "Every. Day."

"And Sophia?" Anjali finally felt she could ask.

"I feel a part of me has been sacrificed, not just for my husband's career but for all those projects and all those countries. Yes, I got a lot in return, but there's a void at the center of my life, a void of what might have been. Nature abhors a vacuum, so the void must be filled. Sophia and I both tried to fill the voids in our lives with busyness. Sometimes it was reasonably productive. Other times, I have to confess, the busy-ness could be downright destructive. Sometimes you'll do anything just to prove to yourself that there's still life in there somewhere."

That did explain a lot of Sophia's behavior, Anjali realized. Not condone it, but explain it. Some women, like Frieda, shrank away when life hurt them. But Sophia was a fighter. And she was impulsive. So she lashed out whenever she felt like it, not really thinking about the consequences, even for herself. If someone got in the way, she was just a victim of Sophia's war.

"I saw myself mirrored in Sophia's face." Catherine framed her own face with her hands, then let them fall. "She wasn't an alcoholic. Her son didn't die. She was more talented and giving than I can ever be. But we were alike in another way. We were survivors, Sophia and I, and that's what brought us together. We were an unlikely pair of friends. She was beautiful. I am...ordinary. She was full of life and energy. I prefer a more quiet existence. She loved the diplomats, and they loved her. I don't care if I never see another diplomatic reception. They're such a bore, both the diplomats *and* their receptions."

Catherine's face fell. "Forgive me, Anjali. You and KB may be diplomats, but neither of you will ever be a bore."

"No apology needed. No offense taken. I think a lot of the diplomats are boring too. But you were talking about Sophia…"

"Despite the differences between us, we had a lot in common. Sons who preferred drugs to studies. Hard-working and often-absent husbands. The void. A life of dreams deferred and dreams denied. A love of poetry. I accepted Sophia as she was, strengths and weaknesses alike."

Anjali realized that Catherine was seeking approval for her lost friend. All Anjali had to do was show some interest, an interest which she genuinely felt. "How did you two meet?"

The Lao Aviation plane lifted off the tarmac at Vientiane International Airport and was immediately rocked left and right by the monsoon.

Catherine gripped the armrests and pushed her feet hard against the floor, pressing her back against the seat, trying to keep her body as still as possible. Something was rising in her chest, and she kept swallowing to hold it down.

Why did she take *this* flight? She looked past the open cockpit door at the Finnish crew laughing and joking. They probably thought this was mild compared to the blizzards they usually flew through.

Finnair had sold a few used planes to the Lao national airline, so flight and cabin crews were mixed as the Finns trained the Lao how to operate the craft effectively.

Catherine glanced across her seat mate and out the window. She immediately wished she hadn't. The wings were shuddering in an effort to lift the plane above the tumbling dark clouds.

She'd known better than to take a turboprop. She should have waited for the Thai jet. They were much more stable. Thank God it was only a little over an hour to Bangkok.

Catherine tried to calm her stomach by inhaling slowly and deeply, but she was instantly thwarted by that old-plane smell of stale air, too many bodies, too many spilt meals.

Several dings sounded on the intercom. Catherine started. Then the stewardesses got up and started to prepare drinks. That was a good sign. Maybe the turbulence was over.

The plane began to buck up and down. Even the Finnish hostess grabbed for something steady. "Cabin crew, take your seats," said the unemotional voice that pilots always use. So annoying, that voice. How were you supposed to know when things were really bad or not?

Catherine shut her eyes and began to hum. Long ago, someone had told her that humming helped fight the nausea and fear. For reasons she couldn't fathom, she always hummed "I'll Take Romance." Such a frivolous song for these times of sheer terror.

God, she hated to fly. Mustn't think about that. "I'll take romance. While my heart is young and eager and gay…"

The plane lurched sideways, and Catherine's eyes involuntarily flew open in the direction of the tilt. She found herself looking at her seat mate, who was now clearly below her as the plane dipped to the left. The woman was calmly working on a piece of needlepoint.

The plane pitched back in the other direction, and her seat mate was thrown against Catherine's shoulder. The woman smiled apologetically and resumed her handwork.

What an extraordinary woman, Catherine thought. And beautiful.

The whole plane was shuddering now, and poorly-secured hand luggage began to fall out of overhead racks.

Catherine went back to humming with closed eyes. "I'll give my heart away. I'll take romance…" She was trying to remember the rest of the words when the plane broke through into sunshine. She could sense the darkness brightening behind her closed lids.

The plane settled down to the bounce normal in monsoon

conditions. Catherine continued to hum in an effort to get herself under control.

"Something to drink, madam?" said a singsong Scandinavian voice.

Oh, go away, Catherine thought but opened her eyes to see a thick blond pigtail swinging above a tray. "Pepsi, please." That always calmed her stomach.

Her seat mate put down her needlework and asked for white wine.

"Here's to us," the woman said and raised her glass. "We made it." Her smile shimmered.

They sipped their drinks, and the woman held out her hand. "I'm Sophia Powell. You must be new to Vientiane."

As the plane bumped toward Bangkok, Catherine found herself telling Sophia all about her efforts to set up house for the umpteenth time in yet another new country.

Sophia waved for a second glass of wine as the stewardess went by. "Then you're a real pro. Are you finding everything you need?"

They chatted as the plane began to descend, Sophia relating funny stories about her own adventures in Vientiane. The aircraft was on the ground before Catherine appreciated that it had been as shaky going down as on takeoff. Sophia had distracted her so the fear couldn't take hold.

They unbuckled their seatbelts. Sophia reached in her purse and took out a creamy card engraved with her name, address and phone number. "I've enjoyed talking with you. Why don't you come next week for tea?"

Catherine scribbled her own number on a scrap of paper. "I'd love to."

"That became a weekly, even a twice-weekly ritual," Catherine said, offering Anjali the plate of grocery-store sweets. "Sophia's teas were more elaborate than mine—lovely cakes, beautiful linens and china—but so what? I always invited Sophia when it was cook's day off, so we could have some privacy. That meant travel-worn cups and tinned biscuits with paper napkins. Such things weren't important. She was herself, and I was myself, and that's all that mattered. We were just ourselves."

Anjali was too interested in Catherine's view to want anything more to eat. "That's unusual. Sophia didn't seem able to be herself with other people."

"No, she was very self-protective. Over time, we talked less about trivia and more about things that mattered. About our children and our husbands, about the efforts to help both, some ending in failure, some in success. About surviving while following husbands here and there. She talked about her dreams for WIVS and all the people who'd hurt her."

"Karen and Jackie," Anjali said.

"Absolutely. Sophia was terrified that Karen's fundraiser was going to flop. And she tried to help Jackie, but that woman couldn't bear to accept it." Catherine grimaced and changed the subject. "I told Sophia about Andrew and my battle with alcohol. No one else in Vientiane knew those stories, just we two."

We all need someone to confide in, Anjali thought, even Sophia.

With a pang, she realized that she hadn't been confiding in anyone for weeks. Not with Suneeta. And not with KB. Why was she afraid to tell her best friend and her husband her deepest concerns?

She resolutely pushed those thoughts to the back of her mind and concentrated on Catherine.

Her hostess looked a bit embarrassed. "I know this is going to sound corny, but Sophia and I read poetry together. I don't mean we sat for hours like two Victorian maidens taking turns reading Tennyson. But we both liked poetry, and when one of us found something meaningful, she'd bring it along and read it during tea. That's all. More like a couple of men talking about perseverance on the playing field than a couple of aesthetes trading lines."

"You're describing a Sophia whom no one else knew."

Certainly not me, Anjali thought and felt ashamed. She'd only seen Sophia's surface. If she'd looked deeper, tried harder, would she have seen more? Might she have helped save Sophia's life rather than questing after her death?

"You're right," Catherine said with some bitterness. "Most people only knew her superficially. Or through gossip. They didn't bother to make the effort to know more."

"Like the gossip about Jean-Claude," Anjali said, thinking ahead to her Monday appointment.

Catherine turned scornful. "She didn't take Jean-Claude as a lover. Not that he didn't try. Let's face it, he's tried with almost everyone in skirts. I think that was part of Sophia's attraction for him. He couldn't get her. Sophia loved to flirt, but it was just one of her many feminine talents. That's all there was to it. We talked about sex very frankly. She knew my secrets, and I knew hers. Through twenty years of marriage, she was always faithful to Tom."

"You said you know what happened the night she died," Anjali prompted.

Catherine lit another cigarette. She drew in the smoke, and it spilled out with her words. "Normally, we'd have come to Sophia's goodbye party in the same car, but she decided to drive alone at the last minute. She needed to drop off some things that someone had bought from the household effects she wasn't taking to Ashkabad. So we met at Il Ristorante."

Anjali realized she'd been holding her breath. Outside, the rain came again, but it was a gentle, nourishing shower this time. She began to breathe normally.

Catherine took another drag and blew the smoke out her nostrils. "It was depressing to see how few women came. I know it hurt, but Sophia never let it show." She paused and sighed, seeming to look deep into her conscience. Then she continued, a great weariness in her voice.

"On the way home, she parked her car beside the Mekong and dove in."

Anjali's heart jumped. She put a hand to her chest. Sophia had killed herself? But why? Surely not just because so few came to say goodbye. What else could it have been? Not daring to interrupt, Anjali listened through to the end.

Catherine smiled to herself and spoke with warm admiration. "I can picture Sophia diving. She was so graceful. I can't imagine she'd have been otherwise, even then."

The cigarette was burning down, unnoticed, in Catherine's fingers. "I often think that if we'd taken my car, it wouldn't have happened. She'd never have opened the glovebox, and she'd still be alive, having followed her dear Tom to his next assignment."

Anjali recalled Tsing's phrase—Tom was Sophia's port in the storm of her life.

Catherine stubbed out her cigarette. "Three days after she died, Frank came in with the mail. There was an envelope addressed to me in Sophia's handwriting. She always had a folder of stationery with her. And stamps. I can see her sitting in front of the post office as her talent for survival ran out, thinking about what had happened and finally writing her last note."

Anjali could also see Sophia sitting there, carefully making up her mind what to do. Just like she'd done when she'd declined the WIVS award. The decision to commit suicide might have been impulsive. Sophia was often rash. But not the act—no dash to the Mekong, no incoherent leap to end it all. And her note wouldn't be incoherent either. Sophia would have needed to present herself as she wanted to be remembered—suffering, brave, whistling in the dark and fully committed to the course she'd chosen.

In the near-silence of the soft rain, Catherine opened the drawer in the coffee table, lifted out a locked box, inserted a key from her pocket and handed Anjali Sophia's letter.

My dear Kit,

How surprised you're going to be when you read this. As surprised as I was a few moments ago when I opened the glovebox.

On the way home——many thanks for being who you are. I felt your love and support from across the room. On the way home, the car started to bump as if I'd got a puncture. So I stopped along the side of the road and started searching for the torch.

I found it buried at the bottom of the glovebox, but I also found something else. A pair of knickers. Not mine, as I'm sure you've figured out already. But I knew whose they were as soon as I turned on the light. I'd seen them often enough in the ladies dressing room at the Club. Hard to forget a tiny red bikini trimmed in black lace. Jackie's. Jackie's knickers.

What a stunner. After all these years, Tom's having an affair. And for his first infidelity, he's picked one of the women who could hurt me the most. I really can't comprehend it. Did she go after him in an attempt at revenge? I have to say that wouldn't be a surprise. I can believe she'd be that vindictive after all the things she said to me over the tearoom fiasco.

But then I have to ask myself, is this his first infidelity? Have all these years been a chimera? Have I always counted on Tom as my rock, when he was really shifting sand? Oh, I can't bear that.

I can't follow him to the next dreary post, needing him to be my rock and knowing he isn't, thinking I'm doing it all for him and knowing it's not worth it.

Kit, dearest friend, I'm going swimming. It just seems like the right thing to do. After all, I first saw those knickers when Jackie and I shared the pool at the Club. Of course, I didn't know then that we were sharing my husband too.

But where to dive in? My first thought was the pool. But it's not deep enough and the sides are too near. I might change my mind at the last minute and lose my nerve. I couldn't stand having people know I'd tried and failed.

So it's the Mekong for me. Sounds like a song title, doesn't it? "The Mekong for Me." Maybe we should have used it in the Follies. I'll hum a few bars as I head down there. (By the way, it wasn't a puncture, just Vientiane's usual rutted roads.)

I'm going to the one place in Vientiane that has any meaning. Remember that dawn when we all sat on the banks of the river and talked about life? Actually, everyone else talked. I, for once, listened. I'm sure everyone thought that was most strange—Sophia Powell not talking? My God, phone the wire services! I didn't talk because I was so struck by what was being said. I surely didn't have the nerve to be that open in public. I can barely manage it with you. Still, a lot of what was said stayed with me. Remember Moira talking about men who'd let us down and churches that hadn't held us up? That keeps running through my mind tonight.

People will tell you it's a sign of weakness to do what I'm about to. Don't you believe it. I'm scared. But I feel strong enough to overcome it. After all, I've overcome so much in life, why not this too?

People will also tell you all sorts of bad things about me. But you've already heard most of them from my own lips, so I have no fear that you won't understand. I know that in the end, you will judge tenderly of me.

Love to thee, dear friend,
Sophia

When Anjali finished reading, she looked up to see Catherine huddled in the corner of her couch, holding herself, cheeks damp with silent tears. Then Anjali's own tears began to fall.

Anjali's mind raced as she drove away from Catherine's house. No wonder Tom was in such a hurry to leave. Sophia had probably sent him a note also. She would've wanted to make him feel guilty.

Anjali had asked Catherine what she wanted her to do with what she'd revealed, and her hostess had said, "Whatever you think best." So now Anjali was following her own conscience.

She heard a commotion behind her and looked in the rear view mirror. A black SUV was swerving through mopeds, the driver honking wildly at pedestrians to get out of the way.

Loose ends first, she thought, steering toward the French Embassy compound to cancel her appointment with Jean-Claude. She didn't want to know what he'd done, or not done, with Sophia. After a week of tales, Anjali didn't need any more gossip. She was filled to the brim with the bile of it.

Jackie was just closing up for the lunch hour when Anjali arrived. "Great to see you. I'm about to have some fruit and cheese. Will you join me?"

"I've just had tea and too many biscuits, but I will come up and talk, if you don't mind."

They climbed the stairs to the apartment, Jackie chattering away about her morning. Anjali kept silent, marshaling her forces, preparing herself for what was to follow. Jackie took her lunch from the fridge and poured them each a glass of cold hibiscus tea. They sat down at the dining table beside the window.

Anjali looked out and saw the sunlight glinting on the waters of Nam Phou Fountain. How could the world sparkle on such a day?

She spoke without preamble. "I know, Jackie. I know what happened to Sophia."

Jackie stared at Anjali for a moment, her face stricken with agony. She wiped her mouth, as if to clear a bad taste. Anjali looked her squarely in the face. She meant Jackie to see her certainty of the facts and her determination to confront the woman with her own iniquity.

Anjali was surprised to find herself in pain. She'd always been fond of Jackie, and now she had to force them both to confront what the younger woman had done. But regardless of how much Anjali hurt, she meant to see justice served.

Jackie set her tea down with shaking fingers. "How did you…" Her voice trailed off.

Anjali continued to look at her, a look that said she wasn't bluffing. Jackie made a visible effort to get herself under control, lowering her head, drawing in a ragged breath and squaring her shoulders.

Her cat seemed to sense her discomfort and leaped lightly into her lap. Jackie's strong arms pulled the cat to her bosom, and she rubbled her cheek against its fur. The cat's gesture of loyalty seemed to soften its mistress.

Anjali waited, never taking her eyes from Jackie's face. She felt still, very sure.

Jackie wouldn't look at Anjali. Instead, she gazed out the window.

"I could have got through Sophia trying to take over the gallery, even the trouble she caused with Customs. The real torment came later, when she tried to destroy me professionally and personally. She was the one in the wrong, but I was the one who got punished. I was constantly confronted with the gossip of how badly I'd treated Sophia. I was even cornered by Pam at a reception." Jackie swallowed hard. "Berated me in public that the whole thing was all my fault."

She looked at Anjali as if seeking comfort.

For a moment, Anjali was touched by Jackie's suffering. Then reason took over. Yes, Sophia had hurt Jackie badly, in more ways than one. But that couldn't assuage the fact that what Jackie did to Sophia was evil beyond compare. She'd meant to destroy the one illusion that had made Sophia's life worth living.

Jackie's face stiffened when she saw the look in Anjali's eyes. "Then I began to hear tales of how she needlessly hurt others. Not just being offensive, but causing real injury. I'm not sure what she did to Freida, but I know what she did to Ralph."

Anjali raised her eyebrows to show interest, and Jackie went on. "When Sophia got ready to leave Vientiane for good, she needed someone to take over the lease of her house. Ralph and his family were in temporary quarters, so he jumped at the chance. Sophia said she was thrilled and promised the house was his."

Jackie pushed her lunch away and lit a cigarette. "Ralph let his temporary rental go, signed a contract with a moving firm, the whole bit. But a couple weeks before Sophia and Tom were due to leave, she announced that the American Embassy was taking her house for one of its personnel. She left that man, his wife, three children and assorted pets high and dry without even an apology."

"Are you sure?" Anjali took a sip of her honey-sweetened tea.

Jackie kept a sinewy hand on the cat as she stretched to reach the heavy glass ash tray and move it to the dining room table. "Absolutely. Ralph's wife told me the story when she came by to ask if I knew anyplace they could live while they started looking for another house."

The corners of her mouth turned down. "Sophia got off on hurting people. When I heard what she'd done to Ralph and his family, that was the finishing touch. Somebody had to teach her a lesson. And who else, if not me?"

Anjali felt a frisson of recognition. How many people had raised this issue since Sophia's death? Herself included. They'd all been wondering why someone hadn't put a stop to Sophia's malicious ways. Anjali saw now that if it was going to be anyone, it would have been Jackie, the strongest of the people Sophia had hurt.

"So you appointed yourself avenging angel?"

Jackie flicked her cigarette into the ashtray as if it were Sophia's hand. "I wanted to hurt Sophia where she was most vulnerable, her darling, handsome Tom. So I set out to seduce him. It wasn't hard. I wasn't his first extracurricular adventure, and flattery was as welcome to him as it was to her."

So the gossip had been true, Anjali thought. Sophia wasted her life following a man who couldn't return her devotion.

Jackie stroked her cat. The contact seemed to soothe them both. "I waited until Sophia went down to Bangkok to buy things they needed for Ashkabad. Then I invited a few friends over for drinks and made sure Tom was among them. It didn't take much to give him the right idea. The next day, I went by his office and cadged a lift up-country to visit one of my villages. I didn't really need to go, but you can accomplish a lot on a long ride in the country."

Anjali had thought that Sophia was devious, but she'd met her match in Jackie. She felt overloaded with what people would do to get what they wanted.

Jackie was oblivious to Anjali's mood. "We took off the next morning. Tom left his driver behind. I packed a picnic lunch, and the champagne did the rest." She shrugged. "I didn't enjoy it. Oh, he's a skillful enough lover, but I wasn't filled with ecstasy. It was victory. He likes big, buxom girls, and he was only too happy to believe he'd given me the greatest joy of my life. It was easy to arrange another rendezvous."

Oh dear, Anjali thought, not sure she really wanted to hear all this. The truth was more shameful than she'd imagined. She felt dirtied by it. But then Anjali thought of Sophia—pitiful, sad, talented Sophia. Despite her sins, she didn't deserve what Jackie had done.

"You felt no guilt?"

Jackie stubbed out her cigarette. "Nope. Not then. They both deserved it. I asked him if we could go for a moonlit drive in Sophia's sports car. 'That car is soooo sexy.' I milked the line for every innuendo. He leered and suggested the same night. As soon as we got back to Vientiane, he got Sophia's car, and we were off, down a dirt road that ended by the Mekong."

Anjali thought about how people couldn't go far from Vientiane thanks to governmental paranoia. But they could go far enough.

Jackie still didn't pick up on Anjali's mood. She was lost in her memories and the sound of the cat purring. "Afterwards, while he was buttoning up his flies and gathering the blanket, I pushed my knickers deep in the glovebox, under a folder of stationery." Jackie's voice vibrated with bitterness. "I wanted Sophia to find them. I wanted her to know who'd done it with her precious Tom in her precious car. I wanted her to hurt."

The vibrato turned to remorse, and Jackie's eyes were wet. She turned to face Anjali for the first time. "But I never meant to kill her. I never meant it to go that far. I just wanted her to hurt."

Anjali drew herself up. A white-hot light seemed to surround her. She felt full of righteous energy. Now she was Devi, avenging the wrong that had been done. "You didn't kill Sophia. She killed herself. But you *are* guilty, Jackie."

The younger woman's jaw dropped, and her eyes opened wide. She looked surprised, even shocked. She shook her head, as if to clear it from unwelcome thoughts. When she spoke, there was relief in her voice. "What are you going to do? Will you tell?"

Anjali appreciated that Jackie might feel relieved at having released the burden of guilt. "I'm not going to tell anyone. Let Sophia lie with some dignity."

"What about me?" Jackie whispered.

"You'll have to live with it."

The white light flared up. Justice done. Sophia protected. Jackie suffering. Enough. Finished.

Anjali rose and walked to the door. She looked back and saw Jackie, her face slack, her eyes unfocused, lost in the residue of her vengeance, with only her cat for cold comfort.

The white light followed Anjali down the steps and out into Nam Phou Square, where it was lost in the midday heat. Suddenly, she felt exhausted.

But she couldn't rest yet. She still had the problems of Cyril's alleged smuggling and how to clear KB's name.

Anjali's eye was caught by a black SUV parked in front of Il Ristorante. The second one today, she thought, giving the unusual color a second look. The car had Thai plates. Thai tourists on a day trip, she decided and got in the Deux Chevaux.

She put the key in the ignition and hesitated. She didn't know what to do about KB. The decision not to sully Sophia's memory had just come naturally. It still felt like the right thing to do. But Anjali was left with the puzzle of how to stop the gossip linking KB to Sophia's death. That required more thought. Meanwhile, she could do something about Cyril.

"I am sorry, Madame, Mr. Cyril is still in Champassak," his houseman said, standing in the open door.

Well, Anjali thought, that was one question answered.

The houseman looked at Anjali's tired face. "Madame, it is very hot. Perhaps you would like something cold to drink?"

Anjali realized how much she needed energy. "That's very kind. I believe I would."

She followed him into the shuttered house. He showed her to a stuffed chair in the living room and turned on a lamp as he went out to the kitchen. Cyril's butterflies flamed in the light, trapped in their cases on the white wall.

The houseman reappeared with a glass of lemonade and some chocolate biscuits on a silver tray. "May I get you anything else, Madame?"

"When will Mr. Cyril return? I must speak with him." Anjali took a long pull from the glass and felt the sweet-tart liquid begin its magic.

"He did not say, Madame." Anjali's spirits fell, and she took another drink of the lemonade. "But you can telephone him," the houseman said.

Her sinking spirits took a U-turn. "Oh. Do you have the number of his hotel?"

He smiled. "I have the number of his cell phone."

"His cell phone?" Anjali was astonished. Cell phones were so common in Bangkok that it was impossible to escape the sound of one-sided conversations. But virtually no one had a cell phone in Vientiane, even though the Thai system reached some way across the river into Laos.

The houseman nodded. "When you are ready, perhaps we could use the telephone in the kitchen?"

Anjali finished the lemonade in one swallow. "I'm ready now." She left the biscuits untouched and followed him out to the kitchen. The houseman's finger was busy for a few moments with the dial of the old-fashioned black phone. Then he handed her the receiver and discreetly withdrew to the living room.

A couple of rings, and then she heard the unmistakable voice. "Hello? Witherspoon here."

"Hello, Cyril."

There was a discernible pause, accompanied by the sound of a motor. Then Cyril said, "Anjali." He paused again. "Sorry, I'm so surprised to hear from you. How did you get this number?"

"Your houseman. I told him I had something important to ask you."

Again she heard the motor before Cyril spoke, and this time there were voices in the background. Speaking Lao, or perhaps Thai. She couldn't tell the difference without being fluent.

"Something important?" Cyril's voice sounded strained. "What is it, Anjali?"

She carefully mobilized her strategy. "You haven't had an altercation with the Embassy's night watchman by any chance?"

"Of course not," Cyril scoffed. "Hardly know the man Just wave when I leave after hours. I doubt if we've spoken two words." His voice became wary. "Why?"

"I'm afraid it's my turn to relay a rumor."

"Really? What, I wonder?"

"Someone came to tell me you're helping the smugglers in Champassak."

Cyril laughed. A laugh of tension that persisted until it turned slightly hysterical. Anjali wasn't sure what to make of it.

Cyril gasped for breath. "As a matter of fact, I am."

Anjali couldn't believe her ears. "I beg your pardon?"

"I am. I am helping the smugglers." Cyril sounded a bit giddy. "That's why I've got this cell phone. They gave it to me so we could keep in touch." He giggled. "We're halfway across the Mekong now."

Anjali looked for a chair. She needed to sit down. "Oh, Cyril, why?"

"I already told you. When I invited you over for tea. I've led a useless life. Nothing to show for it but a terribly inadequate government pension." He giggled again. "Well, I'll be living in the lap of luxury now."

Anjali hooked a foot around the leg of a kitchen chair, pulled it over and sat down. "The tea...when you asked me to find out how Sophia drowned?"

Cyril's voice seemed to smile. "The very one. All a smokescreen, I'm afraid. Couldn't care less how Sophia drowned."

Anjali found her fury rising. "So what do you care about?"

"Not getting caught, of course. I knew it was just a matter of time until there was gossip about the smuggling. And I knew your bright intelligence was bored. I was afraid you'd turn your searchlight on the rumors. Sooner or later, you'd have found out and told KB. I needed a little time."

"So you tried to distract me with Sophia's death."

"That's the long and the short of it, Anjali."

His voice went silent for a moment as the motor in the background coughed. Then came the sound of a Thai voice swearing and a foot hitting the boat's motor. Anjali recognized those sounds, sure now that the voice must be speaking Thai. She'd heard coughing motors often enough as she crossed on the ferry to Nong Khai. Those old riverboats were always breaking down.

The motor caught again. Cyril heaved a sigh and continued. "Sorry in a way to use Sophia like that. But when I remembered how she used to make fun of me behind my back, I realized I wasn't so sorry after all."

"And the gossip about Sophia and KB?"

"Oh, Anjali, I was so afraid you wouldn't fall for it. I made it all up. Of course no one's gossiping about KB. Mr. Paragon-of-Virtue, your husband."

How pathetic to have been taken in so easily, Anjali thought. How badly she must have needed any excuse to keep investigating. Especially with KB against it.

Cyril went on, "That's why I didn't want you paying attention to what was happening down at Wat Phou. World Heritage Site. U.N. jurisdiction. You'd tell KB, and it would be all over." He giggled. "Couldn't have that, could we?"

Anjali was tossing ideas back and forth in her head as she listened, trying to decide what to do, how to stop Cyril.

Her thoughts were interrupted by him saying, "It's been nice talking with you, but I must ring off. We're about to dock, and then it's on to my old age in paradise."

She started to speak, to ask Cyril where he was, but the line went dead. She sat very still in the kitchen chair. She could hear Cyril's houseman running the vacuum cleaner in another part of the house.

Cyril had used everyone, she perceived. Sophia, KB, herself. She stood up. Well, she wasn't going to let him get away with it.

But once she was back in the car and driving out Cyril's gate, Anjali realized she didn't know what to do. She let up on the accelerator and allowed the car to coast down the lane while she thought.

KB was away, so far up-country she couldn't contact him. And even if she could, he wouldn't be back until tomorrow. Far too late. Cyril would be long gone on a plane from Bangkok to whatever hideaway he'd chosen.

Probably someplace where he couldn't be extradited. Sure to change his name too. Regardless, poverty-stricken Laos didn't have the resources to go after him.

She considered going to the Lao police so they could at least try to get Cyril before he left Southeast Asia. But she had neither the language nor the connections to get to the top in a matter of minutes. And every minute was precious.

Raj, she concluded and hit the accelerator. A scrawny dog jumped away from his scavenging as a black SUV followed her around the corner.

Anjali pulled up in front of the Indian Embassy in record time. Across the street, some WIVS members paused on the steps of the

Ministry of Foreign Affairs and stared. Their round eyes, open mouths and exchanged glances spoke volumes.

Gossip be damned. Anjali entered the Embassy.

As soon as the receptionist had announced her presence, Anjali was ushered into Raj's waiting room. His male secretary, long white *kemiz* fluttering below his vest of synthetic fabric, stuck his head into the hallway to shout, "Tea for the Ambassador's guest!"

Raj himself threw open the door to his office. "What a pleasant surprise. Do come in."

"I'm afraid it's not a social call," she said and stepped past him.

He smiled at her fondly. "It never is with you. What is it this time? Collecting for refugees? The arts?"

He closed the door and led her to the taupe velvet couch. Then he sat in an adjacent chair of burnt orange silk. A fresh bouquet of creamy orchids was on a low table before them. All around were displayed the arts of India—painting, textiles, metalwork, statuary.

"Smuggling," Anjali said.

Raj's handsome face took on a frown of consternation. "I'm sorry?"

"Smuggling. Down at Wat Phou. Cyril's the one who's been helping get the stuff out."

"Oh, my God."

There was a discreet knock on the door, and Raj's secretary opened it to admit the server with the tea tray.

Not now, Anjali thought but knew it was too late to stop them. She resigned herself to wait patiently until the tea was served.

"Just leave the tray," Raj said. "We'll serve ourselves."

The secretary looked startled. The server kept his head down. Both rapidly withdrew.

Anjali looked at Raj with gratitude and told him the whole story. Before the last words were out of her mouth, he'd jumped up and headed for the phone on his ornately carved desk.

"Minister of Internal Affairs, please," he said to the Embassy operator.

Anjali watched him, standing there in his raw silk vest with its rose bud. He looked every inch like he'd been cast for the role by some movie director.

"Puongpun?" he said. "Raj here. I have something of vital importance to discuss with you. It's just come to my attention. May I come over now?…Right. Ten minutes."

Raj put down the receiver. "Come on, Anjali, we're going to stop the bastard."

Anjali stood outside the Indian Embassy after she and Raj had returned from their meeting with the Minister of Internal Affairs. She felt like a fool. Cyril had told her half-truths to reel her in.

Just like Jackie, she realized.

She remembered how she'd been suspicious of Jackie at the time, comparing her behavior to her own brothers when they'd wanted to avoid punishment. Jackie had told Anjali everything that had led up to her revenge and stopped.

Anjali berated herself. Why hadn't she followed her instincts? What if Jackie was still telling half-truths?

Anjali pounded on the gallery door directly above the "Closed" sign. It was early for Jackie's gallery to be shut, but she probably couldn't face having it open after her noon-time admissions. Despite the racket, no one came.

She stepped out from the portico and into Nam Phou Square. The smell of garbage wafted from the alley between the Square's two restaurants. She looked up at the windows of Jackie's apartment. They were open, and the curtains blew out in the breeze. Jackie would never have left the windows like that if no one was in the building.

"Jackie!" Anjali called. "I know you're in there. Open the door!"

Passers-by began to gawk. There'd be more gossip tomorrow, but Anjali didn't care. "Jackie! Open up!"

She returned to the door and pounded again. Through the glass she saw a shadow move toward her. The shadow became Jackie. Her face was puffy and streaked with mascara.

Jackie opened the door a crack and leaned against the frame. "I really don't want to see anyone right now."

"You're going to see me." Anjali pondered how she'd get by the athletic Jackie if she resisted.

The tall Aussie and the short Indian stood on either side of the door, each staring at the other with determination. Then Jackie looked at the gathering gawkers and opened the door enough to let Anjali slip through.

Jackie closed the door's curtains. Her voice was weary. "What do you want? I've already told you what happened."

Anjali looked up at the woman in the gloomy light. "But you didn't tell me everything, did you?"

Jackie sighed and rubbed her forehead. Her jaw sagged, and her eyes drooped. "Come upstairs," she said and locked the front door.

Anjali crossed the gallery behind Jackie and followed her up the steps, conscious that she'd acted hastily. She was now alone with a possible murderer. When they entered the apartment, she headed for the dining table beside the open window, but Jackie cut her off and gestured toward the couch and chairs. Jackie took the chair near the door, and Anjali had to accept that, for a moment, no one could see her, and her escape route was blocked. She leaned back against the couch's batik cushions and tried to breathe calmly.

"Scoped it all out, have you, Anjali?"

"I think I have a pretty good idea of what must have happened."

Jackie crossed her arms. "Okay, you tell me."

She glanced toward the bedroom door, and Anjali's eyes followed hers. A half-filled suitcase lay on the bed, clothes strewn around it.

Anjali turned back to Jackie. "You like to go for late-night walks when you can't sleep."

Jackie looked startled.

"You came upon Sophia down by the Mekong."

Jackie stared at Anjali for a long while. Anjali could read her thoughts in the emotions sweeping across her face. Fight? Flee? Give up?

Finally, Jackie's shoulders slumped. She bit her lip and acted out the rest of the tale.

The river's breeze drew Jackie through the hot and humid night. Wondering if she could afford air-conditioning, at least for the bedroom, she stepped into the narrow park beside the Mekong. The breeze rocked the empty swings and carried the scent of jasmine from the hotel garden. She stood still, head up, eyes shut, and let it caress her. The day's tensions drifted away. She swayed gently from side to side.

The night's serenity was broken by a soft moan. Jackie opened her eyes and saw a pale figure on the edge of the bank, half-obscured by the giant crotons growing there. Who else would be here at this hour? And why were they crying?

She walked forward, hoping to help, and saw it was a *farang* in a silk dress, her long scarf trailing in the mud. The figure turned. Jackie blinked. It was Sophia.

"You bitch!" screamed Sophia, bent forward, fists clenched, face contorted.

Jackie sauntered toward her. "Well, it takes one to know one, honey. How does it feel to be on the receiving end?"

"Whore," snarled Sophia.

"Aw, it was easy," drawled Jackie. "He can't keep it in his pants."

Sophia screamed and reared back, raising a hand to slap her. Jackie threw her own hands forward, striking Sophia on the shoulders.

For a moment, Sophia teetered on the rim of the bank. Then, arms whirling for balance, she fell.

Jackie flew to the river's edge, but all she could see was roiling water.

"I never meant to kill her," Jackie said. "I was just trying to protect myself." She sagged forward. "I wrecked her life and mine, too."

"It's not too late," Anjali said.

Jackie looked up. "What do you mean?"

"It's not too late to save your life. If what you say is true, it was an accident. We can go to the authorities…"

"No way," burst in Jackie. "I couldn't stay here after that. I can't face starting all over somewhere else."

Anjali nodded toward the bedroom door. "Isn't that what you were planning to do anyway?"

Jackie eyed the heavy glass ashtray on the coffee table. "Yeah."

"If you run away, your conscience will run with you." Anjali smiled to ease the harshness of her words. "I've seen that conscience. It's a good one."

Jackie picked up the ashtray and hefted its weight.

Anjali could feel her heart beating against her breast bone. She took up a batik cushion and held it on her lap, just in case. "What if we call your Ambassador, tell him the whole story, and let him take charge of what happens next."

Jackie looked at her, bouncing the ashtray in her hand.

Anjali continued, "He won't get you off the hook, but he'll deal with the authorities and see that you get a fair hearing."

Jackie looked down at the ashtray, her knuckles white with a desperate grip. Then she stared at Anjali like she'd never seen her before. Her arm came up a fraction, bearing the weight of the ashtray. Her face twisted and collapsed. "Will you stand by me?"

Anjali held out her hand for the ashtray. "Of course."

They were waiting for the Ambassador and the Chief of Police to arrive. Jackie seemed paralyzed in her chair, so Anjali got up to make a pot of tea.

No need for Devi anymore, she thought. If Jackie was going to follow through with this, she needed Sita by her side.

Anjali found a commercial packet of brownies in a cupboard and put some on a plate. When she returned from the kitchen alcove, Jackie was curled up in her chair, hugging herself.

"Where are they?" she fretted. "I can't stand this waiting."

Anjali put the tray down on the coffee table and went to the window. The black SUV with Thai plates was still outside Il Ristorante, the driver talking on a cell phone. Must have been a very long lunch, Anjali thought and looked across the square toward the road that lead from the Australian Embassy. "Won't be long now," she said.

She poured them each a cup of tea and made sure Jackie's had lots of sugar. The exhausted woman was going to need energy in the coming hours.

The kink-tailed cat crept out from under the bed and came to sit in Jackie's lap. As before, it seemed to give her comfort. She sat there, stroking the cat with one hand and drinking her tea with the other. After all the emotion of the afternoon, she seemed to need just to sit quietly, and Anjali left her alone.

After a while, Anjali heard cars pulling up outside. She went to the window and saw the Ambassador and the Chief of Police. A crowd was gathering, drawn by the official cars, and the Police Chief gestured to a couple of his officers to keep them back.

Anjali went down to let them in. The Ambassador nodded and led the way upstairs. He looked grim and shook hands with Jackie, but didn't say anything. The Chief spoke to an accompanying officer, who came toward Jackie with handcuffs.

The Ambassador said, "I don't think we'll need those. We'll come in my car." He put out an arm to indicate that Jackie should follow him.

Jackie's jaw tightened, and her face looked frozen with the effort not to cry out.

Anjali stepped to Jackie's side, put an arm around her waist and walked with her down the stairs. The crowd surged around the police officers, shouting in Lao, English and French. Anjali could see several WIVS faces among them.

"What's happening?" shrieked Pam. "Did Jackie do it?"

Jackie lowered her head and shrank back. The Chief came forward to move her along. Anjali kept her arm around Jackie's waist and guided her to the Ambassador's car. Then she sat beside her all the way to the police station.

Anjali sat in the family dining room of the Indian Residence and let her mind wander to the events of the afternoon. The Minister of Internal Affairs had immediately contacted his Thai counterpart during their meeting. Afterward, Raj had said they'd done all they could for now and suggested Anjali join him and Suneeta for dinner that evening. Anjali had accepted with pleasure, but then she'd had second thoughts about Jackie and gone to confront her.

She glanced around the informal room, decorated with family items Suneeta and Raj always brought with them as they moved from embassy to embassy. A set of antique tiffin boxes gleamed on the sideboard, their brass polished to mirror-sheen. More antique arts hung on the wall, simple but evocative folk paintings from Hindu mythology. The table was set with Suneeta's everyday dishes and stainless-steel cutlery. Granted, they were designed by a well-known Indian craftsman, but the total effect was homey and intimate. Exactly what was needed after a trying day.

"More pilau, Anjali?" Suneeta asked. The servers were still in the room. Anjali could appreciate that her hostess didn't want to talk about Cyril in front of them. She also wondered how much she could, or should, say about what had happened with Jackie.

In any case, Raj had just been called to the phone to speak with the Minister, so there was no need to say anything until he returned and the servers departed.

Anjali refused a second helping of the savory rice and turned her thoughts to the difficulties faced by the Lao and Thai police now combing both sides of the border for Cyril.

The Minister had said the search would be difficult because the Mekong flowed inside Champassak province. It didn't form the border between Thailand and Laos as it did at Vientiane. Cyril had been registered in a hotel on the eastern shore. So he and his cohorts could have travelled upriver to Thailand or crossed to the Mekong's western shore and then driven to the Thai border.

Raj returned to the table and dismissed the servers.

Anjali watched his face. "Good news or bad?"

He took the wilted rosebud from his vest. "Both. The Lao police found where Cyril's boat came ashore…"

Anjali felt the beginnings of a thrill in her chest and a smile on her face.

Raj lay the wilted bud down on the table. "…but a local man said he saw them head off in a four-wheel drive toward the Cambodian border."

"Cambodia!" Anjali and Suneeta exclaimed together.

"It makes some sense, actually," he said. "The country's still politically unstable. They could maybe get the stuff out easier there than through Bangkok. The Thais would use Cyril as the courier. His diplomatic passport would get him through Customs without a search. Then the smugglers could disappear back over the border into Thailand with no one the wiser."

Anjali's heart sank. They weren't going to catch Cyril after all.

Suneeta looked from one glum face to the other. "Come on, you two. It's not over yet."

Raj put on a smile. "No, it's not. The Ministry has contacted the Cambodian authorities, and they're on the alert too."

"So we mustn't give up hope," Anjali whispered.

Suneeta smiled at Anjali. "Never give up. Wasn't that the mantra we used when we organized the raffle for the women's club in Botswana?"

Anjali smiled and chanted, "Nevergiveup. Nevergiveup. Nevergiveup. Just like it was all one word."

Suneeta rang for the servers to clear the table and deftly changed the subject. "Speaking of which, I've been on an unending search for a new driver. Tan's father is gravely ill, and he has to return to his village. He'll have to assume his obligations as new head of the family."

Anjali grinned. "I've got just the man for you."

When she'd finished telling them about Tom's driver, Raj said, "Looks like we'd better contact this Kham-pun tomorrow."

"That's the second favor you've done me," Suneeta said and passed the fruit plate left by the servers.

Anjali looked at her hostess over the pomelo and coconut. Involuntarily, her chin pulled back, and her eyebrows crinkled. She hadn't a clue what her friend was talking about. Her attention still on Suneeta, she began to serve herself.

"You've had a lot on your mind," Suneeta said. "I'm talking about your advice about how to handle the gossip." She looked fondly at her husband.

Anjali's hand stopped for a moment in mid-air, the serving plate suspended in limbo. Then she passed the fruit to Raj.

He beamed at his wife. "Once a team, always a team." Then he turned his gaze to Anjali. "We're going on as if the infidelity-mongers never said a word."

Why was she feeling guilty? Anjali wondered. There'd been nothing between her and Raj, despite what the gossips said.

Suneeta burst out laughing. "Anjali, I can read your face." She reached out a hand and patted Anjali's arm. "Of course Pam made sure I heard the gossip about you and Raj. I never believed it for a moment. Told her so, too. In no uncertain terms."

Anjali put her hand over her friend's. "I knew you wouldn't believe it, but I was hoping you'd be spared hearing it. I think Cyril's the one who started it."

Raj sat back in his chair. "Cyril! Why?"

"Just another way to keep me occupied," Anjali said. "Like he did with Sophia's death. He didn't want me paying attention to what was happening down in Champassak."

Suneeta lowered her head and looked into Anjali's eyes. "I can read your face again. You know what happened to Sophia. I heard gossip about what happened at Nam Phou this afternoon."

Anjali suddenly felt every weary. "Yes, but I don't want to talk about it now."

She took a bite of the dessert. The grapefruit-like pulp had been separated into its tiny teardrops. Mixed with fresh shredded coconut, it was the perfect ending to a spicy meal.

Suneeta's chin came up. "Seems to me you've been keeping a lot of things inside lately."

Anjali felt guilt rising again. It was true. She hadn't told her best friend about what had happened in Hanoi, how it had circumscribed her life. She'd kept the gossip about Raj a secret. And now she wouldn't talk about how Sophia had drowned. Time to make amends.

"The whole story's so sordid," she began.

When she'd finished, Suneeta squeezed her hand. "You must be worn down with all the burdens you've been carrying."

Anjali returned her friend's gentle pressure. "Investigating Sophia's death has shown me how empty our lives are—the international wives, I mean. Even if our marriages are perfectly happy…" She smiled at Suneeta and Raj. "…we're reduced by our dependency."

Suneeta sat up straight. "Funny you should mention that…"

Anjali was astonished. "I always thought you were the perfect diplomat's wife. And content to be so."

Raj put both hands flat on the table. "Excuse me, ladies, but if any woman has done well in the international life, it's you two."

Anjali kept her voice gentle. "Appearances can be deceiving, Raj."

He looked from one to the other as if they'd suddenly mutated into the most bizarre of creatures

Anjali said, "I think we need some kind of international organization to support the wives."

Raj groaned. "Oh no, not WIVS writ large."

Suneeta smiled encouragement at Anjali, who said, "Definitely not that. Not busywork without much chance of benefiting either side…"

Raj opened his mouth to speak, but Suneeta's voice came fondly. "Oh Raj, do let Anjali explain before you criticize."

He glowered playfully at his wife, but Anjali sensed he was still uncomfortable with what he was hearing. She warmed to her topic. "I'm thinking about true support services—training, guidelines for survival, a newsletter, an international job bank, career counseling…"

Suneeta interrupted, "Don't forget that not all of us want a job."

"Ladies, if a man may make a suggestion?" Raj's voice was tinged with a hint of condescension. "Perhaps you should look on this as a development project. Do a needs assessment first?"

Splendid idea," Anjali said. "We'll organize a conference of dependent wives and find out what they need."

Suneeta rang for coffee, and the three friends talked into the night, distracting themselves with Anjali's idea. But always there, below the surface, was the pain of Jackie's revenge and the worry of Cyril's escape.

Arm-in-arm, Suneeta and Raj walked Anjali to her car.

"It's after midnight," Raj said. "Do you want me to drive along behind you?"

Anjali kissed them each on the cheek. "Of course not. It's only a few kilometers." She got in the Deux Chevaux and looked up at Raj. "Call me as soon as you hear something?"

He nodded. "Promise."

Thanks to a new moon and broken street lamps, it was quite dark in the Residence's neighborhood. Anjali felt more comfortable once she got downtown, even though the streets were deserted.

But not completely. Headlights hit her rear view mirror, and she glanced up. A black SUV was speeding toward her.

Some idiot with too much to drink, she thought and slowed so he'd pass and leave her in peace.

The SUV kept coming until it was inches from her bumper. She looked up again and saw two men's faces in the light shedding from the nearby hotel. Southeast Asian faces, she recognized, but that was all she could see.

Anjali stepped on the gas. The little Deux Chevaux did its best, but it was only moments before the SUV was on her bumper again.

The two vehicles were careening along the Mekong now. The

black SUV pulled up level with the Deux Chevaux. Anjali stamped on the gas pedal, but her little car was already going as fast as it could.

The driver of the towering SUV twisted the wheel toward her, and the Deux Chevaux shuddered with the impact.

Anjali didn't have time to think. She just hit the brakes.

The SUV shot out in front. Its tires screeched, and the SUV began to turn.

She saw the opening to one of old Vientiane's narrowest lanes, and pulled the steering wheel as hard as she could. Her beloved Deux Chevaux responded and shot down the tiny alley.

Anjali looked in the rear view mirror and saw the SUV pull up at the entrance, then drive by. The alley was too tight for it to enter.

Worried they'd come round the block and catch her at the end of the cramped lane, she turned right into another alley, then left and right in a zigzag until she was out of the old neighborhood and almost home.

She was nearly to her compound when she saw headlights turning into her street. Anjali honked her horn and shouted at Vong to open the gate, worried he'd be in the back garden and not hear.

She pulled up to the gate, but it didn't open. She looked down the street. The black SUV was racing toward her.

Oh God, she thought and hit the horn.

The gate swung open, and Vong's frightened face peered out.

The Deux Chevaux roared through. "Close the gate," Anjali shouted. "Bolt it!"

She jumped out of her car. She could hear the SUV's engine idling on the other side of the gate. "Tell them I'm calling the police," she said to Vong.

He called out in Lao and then in French for good measure.

The two of them looked through the crack between the gate and the wall. The men were scowling back from inside the SUV.

"Tell them again," Anjali whispered, and Vong shouted the words as loud as he could. Lights began to come on in nearby houses.

The SUV pulled away, but not before Anjali saw it had a Thai license plate.

Anjali was shaking when it was all over, and concerned neighbors came to help. She told them not to worry, it was just a couple of drunks acting up, and they'd driven away.

Vong nodded to show he understood she didn't want to say more. He locked the gate behind the neighbors and began to patrol the perimeter.

She opened the front door, turned on the lights and went inside. She didn't want to call the police just yet. She needed time to think. So much for her belief in the gentility of life in Laos. But the men in the SUV were not Lao. They had to be part of the Thai smuggling ring.

Anjali sat on the couch and switched on a table lamp. Had they wanted to scare her, she wondered, or kill her? She swallowed the lump rising in her throat and pushed her thoughts onward. She recalled the black SUV in front of Il Ristorante and its driver on a cell phone. Who had he been talking to? His Thai boss? Cyril?

No point in calling the police, she decided. What could they do at this point? The men had driven away. Besides, if the bribing rumors were true, how could she be sure the smugglers hadn't got to the Lao police also?

One thing for certain. She didn't want KB to know, not after his concern that she might get hurt. That meant not calling Raj, because he'd definitely tell KB.

The SUV's gone, she told herself. Go to bed.

But what if they came back? The thought startled her awake, and she raced to her study overlooking the gate. The street was empty, lit by bright sunshine. She sighed relief.

Kongkeo was busy hoeing the garden, and Anjali could hear Onhta preparing breakfast in the kitchen. She looked at the clock on her desk. Seven-thirty. With all of yesterday's stress, she'd overslept.

She picked up the phone and called Raj. "Any word?"

"None yet," came his sleep-heavy voice. "I just got up. Let me get to the office and ring the Minister. Then I'll call you back."

Anjali felt chagrined. It was too early to be calling anyone. Distraction was what she needed. She settled herself on the yoga mat, and a happy thought calmed her. KB was coming home today.

After breakfast, she went to inspect the damage to the Deux Chevaux, only to find the car gone. Shocked, she called Thongsy's name, and Kongkeo came running with a *nop* and a smile.

"Thongsy saw the dent and said he'd get it fixed before Mr. KB comes home. We didn't want you to worry."

Anjali's eyes tingled. "You are all too kind."

She went back inside and puttered around, waiting for Raj's call. When ten o'clock came without the phone ringing, she resolved to focus more on the here and now. She went out to the kitchen and found Onhta busy chopping vegetables for KB's favorite dishes, an exceptionally hot curry with a *raita* of cucumber and yoghurt. A chocolate cake was cooling on the counter.

"I was planning to serve it in thin slices with papaya," Onhta said.

"That sounds wonderful," Anjali said, but feeling guilty about her addiction to chocolate.

The cook allowed a look of pleasure to steal across her face.

"Onhta…" Anjali's resolve weakened.

"Yes, Madame?"

"I have been thinking…well, I think I eat too much chocolate."

"They do say it is not good for older people to eat too much. It is difficult to digest." Onhta seemed to realize what she'd said might be hurtful, and she quickly added, "I have recently found it to be so." Onhta looked down at the floor. She was clearly uncomfortable at being too forward.

"We'll have your special cake tonight," Anjali said, gratified to see Onhta's shy smile. "Then you take the leftovers home and share them with your grandchildren."

Onhta was positively beaming. "And after tonight, Madame?"

"We'll have one chocolate dessert a month. It will be more of a treat that way, and I won't be so tempted to raid the fridge."

"I look forward to helping you, Madame."

If only the rest of life were so easy, Anjali thought.

She walked through the house to make sure everything was ready for KB's return. There were fresh flowers in the living room, and a new cake of the soap he liked in the bath. Onhta had washed and ironed his favorite *kurta pyjamas*. The thin cotton loungewear was hanging on his hook in the bedroom.

Anjali reached out a hand to touch KB's *pyjamas*. How could she get through this day? No word yet from Raj and the worry that the black SUV might return. She felt like she was going mad. Now was when she needed to be a gardener.

Kongkeo looked up with the barest hint of surprise when Anjali stepped off the porch and came along the path toward him. She smiled and tried to chat about pruning the cocopalms. But her heart wasn't really in it.

She walked over to the gate and peeked through the crack. Her heart jumped. The black SUV was parked on her side of the street, hidden from the house by her compound wall.

"Kongkeo," she called softly. He dropped his hoe and hurried over. "How long has that SUV been here?"

"Since I arrived this morning. They asked for you, but I said you were still asleep." He smiled. "Then I locked the gate."

Anjali looked down. The gate was padlocked, a practice normally observed only after the household was in bed. "You did well, Kongkeo."

She peeped through the crack again, then swiftly pulled her head back. The two men were getting out of the SUV. She gestured for Kongkeo to move away from the gate, and they slipped to the side.

Footsteps and whispers signaled the men's approach. Kongkeo ran to get his hoe. A shadow slipped through the crack, and Anjali imagined one of the men peeking through just as she'd done only moments before. Kongkeo took up a defensive stance, hoe at the ready, just out of sight from the crack's view.

When the phone rang, she almost didn't hear it. She thought it was a bird's call. Then she realized two phones were ringing—the smugglers' cell and her own.

Onhta came out on the porch and called, "Madame, the Indian Ambassador for you." The housekeeper gave Kongkeo the tiniest look of consternation before returning inside.

Anjali looked at the gate. The peeping shadow was gone. She

gestured at Kongkeo to maintain his position and hurried inside to her study.

"Sorry not to call earlier," Raj said. "I was waiting until I knew something." His normally calm ambassador's voice couldn't control the excitement any longer. "Looks like you and KB have a lot to celebrate tonight. They caught Cyril and the smugglers!"

Anjali hadn't felt this thrilled since the birth of her sons. "Where? How?"

She heard the smile in Raj's voice. "Joint operation. Lao and Cambodian foot soldiers patrolling both sides of the border. And the Thai flying in a helicopter to search from the air."

Anjali heard a motor being gunned and the screech of tires She looked out the window. Kongkeo was running toward the house, grinning and waving his hoe in triumph.

The black SUV was leaving, she realized. Could their phone call have had a message like hers? And they were in a hurry to get back to Thailand?

"Excuse me, Raj. Could you repeat that last bit? I didn't get it all."

"The helicopter team spotted them first. They were on a dirt road between Ban Tahine and Kompong Sralao."

"I have no idea where that is."

"Ban Tahine is on the Lao side, and Kompong Sralao is on the Cambodian side."

"So they're bringing them back to Vientiane?"

"That's the problem, Anjali. All three countries are claiming jurisdiction. It's not exactly clear which side of the border they were caught on, and the Thai are saying they saw them first."

"So what's going to happen?"

"Not clear at this point. Of course the Canadian Embassy has got into the act. Not to get Cyril off, but to ensure his rights aren't violated."

Anjali thought of the Australian Ambassador doing the same for Jackie. "Come on, Raj, who's going to violate the rights of a diplomat?"

"I gather the soldiers roughed him up a bit."

"Oh dear." Despite her words, Anjali realized she was slightly pleased to learn that Cyril had received a little corporal punishment. Just as long as it wasn't too rough.

"Seems they caught him red-handed. The soldiers opened Cyril's bag and found a whole lot of small stuff, including a gold Buddha. Once they softened him up, alone, out in the middle of the jungle, surrounded by soldiers, Cyril told them everything he knew."

"So what happens now?"

"Not clear. I'll let you know as soon as I hear more."

That afternoon, Anjali sat in the conference room of Vientiane's jail. Even here, far from the cells, the smell of urine and disinfectant was strong.

She shuddered. What must it be like for Jackie?

Across the table sat the Australian Consular Officer and Jackie's Lao attorney. Mr. Norton, the Consular Officer, had called Anjali to say Jackie had asked for her to be present during this first consultation with her lawyer.

Now Norton sat there, looking too young and bopping his pencil up and down on the pad of yellow paper before him. Mr. Bounxouei was perfectly motionless, gazing into a distant tranquility.

The door opened, and Jackie entered, flanked by two female guards. She was still wearing the clothes she'd been arrested in yesterday. Her face seemed slack. There was a bruise on her arm, and she smelled faintly of harsh soap.

The guards brought Jackie to the table and moved to stand by the door.

Norton started to rise, then fell back and introduced the lawyer from his seat. Mr. Bounxouei did not offer a *nop* but merely inclined his head at Jackie.

She was still standing. Anjali reached up, took her by the forearm and guided her to the chair beside her own.

Norton cleared his throat and asked Mr. Bounxouei to summarize the legal situation.

"I have spoken with the authorities," the lawyer said. "The Lao Government will not charge Miss Baxter with murder."

Jackie's face seemed to come alive. She sucked in her lower lip between her teeth, and her eyes were shiny. Anjali placed a hand on her arm to steady her.

Mr Bounxouei continued without acknowledging Jackie's reaction. "This means they believe that Miss Baxter had no intention to kill Mrs. Powell."

Jackie expelled a pent-up breath.

Norton made a note on his yellow pad.

"However," said the lawyer, "they are considering a charge of *homicide excusable*."

"What does that mean?" Anjali asked.

"The homicide was provoked. A fatal wound without intent to kill."

Norton looked up from his notes. "And the penalty?"

"Six months to a year."

Jackie gasped.

Anjali thought of the stories she'd heard of Southeast Asian jails—prisoners covered in welts from bedbugs and sores from poor nutrition, fighting rats by day and guards' rape by night. "Is that the only option?"

Jackie slipped her hand into Anjali's and gently squeezed.

Mr. Bounxouei bowed his head in Anjali's direction. "I am going to enter a plea of *homicide justifie*. Self-defense. If we prevail, Miss Baxter goes free."

Jackie gripped Anjali's hand harder.

Anjali tried not to respond. It was difficult to find the right balance between justice and support.

Norton struck the point of his pencil at the end of his notes. "Right. So what should the Embassy do?"

Jackie smiled across the table at Norton, and he smiled back. Anjali watched the exchange and wondered how so large a woman could look so helpless.

For the first time, Mr. Bounxouei gave a hint of emotion, the barest twitch of the lips. "Your Ambassador could speak to the Minister, inquire if the death might be *homicide justifie*. This would render a trial unnecessary."

Norton underlined a phrase in his notes. "Done!"

Mr. Bounxouei raised a hand in the slightest gesture. "Only inquire…"

Norton nodded and Jackie lowered her head. The corners of her mouth turned up, and she didn't look at anyone.

Anjali undressed, turned on the shower and stepped inside. She felt uneasy about the look she'd seen on Jackie's face. Was the woman still telling half-truths? Had she been subtly manipulating everyone at the table?

Anjali shrugged her shoulders. There was no way of knowing what had really happened that night by the Mekong. And once again, everybody seemed to want this contretemps resolved in the quietest way possible.

She thought about Wilhelmina's plea for social harmony. Maybe that was the best anyone could hope for in this mess.

Leave it alone, she told herself. There's nothing more you can do.

She tucked her head under the shower and reached for the shampoo. Part of her unease, she realized, had to do with KB coming home. How to tell him about everything that had happened? She turned the water up as hot as she could stand it and tried to rinse away the tension of not knowing what to say. She'd never been so independent, never taken such chances before.

He loves me, she reminded herself. But would he understand?

She dressed in KB's favorite sari and spritzed on a bit of the perfume her youngest had sent from London. Anjali's reflection in the mirror brought back memories of her dream about Sophia after Cyril had told about her drowning.

Sophia wasn't unique, Anjali realized. One found Sophias in every expatriate community, talented women who were frustrated, who acted out in inappropriate ways, who bossed and hurt others, who drove almost everyone wild. Anjali sighed. Sophia was a clear example of why international wives needed support.

She walked over to the vase of orchids on the bedside table, wondering about Sophia's reincarnation. How would she lead her next life? Anjali straightened a fallen spray of the pale flowers and thought, I wish her well.

She heard KB's car and felt her heart beat against her breastbone. She still didn't know what to tell him. He loves me, she repeated to herself and went out to greet the man to whom she'd given her life.

After KB had soaked away his travel-fatigue and changed into his *kurta pyjamas*, they sat on the veranda with their glasses of gin-and-tonic. The two cats came to join them, and tough old Traveller began to groom the little gray female.

KB smiled down at them and asked, "Have you decided what to name her?"

"Devi," Anjali said without thinking and surprised herself. She realized she wanted Sophia's cat to be more than just a survivor.

"Good name," KB said and sipped his G&T.

They chatted on, having learned long ago to leave serious topics until after they'd re-established the harmony that was central to their lives.

After a while, Anjali said, "You're looking especially satisfied. Did things go well with the project?"

KB smiled over at her. "Lots of worry, but it all worked out in the end. For the first time since coming to Vientiane, I feel really hopeful."

Anjali felt relief wash through her. The past week had ended well for both of them. Maybe that was where she should start her own story.

KB inhaled a deep breath of contentment. "And you're looking quite fetching. You know I love you in that blue-and-gold sari. Remember when I brought it back from Delhi?"

"I wore it for you."

He looked so handsome, the white of the *pyjamas* against his almond skin, his silver temples gleaming in the lamplight.

The mood was broken by the phone ringing. Anjali started. It might be Raj, and she hadn't told KB the first thing about what had happened.

She began to rise, but KB said, "Let me get it, darling. Probably something to do with the office." Anjali sank back into her pre-shower worries. KB had gone into his study and shut the door. She couldn't hear a thing.

After a while, he came to the veranda door and said, "That was Raj. They want you to make a deposition." His lips compressed into a tight line. "Anjali, what the hell is this about?"

She didn't know where to begin. So many things to focus on. "A deposition? Why?"

KB came forward and rested against the back of his chair. He was visibly struggling to maintain his self-control. "Raj says the Thai Government isn't willing to give up Cyril. The smuggling ring is based in Thailand, and they're claiming jurisdiction. Besides, they've got Cyril down in Bangkok. Put him in the helicopter and flew there straightaway." He leaned toward her, his voice overly reasonable. "Could you kindly tell me what this is about?"

"And the Lao Government went along with it?"

KB came around and sat down. "What power do they have against their stronger neighbor? They'll save face and say it was a joint undertaking."

Anjali looked at his hands, always an indication of what he was feeling. Even though he had clasped them tightly between his knees, they were trembling.

So was his voice, ever so slightly. "Anjali, I've only heard Raj's version. He says you're the heroine, and I should ask you to tell the story. That's what I'm trying to do, get you to begin at the beginning." His voice changed from tremor to command. "Can you please do that now?"

With difficulty, Anjali moved her focus from Cyril in Bangkok to herself in Vientiane. "It all started with Sophia's death."

"Sophia?" KB wasn't shouting, but his voice was definitely raised. He rarely used that tone in the family, and Anjali was shaken. "I thought we were agreed that you'd stay out of that."

Anjali gulped air. "Well...that's what you advised..." She looked at the fury in his face. "And I did think about it. Carefully." She raced on, yet somehow the air inside felt trapped. "But you weren't here. You didn't have all the facts. I just felt like I had to go on with it."

KB's hands fell open. "But Anjali, why?"

Oh dear, Anjali thought. "I've had a wonderful life in many ways—living in so many countries, seeing you move from success to success, watching our boys grow into men we can be proud of..."

KB interrupted. "What does all that have to do with Sophia?"

Now Anjali was feeling a bit angry. "I'm trying to explain, KB. Please let me tell it my own way."

KB threw himself back against his chair. "All right. Tell it anyhow you want, but tell it."

Anjali felt her breath returning to normal. "It's been a wonderful life, but, well, since Hanoi, I've felt I had to keep a low profile."

KB shook his head, and his voice had an edge. "I never asked you to do that."

"I know, but I felt I ought to. Just be the perfect UNDP wife and help us get through this."

He raised an eyebrow over a dark eye fringed with thick lashes. "And…?"

"I found it didn't suit me."

"That's no surprise."

Anjali was startled by KB's perception. "It isn't? No, I guess it isn't. Anyway, you were gone, and I was feeling terribly depressed, nothing to do, useless. I was ripe for the plucking."

A smile played on KB's lips. "So who plucked you? Cyril?"

Anjali read his joshing smile. "He was afraid I'd start focusing on what was happening down in Champassak, so he tried to distract me into investigating how Sophia drowned."

"And you fell for it."

"Yes, I did," Anjali owned up. "But I also discovered a lot of things—about Sophia, about Cyril and about myself."

"So how did Sophia drown?"

"It's all so squalid." Anjali sighed. "Can we talk about it later?"

KB threw back his head and laughed. "Anju, you are the most complicated person I've ever known."

Anjali was a bit taken aback. She wasn't sure how he meant that.

He continued. "Life with you is always an adventure. I'll never tire of you in a thousand years." He'd broken the tension between them.

"A good thing," Anjali joked, "because you're stuck with me."

"Let's leave Sophia alone and come back to you," he said. "You needed something to do, so you started investigating. Then you found out about Cyril. So what did you discover about yourself?"

"Not just myself. All the wives. We need more meaningful lives."

"Anju, everyone wants that. A lot of life seems meaningless."

Anjali hated that tone of reasonableness in KB's voice. This wasn't an intellectual discussion, she thought. This was about feelings.

KB picked up his glass and finished the dregs. His voice took on a new tone, more full of emotion. "Look, Anjali, it hasn't always been perfect at UNDP—I'm not talking about Hanoi—I mean it just hasn't always been a life of meaningful work."

That brought Anjali up short. She hadn't realized that. She'd thought most of KB's career had been fulfilling. This conversation wasn't easy for either of them, she realized. They were both revealing things they'd never discussed before.

KB opened his mouth to say more, but Onhta came through the kitchen door to announce that dinner was ready. He closed his mouth and stared at Anjali for a moment, a look that changed from perturbed to loving. The ice in his glass rattled as he put it down.

He stood and beckoned to Anjali with an outstretched arm. She slipped underneath and felt it wrap around her shoulders.

KB tightened his grip. "I don't know where you're going with all this, but I'm willing to go there with you. But first, can this weary traveler have some supper to fortify body and soul for the voyage?"

Anjali basked in his touch and knew he was right. "Onhta's made us a lovely meal. Let's enjoy it."

KB left his arm where it was and led Anjali to the table. He sat down and turned a boyish grin to his vegetable curry.

Over dinner, Anjali found a way to tell the whole story, how it all fit together—Cyril's smuggling, Sophia's death, her own life and her idea for an international organization. The only thing she left out was the black SUV, but that was to save KB from worry. Or so she consoled herself.

They lingered on the veranda after dinner, reluctant to spoil the tranquil mood created by good food and understanding. Onhta came to say goodnight, then they heard her bicycle rasp by and the creak of the gate as Vong opened and closed it behind her.

They sat silently, the sounds of the tropical night all around them. The scent of frangipani drifted in with the breeze. Nearby, a bird called, and the singing insects stilled for a moment. KB turned to Anjali with a look she knew so well. He held out a slender hand, and she put her plump one inside. They left the veranda, crossed the darkened living room and glided through the shadowy hall to their bedroom.

KB unwound Anjali's sari with deft hands, unwound it as he had so many times before. He opened his *kurta pyjamas*, and they let their garments fall to the floor.

They made the love that only old lovers can, the love of knowing one another so well that giving pleasure is a visit to a favorite land, a visit where one falls deeper and deeper into a communion far beyond words and intellect, a communion of feeling and spirit.

Turn the page for a preview
of Nancy Swing's next mystery,

Child's Play

Available in late fall
through Amazon.com

Nancy Swing's next novel is set in small town West Virginia, where she grew up. Two unlikely sleuths must team up to solve a puzzling mystery: How did their loved ones come to be found in the same place at the wrong time? Here's a preview from the first chapter of Child's Play:

When the news come over the TV about how Miz Gravesly's car went into the lake, I just couldn't believe it.

I could feel the wind beating up our trailer, one of them early summer storms trying to come over the ridge. Saw a program once on how West Virginia mountains are really good at brewing up that kinda storm. But that ruckus outside didn't mean nothing to me, 'cause I was thinking, How can that be? Not the part about Mary Margaret Gravesly. Who cares what that stuck-up old biddy done? But they found Ray-Jean strapped as tight as she could be into that woman's swanky car.

Now, I knew Ray-Jean hated seat belts. Never wore 'em. Not even after her Daddy got a ticket 'cause she was riding in his front seat without one. That was afore he run off with that tramp over to Moorestown-way.

I remember it really well, 'cause he took a stick to her, but it didn't do no good. She still wouldn't wear a seat belt. "Eden," she said, "I can't abide 'em." That Ray-Jean Shackleford was one tough girl.

Well, I couldn't take it all in. My best friend dead? That scrawny tomboy with hair so short it didn't even ruffle in the breeze? So full of life I just had to follow her round. I was always trying to get outta phys ed 'cause I was too fat to run. But she only had to say, "Come on, Eden!" and I was ready to dash off to the ends of the earth. If she'd just let me stop now and then to catch my breath. And she always did. That's exactly how good a friend she was to me.

I musta set there pert' near an hour, rocking myself back and forth on the sofa bed. Keeping time with the squalls wailing through the trailer park. We was in some kinda weird storm, no rain, just wind. Dust swirled up from the dirt road and coated all the windows, but it didn't matter none.

Nothing mattered. Not even my baby brother crying in the other room. Now that Lewiston Junior High was let out for the summer, I was supposed to be taking care of Cruz while Momma took her shift down at the mill. But I couldn't do a thing for him, and that's the truth.

Anyhow, I finally come out of it and started thinking about what that TV man said. And the more I thought, the more I knew I just had to do something.

Bethanne stared into the open casket and tried to convince herself that all this was real. Mary Margaret lay there in her pale-blue linen like she was just asleep. The undertaker had painted her sister so she looked like a faded rose, all cream and mauve. Bethanne touched Mary Margaret's hair, as perfectly coiffed as it had been in life, ash blond masking the gray. But it didn't feel like real hair anymore. Even so, Bethanne's heart said her sister was going to wake up from a nap and start scolding her for smoking in the house.

That made Bethanne crazy for a cigarette, so she went outside and lit up. Thank God the police were keeping the media half a block away. TV and press had latched onto the story like a puppy after a rawhide bone. Wife of prominent West Virginia lawyer found dead in her own car with a poverty-stricken young girl—helluva a story, you had to admit. But Winston's friendship with the police chief was paying off, and the media couldn't get near enough to poke their cameras in anybody's face. Bethanne didn't like Mary Margaret's husband, but at least he had the connections to get things done.

The crush of mourners just kept coming, doctors and lawyers, preachers from churches Mary Margaret hadn't even gone to. A full busload of senior citizens from the old folks home where Mary Margaret had headed up the volunteer committee. Bethanne didn't know a one of them. Her sister's entire bridge club had shown up, cried over the casket and hugged Bethanne until she couldn't breathe. Out at the lake, someone had hung a wreath on the dock, and the neighbor's kids had picked wildflowers and cast them in the water.

All this emotion made Bethanne want to throw up. None of these people had really known Mary Margaret. Not like she had. They didn't know how Mary Margaret had grown up in a small clapboard house on the wrong street, how the two sisters had shared the second bedroom until they were full-grown, how they'd whispered hopes and dreams when they couldn't sleep in the hot Alabama night. These people just knew the woman Mary Margaret had turned herself into, not who she really was.

Bethanne put a hand to her queasy stomach. Jesus, she needed a drink. And there wasn't going to be one until after the funeral, after the graveside ceremony. Then they'd go back to that big house where Winston had brought Mary Margaret as a bride. All these people who didn't know Mary Margaret would crowd around, drink Winston's bourbon and tell everyone how sorry they were. After that, they'd go home and forget Mary Margaret in a week. Or maybe a month. For the rare few, maybe even a year.

36153939R00177

Made in the USA
San Bernardino, CA
15 July 2016